W9-BHB-027

Critical acclaim for *Like Rum-Drunk Angels*

"A fabulist feast.... Cormac McCarthy meets
Gabriel García Márquez." —*Winnipeg Free Press*

"A surreal, often hilarious fracturing of traditional western tropes,
imbuing classic elements with a spirited post-modern awareness....
Like Rum-Drunk Angels is a hoot, with a tender heart at its core."
—*Quill and Quire*

"A wildly funny, wildly entertaining western.
It made me laugh. It made me cry. Buy it for the person that
you bought Patrick DeWitt's *The Sisters Brothers* nine years ago."
—CBC *Day 6* Book Guide

"With a yarn like this, you don't always know what you're hearing,
where it's coming from, and certainly not what it means,
but there's little you'd rather do than sit on your horse and
listen for a while." —*Literary Review of Canada*

"A truly mesmerizing work." —*Edify Magazine*

"Employing traits from the playbooks of both the Coen Brothers
and Walt Disney, this Western stars 14-year-old gunslinger Francis
Blackstone on a journey to make his fortune and win a young
lady's heart. A buddy-novel with bandits, bank robbing
and adventure a-plenty." —*Globe and Mail*

"Beautifully cinematic, with surprising story breaks that create
a long-lasting controlled suspense." —*Hamilton Review of Books*

"*Like Rum-Drunk Angels* turns the historically mundane into
the psychedelically evocative, and the far less mundane
into something even more grandiose." —*Town Crier*

LIKE RUM-DRUNK ANGELS

a novel
by **TYLER ENFIELD**

GOOSE LANE EDITIONS

Edited by Bethany Gibson.
Cover and page design by Julie Scriver.
Cover illustration by Julie Scriver with thanks to
sababa66 (shutterstock) and ioanmasay (iStock).
Printed in Canada by Numérix.
10 9 8 7 6 5 4 3 2

Library and Archives Canada Cataloguing in Publication

Title: Like rum-drunk angels / Tyler Enfield.
Names: Enfield, Tyler, author.
Identifiers: Canadiana (print) 20190187905 |
Canadiana (ebook) 20190187948 | ISBN 9781773101309 (softcover) |
ISBN 9781773101316 (EPUB) | ISBN 9781773101323 (Kindle)
Classification: LCC PS8609.N4 L55 2020 | DDC C813/.6—dc23

Goose Lane Editions acknowledges the generous support of
the Government of Canada, the Canada Council for the Arts,
and the Government of New Brunswick.

Goose Lane Editions
500 Beaverbrook Court, Suite 330
Fredericton, New Brunswick
CANADA E3B 5X4
gooselane.com

Like Rum-Drunk Angels

CHAPTER ONE

When Black Night and Its Genie

Spring, 1884
Nowhere, Arizona

It's well after midnight when the boy named Francis Blackstone urges his horse up the limestone ridge. There's no trail. He just looks for open channels in the stark, mean brush — so dense it rakes at his shins. Clouds pass over the moon. The terrain falls dark, almost black. When the moon's glow returns, agile and bright, Francis finds himself atop a bone-white crest, gazing down upon the distant lamplights of Nowhere.

Francis sits a moment, leaning forward in the saddle. He can smell the sage he just rode through, on his clothing, on the horse. He's considering all that awaits him below, and whether the girl might be among those things waiting, when it occurs to him that home will never twinkle, truly twinkle, like it does from afar.

There is a series of steep switchbacks leading down to the desert floor. Francis dismounts his horse and leads it down the escarpment. He talks to the horse. He murmurs in a gentle voice, praising the animal for its skill. Its beauty. Its many accomplishments on their long journey home.

"You are the sorriest, ugliest horse I've ever seen in my life," he croons. He strokes its damp, muscular neck. "You don't normally think of horses as being ugly. But you, my friend, are a bucket of glue. You are a skunk's rear end."

The horse is a jet-black mare. She is built like a woodland god. No boy on earth has the right to such a beast and Francis knows it. He rubs her moist nose and she blusters and snorts. The steam from her nostrils could power an engine.

The road picks up again at the bottom of the switchback and Francis mounts his mare. They ride slowly in the dark. The sandy plain surrounding the town is raw and featureless. Francis' father once said this stretch of land was like a prototype of the earth, awaiting completion. A hastily sketched world without detail. Why then did his father never leave?

Francis could ask but it wouldn't do any good. His father has no love of questions, or the sort of people who ask them. He is a circuit judge. He values the essential order of things. He imagines he has a hand in that order.

Francis, however, was born to prove him wrong.

The Window

Even small towns get the papers. It doesn't really matter which edition. Anyone who's picked up the *Herald* or the *Post* or anything else that prints in English has learned something of Francis and his legendary year of adventuring. It's been chronicled in the headlines from coast to coast.

So Francis does not go prancing up to his father's gate and freely announce his return. That would be folly. If his father did not detain him, the sheriff would.

He instead makes his way through rutted streets, past the schoolhouse, the mercantile, past the saddler and the church, halting his horse before a public trough at the far end of town. He is within view of the Hotel Whitmore and that's no mistake.

There is a warm, desert breeze, and the town's streetlamps jitter in unison. Hardly anyone is about. Francis brushes the horse with his only brush, and then turns that brush upon himself. All the while he gazes up at the windows along the third floor of the hotel. Then at one small window in particular.

He tries to recall her voice.

It comes to him easily. Her voice is so unusual. It has a way of curling around things, as though caressing each idea, or exclamation, or fat little baby it describes. Francis wonders if she can sense him now, reaching out with his thoughts. He imagines she can. But then he imagines many things. He is a boy after all, which makes him something of a god, for he can still make anything in the world happen in his head. And after a year apart, with the girl so close — just a short climb away — could such a boy ever wait around for the morning?

No.

❧

It's nearly dawn when Francis remounts his horse, searching for shelter just beyond the edge of town. He elects to stay within view of the hotel, making camp beneath a gnarled, lightning-struck juniper. He hobbles the horse and removes its saddle. He unhitches the saddlebags and lays them in a heap beside the tree.

Then he just stands there, looking at the horse.

The horse holds herself rigid, her long velvet jaw turned heroically to the breeze. Out of curiosity, Francis tries to follow her line of sight. A ghost? A rabbit? He can make nothing of it. Just darkness out there, and further on, the faint glow of stars against a whip-bright night.

"You see?" says Francis, scratching the horse's side. "Staring at nothing. Dumb as glue."

And then a line of wagons comes trundling into view. Their faint, shadowy silhouettes gain solidity as they approach the town from the north. Francis digs out his telescope. He can make out the colourful logos of a carnival or a circus upon their ribbed canopies as they draw nearer the town's light. He realizes they are not passing through but circling, hunting out land to begin their fantastic enterprise.

Within minutes, the air is ringing with the dry, muted hammerblows of pegs driven into the earth. Canvas pavilions pop up as though inflated by the wind. Roustabouts appear and disappear as they saunter between lanterns,

10

shouting to each other, erecting arcades, galleries, all manner of entertainment to be discovered by the townsfolk upon waking. But it is all far away, and when the wind changes direction Francis can hear nothing at all.

Francis stretches his arms and yawns grandly, as one does when alone or with animals. With the instep of his boot he kicks out a flat area in the dirt. He unrolls his bedding beneath the tree and stretches out on the blanket. He places his hands behind his head and then jerks upright again, hissing with pain. In his exhaustion he keeps forgetting the finger. He's continually grabbing for things, or in this case lying upon it, as though a forty-five calibre round had not knocked the ring finger from his hand. That was barely four days ago. He gently repositions the denim strapping that holds the bandage in place and lies back on the blanket.

Presently he gazes up at the night sky, stars burning in their sockets, and he thinks, I said I'd come back. And here I am.

Francis tries not to think about his brother, gone. Their closest friend, gone. It was this same time last year they all set out for California. They were exuberant and naive. They were visionary. He tries not to think about the six men dead, or the trains and the trains, and the buckets of money, and every lawman in the state converging on the very dirt beneath his head.

He will return to the girl when the sun rises, and beyond that nothing really matters.

He closes his eyes and is out on the instant, maybe faster.

If Mozart Were a Meteor

Somewhere around mid-morning, Francis wakes to the sound of a cherrywood piano dropping from the sky and landing with a colossal thud about five feet from his head. By some marvel the piano lands upright and sticks as though planted there amid a cloud of ochre dust, fully collapsed in the middle, its keys jutting upward on either side like the teeth of a hideous grin. The resonant clamour of its strings is incredible, otherworldly. It hangs in the air like an exploded song.

Francis coughs on the dust and sits up from his bedding and rubs his face with his good hand, noting this phenomenon. For most of a minute he debates whether he's woken.

After this period he rises to his feet and goes tentatively to the piano's sideboard, leaning against it. He reaches down and twiddles two keys in succession. Neither key is linked to anything, and they make a dull clacking sound as he gazes at the sphinx-like presence of the catapult — newly arrived with the circus — standing between the Whitmore Saloon and the church-house. Francis considers that, squaring it with the dubious arrival of this broken, spectacular contraption at his feet, and then turns his attention to the surrounding desert and finally the clouds above, only to discover someone has launched a second piano. It arcs gracefully across the morning sky.

Most people would not think a piano could soar with such containment, such poise. There they would be wrong. It's like a stout ballerina. There is only sincerity.

The piano crashes a few yards from his bedroll and goes apart in a hundred different ways and almost immediately a third piano is aloft. This one is incendiary, having been doused in lamp oil and set ablaze. It cuts a path through the heavens like a wounded sun.

There it is, thinks Francis, his eyes turned skyward. The last thing on earth I ever thought to see.

He thinks, Today I will speak with her father.

Francis saddles his horse and mounts it and starts toward town, sidestepping the hail of flaming pedals and ivory keys and hissing, whipping piano cords beating the earth all around.

How It All Began
(one year earlier)

CHAPTER TWO

Climb Slow over Walls, Windows

It's the hour of night when the moon sits like a glowing rind upon the darkened windowglass of the Hotel Whitmore's west face, replicating itself in rows. Below, the saloon is buzzing with commotion and the odd celebrant stumbling out the swinging doors and onto the road upon which light opens and closes with the doors. Somewhere in there, a piano. Also a guitar and singing.

When nobody is about, young Francis Blackstone sneaks to the veranda. He scales the awning, and from there climbs the facade to the uppermost tier where the governor and his family, and most importantly the governor's daughter, reside for a month of leisure and adjournment each spring. Francis peeks through the window.

Along the walls, a bureau and a nightstand — all the effects of a young lady, everything alive and flickering in the light of stub candles.

Also the young lady herself, seated upon the canopy bed. She combs her hair before the mirror, more intent on the image than the combing. To Francis' dismay, she is still quite decent, in a short-sleeve blouse and long blue skirt. A dozen times he's stood before this sill, peering through her window. And a dozen times that same white blouse, just waiting to confound him. What are the odds?

But really he loves the blouse. He loves the blouse because it's hers. Because it touches her. It knows her body in a way he can barely fathom. And so he despises the blouse too. Of course he despises it. A youth's tenderest feelings are always conundrums. They are dreamworld animals, leaping about, babbling in strange tongues. No one can make any sense of them, least of all a boy. Francis once stole a pair of her Sunday shoes just to smell them.

Presently the girl's hairbrush hits the floor with a bang. She stands up in surprise. "Who are you? What are you doing here?"

Francis is equally surprised to discover he has dropped down through her window and is now standing before her. He had no intention of doing so, and yet here he is. Staring back at her, mute with awe.

"I said what are you doing here? This is my bedroom."

For lack of an answer, or any real sort of plan, Francis fumbles in his satchel. "Here," he says. "I guess I wanted to give you back these."

The girl looks at the patent leather shoes in his outstretched hand. She takes them slowly. She studies their laces, their eyelets, their soles, as though she has never seen these or any other shoe before in her life. "I don't understand," she says.

"Me either," says Francis, shrugging with bewilderment. Because this isn't at all how he imagined their first meeting would go. Not even close. He can't believe how much better it is.

"But Who Are You?" Asks the Girl.

"Francis," he says. "I'm Francis Blackstone."

When this fails to register he adds, "My name may not mean much yet, but someday you'll remember this as the night we met."

The girl blinks in surprise. She stares a moment, and then carefully, slowly, sits down on the edge of her bed. "What an odd thing to say. You standing here like I know you."

"All right, granted," he says. "So how about this. I know you love to read books about outlaws. And angels. And your favourite candy is butterscotch. I know on cool evenings you stroll through town with your mother. You stop at *Landry's* on the way home for vegetables."

The girl's bafflement deepens.

"There's more," he says. "I know you don't like to go to church but you read the bible on your own. I know you own three hairbrushes but only use the one. Right there on the floor. And I know your moods, all of them, by the way a ribbon holds up your hair, or pulls it back in a ponytail."

"How do you know all this?"

For the first time, Francis' embarrassment shows a little. "I've been watching you. For a long time I've been watching."

Unexpectedly, the girl smirks in delight. "You have not."

Francis says nothing.

"Watching me. Well. If that is meant to impress me I'm not impressed. Why are you smiling?"

"Nothing."

"Then stop smiling."

"All right."

She pulls at a bit of fuzz on the bedspread. "So where have you seen me?"

"I thought you weren't impressed."

She smiles, though her face has gone red. "There is a big difference between curiosity and —"

"I am hands-down, flat out in love with you. Do you understand? I'm a goner. That's why I'm here right now. To tell you that. And also to give back those shoes."

The look on her face says she recognizes flattery when she hears it, and could perhaps tolerate a bit more. She waits.

When it's clear no poetry is forthcoming she narrows her eyes. "But how old are you?"

"Doesn't matter. We're going to be together a long time."

"Just tell me."

"Fourteen."

"Me too," she says. "I'm fourteen too."

"I know that," says Francis. "I know just about everything about you. Except probably your name."

She appears to think on this. As in really considers him this time.

She says love is a start, but without money her father will never consent to courtship. Plus Francis is a rogue.

"That's all fine."

"It is not fine. I mean it. My father is Governor Whitmore. He owns everything. This hotel, everything. He won't allow some poor nobody to come sweep me away."

"Then I'll find money."

"Just like that?" she says.

"Just like that," he says.

Francis promises to return with money. There is no obstacle, he says, that can impede his heart and the pledge he now makes to her. He asks for a token of her commitment to keep him going.

"What kind of token?"

"Let me see them."

She laughs in surprise. "Did you say —?"

"Yes I did."

She regards him a while, incredulity plain upon her face. "You are something else, you know that? I suppose this is your idea of gallantry."

"Maybe."

"And had you asked for a small kiss I might have even considered it."

"I say never start small. With anything."

The girl opens her mouth with yet another retort, and hesitates.

Francis just looks at her. She looks back.

A subtle something ripples through the air. Call it a pinkness.

She says, "Well. That's just silly. Why would I do such a thing?"

Francis looks at her.

She looks back.

They look at each other.

"Anyhow it's you who wants a peek. And you haven't given me one good reason."

After a long, lovely moment, Francis lifts his chin. The tiniest of gestures.

Still meeting his gaze, she unbuttons her white blouse, bottom to top. She then opens its sides, revealing to Francis what lies beneath. What does Francis see?

Space. Time. The harmony of the planets.

He is destroyed. He is inspired. He is confounded beyond all account.

The girl is visibly shy but no less engaged than he.

A tremulous magic, then. A shared wonder. He watches her, and her eyes never leave his.

A noise in the hall, just beyond the door. She gasps and twists away to button her blouse and Francis is out the window to the road, running, running.

He has never run so fast.

He doesn't know where he is going, though he is firm in the belief that speed is somehow necessary. Everything is imperative. There is no time to lose. He is lost and clueless and utterly alive.

While across his face, tears of glory.

The Fortune

For the next two weeks Francis wanders about in a daze. He eats oatmeal or nothing. His sleep is all wrong. His skin grows sallow. He can sit for hours at a stretch — on a grain sack in the pantry, beneath the thick limbs of a tree — simply watching a girl open her white blouse, one button at a time, across the double-page spread of his mind.

His elder brother Samuel takes notice. "I'm concerned you might be dying. Are you ill?"

Of course he is ill. Francis is in love. There is no pestilence, no parasite on earth like the havoc of first love upon a young man's body and soul.

Their father says nothing. He sits at the far end of the table, quietly sipping his soup. He is a stranger to affection. It is a foreign condition — like typhoid. The nearest their father comes to sentiment is that brief moment each night before he settles into bed and determines, whether by will or by habit, to sleep on one side of the mattress. When there is really nothing in the world to keep him from the middle.

"You've completed your chores?" asks their father between slurps.

Francis nods.

Francis hasn't completed a chore in days. He doesn't even know what a chore is.

From the moment he wakes Francis is like a tuning fork pitched to the resonance of some moon-mad fortune he cannot see but nonetheless jangles like a doorbell in his bones. By the girl's account, everything hinges upon his finding it.

So where is this fortune?

Francis can almost hear the money, calling to him. Reeling him in like the sweet trilling song of a yellow bird.

In this fantastical phase of his life Francis never stops to wonder if any of this makes sense. He is done making sense.

There is only the girl in the white blouse, and the whatever it takes.

So It Is

that the following morning Francis finds himself one of three boys standing side by side on a dirt road. All three stare through the open doors of the Whitmore Saloon and into the darkened interior where men drink and smoke and speak and so on.

"Which one is he?" asks Francis, peering closer.

His brother Samuel leans in, pointing through the saloon's front window. "Right there," he says. "The big guy. With the hat on."

"On the barstool?" asks Francis.

"That's him. He just took a sip."

"That's Bob Temple?"

"That is Bob Temple. I told you he's in town."

Francis just looks a while.

The third boy, Ned Runkle, finally shakes his head with professed doubt. He's a lanky kid, ever grinning and somewhat funny to look at. He spits in the road and kicks it over with dirt. "Doesn't look much like the poster."

"Well it's him," insists Samuel. He's big for his age, already bigger than their father, his broad cheekbones still dusted with black freckles. "It's definitely him."

"What would Bob Temple be doing here?" asks Ned.

"Why not here?" says Samuel. "Every living man has to be somewhere."

"That is some cockeyed logic," argues Ned, "and it sure doesn't put Bob Temple here over someplace else."

Amid this debate, Francis starts for the saloon. He's barely two steps along when his brother claps his shoulder and spins him about. "Where you headed, Francis?"

"I'm going to talk to him."

"Talk to him? I'm telling you that is Bob Temple. That man is a killer."

Francis regards the swinging doors to the saloon with something like heedless curiosity, as though the doors themselves hold some glamour or charm. He has moreover the clean, animate gaze of one who sees what is before him and nothing more — not his brother, not Ned, not the warning in his blood, and certainly not providence in its entirety, though its promise hangs like an obscure glow upon the saloon's dim entrance.

"I'm going to talk to him." Francis shrugs free of Samuel's grip and heads for the saloon.

"Damn, he's going to do it," whispers Ned.

"Course he's going do it," says Samuel, staring sullenly after his kid brother. "That's the problem with him. He's always going to do it."

But If Francis Could Do It Over Again,

he would not ask for the blouse. Not at all.

He would ask to see her toes. Her naked toes.

Ten perfect little toes, dangling freely from a swing. A girl's pale toes to carve shapes in the sand. Toes he could sing to, and die for, and cherish.

There is a reason for this obsession, belonging to another time, back when Francis first discovered the Northwestern Passage to her window. It was something he witnessed at the time, and hopes to share with her one day. Or perhaps he'll just put it in a letter.

Enchantment aside, Francis' feelings are bolstered by a strange new assurance. It has to do with what the girl is, and what Francis is, and what is the glue that holds them together. Certainly there is the curve of her cheek, and the white of her smile. And her toes. Naturally her toes. But all that will disappear one day. Altered, or tarnished, or just plain forgotten. There are the girl's opinions and her beliefs, none of which concern Francis. And then there's the compatibility of two sweethearts who have agreed to move as one through the world. To share certain feelings for each other, and no other. But all this, too, is subject to drift. Francis has the dreadful loneliness of his father to prove it.

So what is there really between them? Between any two people?

It can only be something that remains when all else turns to dust. Certainly not Francis' thoughts then. Nor his feelings. Nor even the outrageous warmth that coasts through his veins when she rattles down the street in her father's wagon.

It is her soul Francis loves. And this is the most dangerous love of all. Because it comes up from the deep, and regards only the deep, and has no regard for any conventions in the world.

If this bond could gallop a white horse and fly a banner in the sky, it would read:

Anything for Love

It's this banner Francis carries. The one he waves about, like a mad drummer on the field, as he saunters into the Whitmore Saloon.

Someone Like You

Bob Temple sits on a barstool facing the shelves with their many bottles. He dabs mindlessly at a wine spill on the counter, scribbling out shapes with the pad of his finger. A spiral. A diamond. A noose.

The barkeep is playing pinochle with a Mexican woman in a blue dress, and a slovenly gentleman, either drunk or unskilled, is casually pestering the keys of a derelict piano. Everyone else is quietly engaged around chipped, polished tables, blowing smoke through mustaches, discussing the blue-sky heat.

Francis pulls up just behind the big man with the split-tail coat, greasy hat, and dark reddish sideburns.

"You're Bob Temple?"

Bob Temple sets his shotglass on the counter beside his wineglass and twists over his shoulder, looking a little bleary-eyed.

"I am."

"You're the one they say shot Jack Glover? One-Eyed Jack, straight through the heart?"

Bob Temple's jaw goes stiff. "You got something to settle?"

Francis considers the question. He has no plan, no strategy. Not even a goal really. Just a vague tickling sense that everything he's after—namely the girl, the fortune he needs to get the girl—it all starts here. In this very moment.

"I don't know what I got," says Francis. "I guess I'm here to find out."

They look at each other. Bob Temple glances down at Francis' hip.

"Look, son. If I had a dime for every kid walked up with pistols swinging, wanting to test his mettle, I wouldn't be sitting here in this no-account shithole drinking poor whiskey. Why don't you go on home."

Temple twists back around.

A moment passes. Francis slaps a dime onto the counter beside him.

Bob Temple stares into his glass. He places one finger upon the dime and slides it exactly one inch to the left. "The fact is, I'm not even interested. Just minding my own today."

"That's fine. I just wanted you to have that."

"So you think you're fast? Is that it?"

"I don't know. Maybe."

"You ever drawn against a man?"

"No."

"You just thought you'd start with me?"

Francis shrugs. "Who even said anything about drawing guns? I'm just looking for what's next and now here you are. Biggest next in town."

Bob Temple just looks at him. "Shit. Sit down. I'm pouring you a drink."

"All right."

"You ever drink?"

"No."

"Sit down. This is what we're drinking today. This here's what one man drinks with another."

"All right."

"How you like that?"

Francis wipes his mouth. "Not much."

"How old are you even?"

"Me? I'm fifty-one."

"All right, fine. And that your brother out there watching us? With his buddy?"

"Yeah."

"How old are they?"

"They're same as me."

"They let you come in here on your own? Talk to me?"

"Yeah."

"They know who I am?"

"Yeah."

"Let me see that pistol you got there."

Francis passes him the pistol.

"Oh my, now look at that. A big old Schofield. This your daddy's?"

"Not when I'm wearing it."

Bob Temple handles the pistol, looking at Francis.

"So you think I'm a killer? A real baddie?"

"Honestly?" says Francis. "Looking at you now, I'm not sure you're much of anything."

"All right, bit of advice. That is not what you say. Not to the man holding your pistol."

Francis shrugs. It's moments like this—staring back into Temple's clear, cold eyes—he gets the sense his life isn't his own. It belongs to something else, something more, though what that something is he can't yet say.

"I'm not afraid."

Bob Temple regards him a while. He glances out the window. The two older boys seem to have drifted away.

"All right, well, here's the thing," says Temple. "I could use you. Someone like you." He returns the pistol and Francis holsters it.

"I got something in mind, and if you are game, you just let me know." Temple faces the shelves again and brings the whiskey glass partway to his lips. "Eighty-twenty. That's my usual split. So you just let me know." He completes the sip and sets the glass on the counter.

"What are we even talking about?"

Bob Temple grins, tapping the rim of his shotglass. It's like he sees something glad in there but it's just a shotglass. Just his finger tapping it.

"Talking about a good old-fashioned treasure hunt. Right here in the smack middle of Nowhere."

Wherever You Are, You're
On Top of the World

Three miles from Nowhere sits a small home with a veranda out front, a rambling lilac, and a grand old cherry tree the size of an oak. The house is now vacant, but for most of Francis' childhood it was the home of his uncle.

Francis and Samuel spent much time in their uncle's yard, building forts and climbing trees. But never the cherry. Never the cherry. Francis' uncle had a strange notion the tree would be the death of them, and forbade any child from climbing it.

They begged, he refused. The uncle went so far as to hide all the buckets and ropes and anything else that might inspire the boys to defy him.

Year after year, the legendary tree bore soft pink blossoms, consequently stirring in the boys something they could not possibly understand, while nevertheless redoubling their efforts of persuasion.

After several such years, there came a summer when the limbs went heavy with dark red fruit, and the boys were so convincing in their bid that the uncle finally agreed to a compromise. He allowed that he would climb the tree himself and pick the fruit as the boys directed him from below, pointing here and there. Only the uncle promptly fell from the tree and broke his neck and that was that.

To the folks of Nowhere, the whole event smacked of fate. It appeared that while certain outcomes might be undesirable, there was no outfoxing their arrival. At best, one could hope to delay their appearance by hiding this bucket or that.

And Francis?

He didn't buy it. Any future that was fixed, unwilling to change as we change, belonged exclusively to the nonsense of adults. No matter which way he turned, there was only ever one moment — its shape moulding into something new with each choice.

"I'm in," says Francis Blackstone to Bob Temple at the bar.

The two stand as one from their stools and depart the saloon, shading their eyes as they pass from dimness to light, casting their gaze upon the solitary road leading out from Nowhere toward a wider, wilder world wherein the myriad possibilities lie gleaming like cherries. A shining horizon of cherries. Cherries enough to make you weep.

This Much

Francis Blackstone is five years old. His father sits in the lounge chair of the parlour, reading his paper. Francis stands in the doorway, watching him.

There are many books on the parlour shelves. His father is not only a judge but also a futurist, a member of the Geological Society, and also the Neo-Architectural Movement of Zurich, though he has never been anywhere or built anything. Mostly it's their ideas he is given to. The idea of them. This is what pleases his father most about the world: that you can be so intimate with its workings without ever having to touch it.

Francis enters the parlour and pauses on the rug before the fireplace, working a loose thread with his toes. He gazes intently at the back of the newspaper in his father's hands.

Francis asks his father how much he loves him.

When his father doesn't answer Francis asks a second time and his father sets down the paper, revealing an honest face, not overly happy with the present distraction.

"What are you asking?"

"I want to know how much you love me."

His father rubs his mouth with one hand while assessing his son. Many moments pass. Francis recognizes the look on his father's face. It's the one he gets when working sums, doing his accounting.

"What's your guess," says his father.

Francis throws his arms wide. "This much."

His father studies the gesture, silently nodding while taking the measure in his head. After a time he leans forward and brings the boy's hands closer by half, sits back to assess his work, then leans forward again to make a slight adjustment, spreading the boy's hands an inch further apart, then sits back again.

"That looks about right."

He picks up his paper and resumes reading.

The Thing about the Parlour

There's also a piano in it. It's an old Baldwin. A lordly, stoic, vaguely frightening machine with huge clawed feet and an inch of dust behind it. Francis isn't allowed anywhere near the piano.

He's never once seen it played, not even by visitors.

Where did it come from?

Boston, says his father.

The piano has a wonderful habit however. As though stifled by silence and seasons of neglect, every so often it will intone a single note. Just one. You can hear it all through the house and by the time you get there, nothing. The parlour is empty.

This happens perhaps once a year at most. Francis never does find out why.

Not Just Any Girl

Bob Temple sits his horse. Francis Blackstone walks, keeping pace beside him. They are a good three miles outside town, following the old Newton trail toward the local mine. According to Temple's map, that's where the treasure will be hidden. The surrounding scrubland—cruel and spare—is just the sort of thing you'd expect to find at the municipal limits of Nowhere.

"So that's it?" says Bob Temple. "That's all you want? Nothing else?"

"Yeah," says Francis. "That would do it."

"Well," says Temple. "I don't know I could ever be satisfied on just love itself." He lifts a waterskin from the horse's side and uncorks it and takes a drink. Then drinks again.

"Love," he says, wiping his mouth. "That would be nice though. I confess it would be nice. To be happy with just that. I think I'd need something a little more, however. You didn't bring water?"

"No."

"I suppose you do have a point though. Keep it simple. Not a bad course, in my experience." Bob Temple takes a final sip and corks the waterskin and returns it to its place.

"What are you after then," asks Francis. "If not love then what?"

"What am I after?" Temple sets both hands atop the pommel, one upon the other. He is thinking.

"I guess you could say...I guess I'm what you'd call an opportunity man. I've hired on with mining outfits in the past, out of Nevada City, doing freelance. Protection and so forth. Also out of Thornbrook. Once or twice in Yuma. But that stuff never lasts. The Pinkertons get just about every contract these days, which means folks like myself just aren't in demand. So I take my opportunities where I can. Or make them, such as now."

"That's all interesting," says Francis. "But it doesn't really answer my—"

"Peace of mind!" says Temple with unexpected volume. "That is what I want most. Peace of mind." It's as though a wall has gone up. This line of questioning is no longer welcome.

Francis doesn't pester him. Eventually Temple roots out a handful of peanuts from his saddlebag, eating them loudly from the saddle. Shells go over the side. When the nuts get stuck between his teeth Temple digs them out with a fingernail.

"Listen, how far to these coalmines?" he asks around a thumb. He spits something invisible into the distance.

"Not far," says Francis.

"They don't even have a name on my map."

"I doubt they have one. We just call them the mines outside town."

They walk and ride respectively, the abandoned coalmines drawing nearer. The late April sunshine lays shadows neatly upon the earth. Temple scoops up another handful of peanuts. He tosses a few in his mouth. He observes Francis a moment, walking beside him.

He flicks a peanut at Francis' shoulder.

"So what's this girl call herself?" asks Temple.

"No idea."

"You're kidding me."

"I'm not."

Bob Temple looks down at Francis, then back at the horizon.

"Well," says Temple. "And I suppose you're right on the one point. I reckon when it comes to women, any name will do."

"She's not just any girl."

"None of them are."

"No, this one's different. She let me see behind her blouse."

"Now you're talking."

"And there's just space."

"As in...what are you saying?"

"There's just space. Stars and such. Planets swinging about."

"Huh. Now that does sound different."

"Yeah. Now you see why I got to have her."

"I believe I do," says Temple. "I believe I am beginning to."

❧

The mine itself is a vertical shaft in the desert floor, framed in an exoskeleton of decrepit beams going down into the dim. Francis Blackstone and Bob Temple stand at its threshold, peering at the rope ladder scaling its depths. Temple nudges the ladder with his toe and sends a few pebbles tumbling.

"This is where you earn your keep," he says.

"The shaft is big enough for two," says Francis.

"Nuh uh. I don't do well in such spaces. Besides, you got to win your share. Your twenty percent."

"All right. Let me see the map."

Bob Temple returns to the horse and digs around in the saddlebag for the item in question.

"Where'd you get it anyhow?" calls Francis, still peering down into the gloom.

"From an old dynamiter. An old Chinaman," says Temple. "Lost five of his brothers in the mine explosion happened here. But they found something at the bottom, somewhere in the shaft, before the most of it collapsed. Wrote it all down on this."

Bob Temple produces the map from the saddlebag and Francis looks at it, but doesn't take it.

"That's the map?" says Francis.

Temple nods.

"That doesn't look like any map I've heard of."

"Perhaps the old man did not have much to write upon."

Francis looks at the item in Temple's hand, grimacing faintly.

"I try not to think about it myself," offers Temple.

"But still," says Francis.

"Hence the glove," says Temple.

Francis looks at the glove, then the map.

He takes the one and then the other and starts down the rope ladder into the mine.

❧

The shaft widens at the bottom and Francis strikes the lantern. He ups the wick and observes a low-slung room, roughly the dimensions of an egg. There is a set of iron rails planted in the earth, leading into the dim. Francis can't imagine how they got here. He notes also a slagheap and another of rubbish and where the mine divides into two tunnels, an empty canary cage hanging from the rafter.

Francis goes to the cage and raises the lantern. He looks within. He finds a tiny perch with an antique newspaper beneath it. The script on the paper is Chinese. Where the bird should be, there is now a solitary photograph dangling from a length of string.

The Thing about the Photograph

It shows a busty woman in a corset and bloomers. She is posing in a room with flower-motif wallpaper all around. She holds aloft a cornucopia of fruit, gazing at Francis through the bars of the cage.

Francis places a finger against the bottom corner of the cage. It rotates at his touch, casting a zoetrope of light and shadow against the wall.

And Over Here,

between the dual entrances to the tunnels, Francis finds a Chinese pictogram emblazoned in the stone. A skilled reader of such pictograms might discern what lies ahead, but Francis is no such reader. He refers to the map and selects the tunnel on the right.

It could be the stifling atmosphere but he believes the map is growing more pungent. He doubts it will tolerate much more handling.

❉

The tunnel's circumference is ribbed with old pine beams gone partway to powder. Francis follows the rails on the ground until the way is blocked by an old trolley, frozen with rust. Francis shoves, but the trolley won't budge. Not even a squeak. He climbs into the trolley and then over the trolley and continues on his way, following the rails, his head ducked to accommodate the ceiling, the lantern letting a thin stream of rancid smoke which collects and hovers in confusion against the ceiling. When the path divides he checks the map and determines his course. He does this twice more and eventually comes to the collapse. Broken timber and rubble block the path forward. He turns around and marks his path back, counting steps this time, halting at the count of one hundred forty-two.

He refers to the map and then lifts his head, studying the rift in the ceiling.

❁

Francis gets a foothold on the wall and manages with some effort to wriggle up into the rift. It's more like a crevice. This part wasn't dug, Francis concludes, but rather it was come upon. A natural occurrence in the lay of stone converging with the labours of man. It's a tight space, which is to Francis' advantage, as he requires the walls of the crevice front and back to propel himself higher. The trick is keeping the lantern's handle between his teeth while he grunts along, and then the trick fails and he watches the lantern plummet past his toes and recede down the briefly illuminated length of the crevice to the floor of the shaft in a small, debauched explosion of oil and tinkling glass and then darkness.

A whole lot of darkness.

❁

Francis has matches however.

❁

Feeling glad in himself with the knowledge of said matches, Francis continues to wriggle upward into the lightless crevice until he experiences a broadening of his senses. He feels it primarily in his ears. A kind of inflation of felt awareness that has him turning his head this way and that despite there being nothing to see.

A room, then. A natural cavity. Francis tries not to think about how he's going to return through the crevice. He tentatively feels about him until his hands come upon a small thing on the floor. It's an item of unnatural angles and planes. A manmade item. He decides to use the first of his matches and in the brief flare of sulfur notes the contours of this room, the small thing in his hand, and also the things in the walls.

The thing in his hand is made of clay and shaped like a flat kettle. The nozzle has a wick of sorts, and the body is filled with a liquid, thick to the touch, and Francis rightly presumes it is oil. The markings on the lamp could be Navajo and they could be Hopi. It doesn't matter much to Francis who made it, so long as its sale will contribute toward his fortune once above ground.

The walls of the room have long niches, like shelves, carved into their sides. There are three such shelves. The bones arranged within their beds still hold the rough outline of their occupants as they were placed there long ago. There are also weapons among the remains; a stone tomahawk, an antler-handle knife, and a piece of tooled bone that looks like the sharp end of a scythe.

A second match fills the chamber with light.

Francis glances quickly about, confirming what the first match revealed. Before the tiny flame completes its traverse of the stick, he transfers it to the wick and the ancient clay lamp introduces a soft glow, and then a brighter one as the oil begins to draw.

Francis raises the lamp and surveys the burial chamber. What to take?

He starts with the scythe, giving it a practice swipe through the air. Bob Temple said such artifacts could be traded or sold, so Francis slips it into his belt along with the knife. The tomahawk he leaves behind. He has nowhere left to put it. He sifts through the bones in their niches but finds no coins or anything else of discernable value. His purpose here feels mysterious. There is no obvious treasure that would warrant the creation of a map, and Temple gave him few instructions.

A moment, then, while Francis sorts through his perceptions, the actual from the haunted. He is finding it increasingly difficult to quell certain impressions from flooding his mind and sending him cuckoo.

"All right," he says aloud. He raises the lamp higher and it casts its own shadow upon the floor. The shadow wobbles like a fish.

"All right," he says again, "I'm taking what I have and no more."

He is still thinking about how he's going to get down that crevice. This lamp would remain clamped between his teeth no better than the first. Worse even, without the ring handle. In short, the way down is shut. What to do?

The lamp blows out. Francis' body goes stiff.

"Hello?" he calls out, his voice tremulous, uncertain.

And then something unexpected occurs.

In his wildest dreams, Francis could not have thought to prepare against such a moment.

Audience of One

Francis Blackstone is eleven years old. It's evening and his brother is off with Ned somewhere. His father is still in town.

Francis goes out in the yard, which overlooks the desert. There is stormlight on the plain, roving like ships, and electricity branches through clouds so deep and dark they look like tarsmoke churning the horizon.

Francis is drawn to storms and always has been. They have never frightened him, not even as an infant. Presently the clouds roll inward, heaving, densely strange. Their bellies spark with eerie light like the dawning of our cosmos in a quavering glass thimble.

Francis stands in the yard, watching this. He wonders why he is alone with this vision. Why no one else is out when the heavens are aswirl, detonating in a chemical glow. And then a twister falls out.

It is too fantastic to be real, and yet there it is — a grotesquely whimsical whirling. It unspools across the desert in a train of dust, hungry and quarrelsome, drawing off clouds like fuel. He is spellbound.

The first wind hits him square in the face. It rocks him back on his hind foot. The light on the plain is oddly orange and grey. It has a smell. He can feel it on his skin. The air is trembling, shimmering with anticipation, and just when Francis thinks it will bear down upon him, the twister wobbles and goes suddenly slack and then vanishes —as gone as though it never was.

But is it truly gone?

Francis squats down on his haunches, staring out at the place where a thing has passed.

This is what he knows: there is a record, and he is that record.

He knows that nothing that is real truly dies.

He knows the twister will endure as a cloistered event, a secret merriment deep inside — he is a container. He is a snowglobe. He is a vastly tiered arena with an audience of one. Look beyond his skin, his eyes, and you will find these moments, these eccentric little pets, each fizzing in their lesser eternities.

Francis doesn't ever speak of this moment. Not then and not now.

No one ever asks. And why would they?

Third and Last Match

Francis still holds the lamp in his hands, though he cannot see it. He stands in complete darkness. The sound of his breathing echoes against the burial chamber's walls.

He considers what just transpired. It was something, yes, but what exactly?

He doesn't know. He only knows it defies description — a private moment spinning in his palm. So what next?

The lamp, of course. The lamp in his hands. Should he relight it?

No, he thinks. Don't light the lamp. That's how all of this started.

But on the other hand, he reasons, screw it.

Francis strikes his third and last match and touches it to the lamp and holds the lamp aloft. The shadows careen and shudder.

"All right," he says aloud, turning in place. "I'm on my way for real this time. Except I'm not sure exactly how. Any suggestions?"

He looks about. He awaits an answer. The lamp flame fizzles and spits.

Francis can't say precisely when it occurs, but at some point his attention goes solely to the smoke, which corkscrews up from the lamp and then chimneys sideways into a cleft, a shadowy fissure nearly obscured until one positions the lamp just so.

A good thing, perhaps? Yes. A possible exit route has presented itself.

Or better yet, with no matches remaining and no feasible path back down the way he came, it's now all or nothing for Francis — which is historically the most inspired approach to removing oneself from a tight spot of any order.

Francis emerges from the crevice into full sunlight, coughing on sand, blinking wildly and gazing about at the billowing dunes. He is alone. He is alive. He is glad for many things. Among them: fresh air, freedom of movement, and the knowledge of a nameless girl with burning galaxies in her heart, awaiting him in a canopy bed above the saloon. Also the possibility he has now, upon his person and in the artifacts about his belt, the means to please her father and properly court her.

Before setting out to find Bob Temple he does one thing however. Francis pours the remaining lamp oil into the sand, extinguishing the small flame, and hides the lamp in his pocket.

Now to find Bob Temple.

❧

"Got you something," says Francis, coming up from behind.

Bob Temple sits up in surprise. He's been napping on his saddlebags near the mine's entrance, waiting for Francis to emerge.

"Shit. You nearly scared me."

Francis removes the artifacts from his belt and tosses them, first one and then the other, onto the sand before Temple.

Temple takes off his hat and wipes his brow and puts the hat back on. He crouches and picks up the antler-handle knife, turning it over in his hand.

"Worth anything?" asks Francis.

"Hell if I know. Probably. To someone."

"Who?"

"You didn't find any money? No jewels or...there wasn't any money?"

"Nope."

Bob Temple stands back up and studies him. He sniffs and wipes his nose and leans to the side and spits and then studies Francis some more.

"You sure?"

"About no money? Yeah I'm sure. Indians aren't even money kind of people. Don't really know what you were thinking in the first place."

Temple looks at him. "Can't say what it is, but there is a line in you I cannot figure. Nor do I especially like it."

"That's fine," says Francis.

"No. It is not fine."

"Then I'm sorry to hear it."

Bob Temple considers Francis. "I've a mind to frisk you, you know."

Francis winces with dismay. "It could get awkward," he says. He drums his fingers, twice—*thrat, thrat*—against the butt of his pistol. Temple glances at his own pistol belt, coiled up beside the saddlebags where he slept.

Bob Temple studies him. After a time he clicks his tongue, loudly. This is something he does. Francis doesn't know if it's a mannerism or a tic or what if anything it means. Bob Temple says, "I find out you're swindling me, and I swear to you. You will not like it one bit."

"You done threatening me?"

Bob Temple nods slowly, looking at Francis, then looks down at the artifact in his hand, still nodding, only now that nodding means something different. "Well I reckon it's genuine," he says. "Certainly old. Could be we got something. And what's this one." He stoops to pick up the scythe-head. He looks it over. "Hell, I don't know the first thing about grave robbing. Maybe it's worth a million dollars."

"Maybe."

"All right." Bob Temple adjusts his hat, looking back the way they came. "Let's get these saddlebags loaded, load the horse. We'll go find out."

❧

Francis Blackstone and Bob Temple return toward town along a different trail, wary of doubling their tracks and drawing attention to their exploits at the mine. But Francis still has no horse, and Temple still does, and does not wait, and Francis quickly falls behind on the trail.

Thus Francis is alone when he comes upon the wagon.

The wagon is stacked with gunnysacks full of something. The yellow sun sits lower in the sky, rimming the vehicle in reddening light. The driver is a tall, mournful-looking man with an angular face and a wide straw hat and a long, bushy yellow beard but no mustache at all. He wears a beige, work-stained shirt with suspenders and black pants. Francis doesn't often come upon the Amish but they're around. The man holds the reins in the manner of one who is driving his horse at great speed, though he is quite parked, and openly studies Francis as Francis passes close enough to slap the side of the wagon in a cordial fashion while nodding to the man.

"Howdy."

The man just stares, and Francis continues on his way.

A little further on Francis comes to the levy, and beyond the levy the spring. The spring has water clear as glass with little bubbles rising up through the blue. It's like an oasis without the palm trees. Nothing grows around the spring and Francis doesn't know why because it's the most inviting water he's ever seen or heard of.

To wit:

Happily treading water in the spring are three Amish sisters in homespun, flower-print dresses. The dresses are apparently all cut from the same curtain. Same for the scarves on their heads. The three sisters are in fact identical in every way. They are paddling in place, each equidistant from the next to form a perfect triangle in the water, their dresses ballooning fascinatingly about them.

"Guten Tag," says the one in the middle.

Francis looks at the sisters. They wave in unison.

He doesn't know if this is real or what this is. He waits for something to happen but nothing happens.

They are still waving when he finally waves back and continues along the trail after Temple.

Inconvenience Store

The Hotel Whitmore was the first brick building in the town of Nowhere, Arizona. It was assembled in 1856, during the wave of rebuilding that followed the fire. There was nothing, the town a wasteland of char and blackened dreams, and then in a maelstrom of industry the town refashioned itself, right down to the name.

Directly opposite the hotel is the town's primary mercantile, known as Landry's, likewise erected upon the craters of disaster. It shares a plank wall with the Chinese laundry and another with the law office of Frederick Gateman Esq., all of it fronted by a porch and awning.

Francis halts in the road, observing the above, when he recognizes Bob Temple's horse at the hitching rail outside the mercantile. Francis enters the store. He sees Bob Temple in discussion with the proprietor, the two weapons arrayed on the counter between them.

As Francis comes up, Temple acknowledges him with a nod, raising a hand in restraint as if to say, I got this one, and returns his attention to the following conversation.

Bob Temple: "Go ahead, pick it up. Take a look. I think you'll agree these artifacts before you are one of a kind. Look at this one here. Look at that engraving. That's Navajo. An expert from Virginia told me it's over eighteen thousand years old."

The proprietor, whom everyone calls Landry and has always called Landry, but whose name no one has in fact ever bothered to ascertain, looks at the items arranged before him. He looks at Bob Temple. His eyebrows have an unfortunate, ironic arch to them, giving his face a permanently quizzical look.

"Now I look at you," continues Temple, "and I see a man of intelligence. I see a visionary, a captain of industry who comprehends that Man is hardwired to make a grab at limited and disappearing resources, and knows his customers know this too. I furthermore identify you, sir, as one who recognizes a once-in-a-lifetime opportunity when it presents itself. Now let's try this again. What's your best offer?"

"Well I sell mostly feed is all," says the proprietor. "Bird feed. Cow feed. Horse feed . . ."

The proprietor's mustache gives the impression of nosehairs that have run rampant and colonized the upper lip. It is an altogether ill-starred, vacuous face, one that suggests the man's brains might be replaced by buttons and no one would be the wiser, leading Francis to conclude that this present venture, so far as Landry and his store are concerned, has little hope of success.

"Goose feed. Goat feed. Sheep feed, which is the same. Hog feed. Alfalfa by the bundle. I got vegetables too. White turnips. Blue turnips. Carrots. Cornmeal."

"Let us cut to the chase, shall we?"

"All right."

"I am trying to sell you something. Do you understand that much?"

"All right."

"And this something is of great value. You can make money on this."

"All right."

"Now how much are you willing to offer for these price-less items?"

"Well I'm mostly interested in feed is all."

Bob Temple looks at the man, nodding. He sniffs and turns about. "You got any other stores in this town?"

New Plan

This one involves purchasing supplies from the mercantile and then travelling to some other place where their plunder might fetch an actual price.

Francis is standing about the shop, waiting for Temple to finish with his purchases, when he hears movement behind him. Francis turns about and there they are, facing him, all three in a row.

"We are the Amish triplets."

"Holy Jesus."

"We are here to sell potatoes."

"Well it's a good town for it. We eat a lot of potatoes," says Francis.

He peeks around the triplets and sees through the open door the figure of their father hanging about in the road beside the wagon filled with gunnysacks.

Francis returns his gaze to the girls. Their dresses are still wet from their swim. Springwater is pooling about their feet. These three puddles, positioned as they are, reflect perfectly the flower-print pattern of their dresses and give the overall impression the sisters are melting.

"You'll excuse me," says Francis, noting this phenomenon. He goes to Bob Temple.

"You see those girls," says Francis, nodding in the direction of the sisters. They are watching Francis, patiently awaiting his return.

Bob Temple is skimming through stacks of bluejeans on a shelf. "What of it?" Temple turns about and upon seeing the Amish triplets gives a little jump and squinches one eye as though searching for comprehension and finding none at all.

"They are witches," whispers Francis.

"Good God. Are you certain?"

"Watch this." Francis turns to the sisters, indicating Bob Temple with his thumb. "Where was this man born?"

"Dayton, Ohio," says the one in the middle.

Bob Temple grips Francis' shoulder.

"What's the true algebraic value of the number zero?" says Francis.

"Zero isn't a numeral. It's a placeholder for the infinity of nonexistence."

"How come my friend here clicks his tongue before he speaks?"

"He has a gap between his teeth. His habit is to suck upon it, and the click is an unfortunate spinoff of said habit."

"See?"

"Yes I do."

"I think we should ask them about the loot."

"All right."

"We have about us two items," says Francis. "Two items we'd like very much to sell but aren't too sure —"

"Your fortune lies elsewhere," says the one in the middle, and the two on either side nod in cheerful complicity.

"Okay," says Francis. "And where might that be?"

"You must go far away and come back again."

"Okay. And can you point that out on a map for us?"

The proprietor, who is watching all this with no particular look upon his face, offers up a map of Nowhere and its environs from behind the counter. He scrapes a pencil tip and places that down as well, and for the next few minutes the triplets and Francis and Temple and the proprietor together crowd about the map as they discuss the route ahead and draw a rough pathway across the macho, shiny desolation of America's west.

"Your fortune lies…here," says the middle sister, pointing to a town called Chesterville. It's in California.

"This is very helpful," says Francis, folding the map and nodding to Temple. Then: "Any suggestions regarding the two items we mentioned?"

"They are best left in our care."

Francis and Temple share a look.

Temple leans in to his ear, whispering, "I think maybe that's how it works," he says. "Supposed to give them something in exchange."

Temple and Francis quietly discuss between them the pros and cons of transferring grave-robbed loot to a coven of witches. At worst, they conclude, a bad thing will happen. And people, whole enterprises in fact, have moved forward on softer, less convincing arguments.

"All right," says Temple. "Which one of you wants the knife and which one the double-edged scythe?"

But before Francis and Temple can depart the store, the middle sister calls out and Francis and Temple turn about in the doorway.

The sisters expertly switch places, middle one to the side, side one to the middle. Francis suspects they've been doing this all along.

"When you get there," says the one, "look for the building marked liked so."

She draws the letter *M* in the air. Then the letter *C*.

"Manhattan Company?" says Temple. "But that's a bank."

The triplets just look at him, as if to say, My good friend, where else are fortunes kept?

✿

Standing together in the road, just outside the mercantile, Temple squints into the sun as though pondering the time of day.

"So I guess it's Chesterville then. Off to Chesterville, California."

Francis nods, likewise observing the sky.

Temple says, "We're going to knock over a bank we'll need some assistance."

"I know it."

Temple spits. "I know a few men," he says.

After a moment he adds, "Actually I don't. Most the good bad ones are in jail."

Temple stands there beside Francis, rubbing his jaw. An idea strikes him. He actually jolts at the thought. "There is one fellow," he recalls. "Out of Barlow. Ever heard of John Lake? Used to do banks with a little lapdog on a leash. Wrote poetry. Wore a bowtie on the job, that kind of thing."

"Out of Barlow?" says Francis.

"Not a bad guy, so far as badguys go."

"But Barlow?"

Temple shrugs. "It's a bit of a hike."

"Nah," says Francis. "I think I got something better."

Show Me

Later that same afternoon, Francis is crouched on the sill of his bedroom window, hanging halfway in. He's waving for Samuel to hurry.

But Samuel is not hurrying. Samuel closes the bedroom door and then locks it behind him. He stands with arms crossed, middle of the room. He looks ridiculous, large as he is, like some ironical colossus filling the space between two children's beds.

"If Father finds out you're here," says Samuel, "he'll either lock you in or throw you out. He knows you took his pistol."

"Grab your things. We're leaving," says Francis.

"Where we going?"

"Get Ned too."

"Where we going?"

"Just get your things."

"You still playing at outlaw?"

"It's not about that," says Francis.

Samuel looks at him. "Talk to me."

"Fine."

Francis describes in simplest terms the lay of their future. This includes, as all futures do, the accumulation of many small events into a solitary, larger one that may or may not add up in the final math but nonetheless colours the whole of the project, failed efforts included, with the worthwhile stamps of passion, lunacy, discovery, and the possibility of requited love. A life, in short.

Samuel sits heavily on the bed. "A girl," he says.

"It's not just any girl."

"All this for a girl?"

Francis shrugs. "There is a little more to it than that. But if you like, okay. It's for a girl."

Samuel glances resignedly at Francis, and then past him and out the window. "So does this girl have a name?"

"Probably."

Samuel closes his eyes.

"It's just a name, Samuel. It's not who she really is."

"I want you to listen to me."

"Okay."

"You're listening?"

"I am," says Francis.

"Good. We are not going to California to rob a Manhattan Company bank. I don't care who she is."

"What are you doing that's so important?"

"Nothing at all."

"Then give me one reason why," says Francis.

"Because it's plain stupid, that's why. Plus we don't know how."

"How is a detail. It's not reason in itself."

"How about ten-to-one we'll end up in federal prison?"

Francis sits down on the sill, both legs dangling. He carefully opens the flap of his satchel and peeks within. "I have a lucky charm here says otherwise."

"You have a what?" says Samuel.

For explanation, Francis now reaches into the satchel and removes the lamp. He holds it before him.

Francis says he's made an agreement of sorts, a kind of pact with another—the full nature of which he can't rightly reveal. But this little item holds the promise of it all: his fortune, the girl, and even a bit of special help when they need it.

"It may not be much to look at," says Francis. "But sometimes you just have to —"

"Show me."

Francis looks at his brother. He grins.

❧

A demonstration then, hasty though cogent, followed by a moment of disbelief, another of awe, and finally another of reconciliation, and then the two are out the window together, brothers again; a hat, a satchel, and a clean pair of white socks.

Wild

The first meeting of the gang takes place in a changing room of the town theatre. There is no performance till evening so the room is decidedly private. The garish, plumed dresses and violently elaborate hats of cancan dancers hang from pegs on the wall. There are mirrors. Also a solitary table around which Bob Temple, Ned Runkle, and the Blackstone brothers presently sit in discussion regarding the confluence of their ambitions as professional adventurers.

The meeting is going roundly well until the topic of names comes up. A proper name can make or break a gang, as we all know, and a newly minted venture of this sort cannot always accord on all points.

Here we already see the first signals of disharmony.

Bob Temple slugs back the last of his beer and clicks the empty down on the table and says to the empty, one hand upon it, "I reckon we'll go as the Bob Temple Gang. As my name already has some mileage."

"Nah," says Francis, distractedly touching at the bottle sweat on his bottle.

Bob Temple grins distastefully and furrows his brows. "No?" he says. Temple is seated directly opposite Francis Blackstone, Samuel and Ned to either side.

Francis continues to touch at the bottle.

"You know," says Temple, "you are not required to contest me on every little detail."

Francis kicks the chair back onto two feet, balancing there. He looks at Temple. "I was picturing something different," he says. "A whole other name actually."

"Did you now! You ever rob a bank, son?"

"No. Have you?"

Francis clacks his chair back down.

Temple just looks at Francis. He tilts his head to one side, then the other, squinting as though into some vexatious puzzle he is not at all pleased about having to solve.

"Listen, I'm going to run with a bunch of greenhides then I get to sheriff this thing, and that means my name goes top of the sign. Anyone got a problem with that?"

Temple glances challengingly about the table. Ned shrugs. Samuel opens both palms.

Francis raises a finger. "Right here."

Bob Temple sucks his teeth.

With an abrupt, decisive motion Temple clacks his pistol onto the table, sits back in his chair and then nudges the butt of the pistol around until the barrel, lying on its side, is nevertheless directed at Francis.

Francis looks at him and says, "How you know I don't have one just like it under the table?"

"Do you?"

Francis says nothing.

Temple picks the pistol up and points it proper at Francis. "I pull this trigger and you fall down dead."

"Yeah. But I pull mine and your balls hit the floor. So let's put it to a vote. I vote Francis Blackstone Gang. What do you say Bob Temple?"

Bob Temple's face goes hard and red. His tongue is actively working his cheek.

"You are wild," he says.

After a moment Bob Temple releases his grip on the

pistol and it swings freely on his trigger finger, that finger in the ring, until the pistol rocks ineffectual and barrel down between them.

"We're unanimous?" says Francis.

Temple spits on the planks.

Ned and Samuel mutter, nod.

Francis says, "Admit it, Bob. The name of Blackstone does have a ring to it."

"It is debatable."

"The author of this story appears to feel different."

"I'll grant you that," says Temple, staring sullenly at his empty bottle, tilting it back and forth with one finger.

"Tell you what," says Francis. "We'll go as the Blackstone Temple Gang. Which is, truth be told, what I was after to begin with."

Temple sniffs and thinks on this a moment and sits forward and nods to himself before declaring his feelings on the matter are perhaps in repair. He believes he endorses the name. He tries it aloud.

"Blackstone Temple Gang..." He taps contemplatively upon the table.

Indeed, he endorses it fully. In fact Bob Temple has been thinking on this same name himself, before this conversation even, so there is little need for anyone at the table to recount the day's events, or how exactly — for who could remember such details? — they struck upon the agreed appellation.

"Right. We're a gang proper then," says Francis, scritching the chair back from the table. "Ned, if you'd round up those horses we discussed. I know your uncle's got more than a few. Bob, you may as well see about the tab. And Samuel, if you'd reach me my belt back there. On the peg, just behind Bob."

Samuel passes it to him.

Francis stands and takes the pistol belt with its pistol and secures it about his hips.

"All right. Let's go hit a bank."

❖

The sun is nearly down when they mount up, four horses in a line, clomping down the only road out of Nowhere. The light on the horizon is simmering red. The facade of each building glows in orange isolation, everything is glorious, everything is right.

As they pass the Hotel Whitmore, Francis trailing at the rear, he tips his hat back and glances up at a third-floor window.

Is she watching? Francis can't see inside for the glare.

But there is a Genesis of stars twinkling across the surface of the pane; this, despite there being not a star in the sky to match it.

CHAPTER THREE

Their Slick Muscles Stretched

The first days west are uneventful. The canyons go up and the canyons go down and the horses keep their heads. The Blackstone Templars tread on. Samuel and Ned are agreeable to the journey and talk much but are still wary of Bob Temple. The gunslinger's reputation looms over them like a dank and malodorous blanket.

"I heard he scalped an angel," whispers Ned from atop his saddle.

Samuel looks at him, then looks away. "I don't even know what to say to that."

"Just what I heard. What people are saying."

They ride on.

It's difficult for them not to ponder on Francis as well. For Samuel, it's as though his brother of many years were suddenly replaced by some pluck or charm, some iconoclastic glow. How does this happen?

Or maybe it's only that circumstances, like a spotlight, have at last revealed what was always in place. Whichever the case, Samuel recognizes in his brother a thing or quality he himself does not possess. He can't help but wonder how he got passed over on this.

Ned speculates aloud on what his uncle will do when he discovers three horses have gone missing. And not just any three horses. Genuine Appaloosas, of which there can't be more than a handful in the state.

"Once we have our fortune, we'll pay him back in kind," offers Francis.

Ned's chosen horse is a gelding, sleek, with a blizzardy pattern of stark white on black. Ned names the horse Ned.

Samuel's mare is the opposite, like a Dalmatian, with countless black spots on a field of white. He tries out many names but settles on Sybil. He claims she stares at him in the strangest way, as though she can read his deepest thoughts. Or even his future. She's given Samuel the chills on more than one occasion, making him a bit self-conscious about what passes through his mind.

The standout somehow falls to Francis. A high-heeled seductress in a black velvet coat. The sheen of it literally picks up rainbows in the sun. And stamped upon her haunch is the Appaloosa trademark, a constellation of brilliant white flecks like a starry night.

Francis doesn't name her right off. It seems wrong, somehow, that his mare should have a name before his girl does. He holds off, dubbing her Beautiful in the meantime. Come here, Beautiful. Let me brush that coat. Anyhow who is Francis to say this shining, transcendent creature will be forevermore called Bonnie or Blackie or Tips when she no doubt already holds some title among the pantheon above.

Bob Temple keeps with his chestnut gelding, which he claims has many names depending on his mood. It's served him well enough. Frankly speaking though, Temple doesn't care for this horse or any other. They are animals. They are sweating, stinking mediums of conveyance and no more. He frowns upon any talk of friendship or loyalty or intelligence. He just wants a horse to go where he aims it and be agreeable and make no more demands upon his attention than are necessary.

Toward evening on the tenth day out, they hit a stretch of desert like none before. The saguaro cactuses stand twenty feet high and cleave like weird, green tritons—malformed monuments to an underworld. The ground is anodyne, white. There is water out there, for the gang encounters coyotes aplenty, and antelope too, but the water itself eludes them as they cross one dry wash after another. They make camp in a forlorn, sun-cracked gully. The night is thirsty and miserable.

Lying wrapped in his wool poncho, the firelight crackling at his back, Francis quietly tips the clay lamp out of the sock he keeps it wrapped in. He cradles it in his hands. He touches at the handle. The spout. He thinks the markings are especially pretty.

He runs his finger along its belly.

Something to Hold On To

Next morning, the gang rises to find another camp beside their own. An old Indian man is tinkering about within a makeshift tent not twenty feet away. No one heard him arrive. Ned voices his surprise, and even a touch of alarm, but Francis assures him there is nothing to fear. Presently the man makes a fire and beckons everyone over with a gesture of the hand so subtle as to be imperceptible. The mere whiff of an invitation, which Francis vibes nonetheless. He is first to join the neighbouring fellow and the others soon follow.

The old man's fire is small and the flames near invisible in the quickly brightening sun. He shares water from a canteen, of which he possesses many.

The old man wears his long hair in a topknot gathered toward the front of his head. He carries a tomahawk at his side. The deep fissures in his face are a landscape. He wears several large lobes of turquoise about his neck, and his buckskin blouse is embroidered with seeds and stones and other small, bright things. He is somewhat extraordinary to look upon, beautiful even.

He tells them he is a storyteller. He is on the path of his story—the story of his life. His story began in one place and goes to another, and where it crosses the reader's path, such as here, the two are conjoined. That is why he knows the gang's path too, so far as it can be known at all. Also, he is following a jaguar.

"What's a jaguar?" asks Francis as a bowl of cornmeal goes round the fire.

Bob Temple puts the bowl to his mouth and rakes in a mouthful. While chewing, he says, "It's a big cat, like a cougar. They come up from Mexico. You hardly see them these days, but they cross the mountains sometimes and end up wandering these parts."

The old man says he has been following the jaguar for some days. It too is part of this story.

The old man sets out tortillas to warm on the rocks beside the fire. He sets out a bowl of peppers. Also a bowl of chopped onions, and another of rice or something like it. Ned boils coffee in a broad iron skillet.

It is a generous breakfast. The boys roll tortillas with cornmeal and onions, rejecting the red peppers.

Samuel, somehow, still gets a mouthful. "Hot," he yells. "Jesus it burns. Who did this? You did this!"

Ned is laughing too hard to deny it.

"It's your own fault," says Francis, rolling another tortilla.

"How's it my fault? Give me some water."

"It's your own fault for thinking it won't happen. I can't even believe you're surprised. And just so you know, water won't help."

"Just give me some water!"

Ned, still laughing, passes a tin mug to Samuel, who tosses the water back into Ned's face.

"Give me another, quick!" says Samuel.

Twenty minutes later the meal is finished and Samuel is still griping about his belly. "I know it was you, you bastard," he says to Ned, who dissolves into merriment with each accusation.

"Like Francis says, you brought it on," says Ned. "Always playing mister high and mighty."

"All right," says Samuel. "Well it's a long journey to California. I hope you all sleep well tonight."

"Don't even think about it," says Ned.

"I'm just wishing you sweet dreams is all. And if something should happen you are free to wonder why. Can I take a couple of these for the road?" Samuel shows a handful of red peppers to the old man.

"That's not a bad idea," says Francis. He grabs a heaping handful of his own.

"What do you want peppers for?" says Samuel. "Ned already got me."

"I can think of about a hundred uses right off. And it's not really a game until someone gets hurt."

"Are you looking for war? I'm happy to war. I'll war with you, little brother."

Francis smirks.

"I'm serious," says Samuel.

"That's fine," says Francis, still smiling.

The old man watches all this, appearing to have no opinion on the matter, until he turns his gaze to the sky and says to no one in particular, "No deed stands apart."

Ned stops chewing. He's waiting for a punchline. When none arrives he grins nonetheless, gives a little shake of the head, and resumes chewing.

The old man holds perfectly still. "Do you hear my words?"

"Not really," says Ned, wiping his mouth on a sleeve. "Are we still talking peppers, or are we on to something else?"

The old man nods to himself, his gaze unchanged. "This is our story, yours and mine. But it is their story as well." With a sweep of his hand he indicates all those things perfect and flawed beyond the scope of natural vision, you and I included.

Ned folds a whole tortilla into his mouth. "You're totally losing me," he says around the tortilla. "But I thank you for the grub."

The old man rises and goes to the cargo arranged beside his tent. He rummages through an assortment of small sacks.

"Looks like you've upset our host," says Bob Temple. He sets down his bowl and rises too, stretching.

"Nah, he's fine," says Ned.

"Well I'm going to find me a tree," says Temple. "I'll be back shortly, and then we should pack up and get moving."

Temple goes off for a private moment, and when he returns the old man is again seated beside the fire. The boys are eating an ugly grey mash from a bowl.

"No, don't eat that," says Temple. But they have already eaten it.

Temple shakes his head. "All right, here we go. Hope you boys got something to hold on to."

America Strangely

Within the hour a palpable weirdness descends upon the camp. The old man sits with eyes closed, rocking to and fro. The three boys sit in the dirt, all in a row. They stare unblinking into the desert. They are at once quietly absorbed and acutely distractible. They turn their heads to the least nuance of sound. Also, they are stupid with sensation — mere imprints of humanity upon the softplate of consciousness. This is the first phase.

Renaissance clouds and their shadows pass in tandem over the earth. There are imperturbable beetles, and the pulse of embers in the fire, and other wonders too; tiny, greedy wonders that shock the beam of attention like a sheetsnap.

The wheeling silhouette of a condor blinks against the sun, and it matters. It matters like never before.

Ned laughs abruptly and goes quiet, his eyes wide with fascination. "Whoa..." he says. The others nod in solemn understanding.

Samuel begins sniffing at the air. "What's that smell?" he says.

No one responds.

"What's that smell?" he says again.

Bob Temple is packing his kit. He is not impressed. He pauses to sniff about and then returns to his task. "It's nothing," he says. "It's in your head."

"It's in my head?" shrieks Samuel, his eyes bulging with panic.

"No it's...There is no smell, you're imagining it," says Temple.

"I am sleeping in my belly," says Francis.

"I can smell my brain," says Samuel, pinching at clouds. "I am alive."

"Damn it. Will you all just...let's pull it together," says Temple.

Francis stands up. He doesn't go anywhere, he's just standing now.

Ned is all the while laughing hysterically, his face expressionless, sitting straddle-legged in the dirt.

"I'm going out," declares Francis.

"Out where," says Temple. "There ain't nothing out there. I'm ready to leave."

But Francis is already wandering into the desert. It's as though someone knows where he is going, though Francis is not that someone.

It doesn't matter much to Francis who that someone is. He trusts them emphatically.

❧

Francis walks until he stops walking. He turns in place and the only features in this desert are his own footsteps leading back to wherever he came from. Francis stares at the prints. Francis is breathing through his eyes. He stares at the prints and he is breathing through his eyes, and he stares at the heat sprays on the horizon. It is chanting. The horizon is chanting.

Francis hears a soft padding behind him and when he turns about there is a gigantic cat trotting directly across his footpath, and it watches Francis as it trots, carving an unhurried circle about his person. The cat is gold with black markings. It watches Francis as it circles, and Francis watches it. Francis is a peg planted in the centre of the world. Francis is a peg turning and turning with a fantastical cat going round, and after two such revolutions the cat drifts from its orbit and veers north across the hardpan, glancing over its shoulder once before padding off into the whitely glistening oblivion of wilderness.

Francis stands there for many moments, watching the cat grow stranger in the distant heat.

"Hot damn," he says.

Francis discovers he is waving.

He discovers he is crying with his hands.

❧

Bob Temple finally accepts the day is a wash. The gang is divided, frothing like cretins or else wandering the desert, and there is no use trying to corral them toward anything useful till the cactus runs its course.

He takes his pistol and goes out a ways and stacks up stones.

The sound of his pistol fire has an improbable quality, oddly muted against the hugeness of his surroundings.

His hand is numb and ringing when he stops and stares at the stacks, spilled as they are. He stands in place, looking about. He is alone.

An unfamiliar line of thinking introduces itself. It seems to come out of nowhere.

Bob Temple wonders, for the first time in his life, what it would be like if he were not himself. If he were someone else, per se, though still in this body.

Who would he be?

A wrong question, perhaps. The question is: *What* would he be?

Indeed, what *would* he be?

What would he *be*?

Bob Temple scratches his head with the barrel of his pistol.

Forgotten Worlds
, Remembered

Francis Blackstone is five years old. He is lying in bed, quietly watching the day's first light refract through the window and steal across the ceiling of his bedroom. His brother Samuel is in the next bed over, and Francis knows he's awake without even looking. He can just tell.

Samuel says to the same light on the ceiling, "I had the oddest dream."

"Tell me," says Francis. "I want to hear."

"I can't," says Samuel. "I wouldn't know how. But you were in it," he says. "You were in the dream too."

"I was?" says Francis.

"You were," says Samuel.

Francis lies there a while.

"Oh yeah," says Francis. "I kind of remember now."

Remembered Worlds
, Newly Walked

It's nighttime now and Francis has long since returned to camp. He sits cross-legged at the fire, the old Indian seated opposite. The two have been gazing at each other across the flames for a piece of time Francis cannot reckon. Minutes? Hours? The old man's eyes are objects bearing no relation to his head. They float, independent of the world, in calmly piercing incandescence.

"You have seen the jaguar?"

"Yeah, I saw it."

The old man nods without breaking his gaze. "Where did you see it?"

Francis points and the old man nods again, looking that way.

Francis hears Ned somewhere in the desert, singing at the top of his lungs. A coyote answers, and then a whole chorus of them.

The old man says, "I have seen the jaguar too. Many times."

"Yeah," says Francis. "It's something to see."

"It is good."

"It was interesting anyhow."

"No. It is good."

"All right," says Francis, "it was good." He snaps a twig and tosses half into the fire. "You mean the thing itself, or me seeing it?"

But the old man doesn't say. He's still looking off where Francis pointed.

�֎

Francis wakes the next morning and the old man is gone. His tent is gone, every sign of him gone except for the fire. Bob Temple is already heating water over the old man's coals. The sun is not yet risen, and the horizon is purple and flecked with stars.

There is a buzzing in Francis' head like a solitary bee, which he can almost track. Its movement is that clarified, that vibrant and pure. But he is also groggy, and he lies abed in his blankets, trying to puzzle out how Ned and Samuel, snoring each to a side, could have the identical bad breath. Exactly identical. And then Bob Temple toes Francis in the ribs and announces the coffee's ready.

The gang drinks their coffee in the dark, packs their kit, and loads the horses. They are on the trail by sunup.

While riding, Francis pulls alongside Ned. He's about to ask how his night went when he notices Ned's face is puffed up. His cheeks are an angry red and his eyes are nearly shut.

"Why's your face all swollen up like that?"

The Reason Ned's Face
Is All Swollen Up Like That

Ned and Samuel are tromping through the night, swatting at sagebrush in search of their camp. Despite the brightness of the old Indian's fire they've lost sight of it somehow. They are thirsty and sweaty and quite out of their minds.

The idea arises between them that they should no longer look for the camp but should instead lie down and observe the sky.

They lie down. They watch clouds shape and reshape and grow dusky and bright as they slide before the pale roundness of the moon. Ned becomes increasingly restless.

"It's like I can't lie still."

"Just relax. Get your breath," says Samuel.

"I can't. There's something wrong."

"There's nothing wrong, Ned."

"I think there is though."

"Tell me what's wrong."

"I don't know. Just something."

"Don't think about it," says Samuel. "Just think about something else. Try singing."

Ned begins singing. He sings loudly. The coyotes interrupt and he swats the air in frustration.

"I don't know. It's like I got ants all under my skin."

"Don't even go there," says Samuel. "You'll freak yourself out."

"All right. I'll calm down."

"I'm serious."

"All right."

They are quiet for a while.

Ned sits up. "I'm going berserk."

"You have to roll with it," says Samuel. "You'll drive yourself crazy."

Samuel finally sits up and glances over at Ned and then gasps in horror, his hand covering his mouth.

"What's wrong?" says Ned.

"It's nothing," says Samuel. "You might want to just, just brush yourself off there."

Samuel mimics the motion, brushing at his own face, neck, chest, arms, legs.

"And maybe move a little away from that mound."

Even Outlaws Need Math

Around midday, they're riding the rim of a canyon. There's no trail in these parts, so they just compass to the west, always west. The earth is red and raw with tiny balls of cacti and gleaming buttes and no clouds at all. Sinewy rabbits shade in the chaparral, burst from cover when the horses tread near.

Samuel keeps looking over his shoulder.

"What's up?" says Francis at his side. "What are you looking for?"

Samuel says he hears horses. But each time he turns there's nothing there.

"None of us is yet right in the head," says Francis. "You want some water?"

Ignoring him, Samuel peels away from the trail and trots to the lip of the canyon and peers down into it and then curses and hunches down and jerks the horse away. He gallops back to the others.

"They're down there!"

"Who's down there?" says Bob Temple, pulling up short.

"Don't know," says Samuel, "but they're a rough-looking lot, and there's a bunch of them."

The gang dismount and tether the horses. Bob Temple grabs the telescope from his saddlebags. They creep to the lip of the canyon and peek over the edge. This is what they see:

A trickling watercourse runs the floor of the canyon, and a line of riders moves single file along the bank, following the water upstream. The riders are dusty and bedraggled and moreover armed with pistols, rifles, hatchets, knives. The pinto in the rear is dragging a rough-hewn sledge with a large chest atop it.

"Thirty-eight, thirty-nine…I count forty of them," says Bob Temple, collapsing his telescope.

"That's a big gang," says Ned.

"Must be Stanley Carter," says Temple. "No one else runs an outfit that size."

"The Stanley Carter Gang?" says Samuel. "They the ones that hit a train out of Pittsburgh? And then rode it all the way to Cincinnati in the liquor car?"

"Not the brightest bunch. But they get the job done."

"What are they doing out here?" says Samuel.

"Must be something big," says Temple. "And probably has to do with that load they're dragging."

Temple extends the telescope again and glasses the sledge and collapses the telescope. "Come on," he says. "Let's follow."

They stay low, skulking along the rim of the canyon to keep pace with the Carter Gang. At a sharp bend in the canyon, they lose sight of the riders, who are now directly below, concealed by the incline. Some minutes pass. When the Carter Gang returns to view and resumes their journey upstream the pinto is free of its load, the sledge and its chest nowhere to be seen.

Francis and the others wait some minutes more and when the Carter Gang is thoroughly gone from sight they scout a trail down to the canyon floor. Reaching it, they immediately solve the mystery of the sledge. There is a cave in the wall of the canyon. The mouth of the cave is cunningly hidden with live brush but this is easily pushed aside.

Once inside the cave, the gang finds themselves standing not in a fusty, hollowed chamber but upon a precipice of wonder. A fantastic treasure-trove of loot.

"Light those braziers," says Bob Temple, and when the torches go up, a collective curse of astonishment fills the chamber.

"Looks like old pirate loot," says Temple, sifting through an upturned helmet filled with Spanish coins.

There are bolts of fine linen, candelabras, sceptres, tapestries, open chests of jewels and antique swords. There are oil paintings. The large chest that originally drew their attention rests against the wall of the cave, and Ned immediately crashes at the lock with the handle of an old sword.

Amid the clatter and knocking, Francis saunters among the hoard, eventually finding himself toward the rear of the cavern. From its furthest recesses, fresh routes branch here and there into the bowels of the world. This intrigues Francis, perhaps even more than the treasure. Some part of him is always enchanted by the deep and the dark. The unseen corridors that lead to the bottom of it all.

Eventually the knocking ceases, and Francis strolls back to the chest to learn what's been exposed.

Instead, he finds two men in hats standing in the cave entrance with pistols drawn, pointing at Samuel and Ned respectively, their hands in the air.

Bob Temple remains cool, his hands raised as well, while his eyes take in Francis' approach.

Francis steps cautiously forward, his own pistol levelled before him.

The taller of the two men nods at Francis and Francis stops.

"You're with them, I take it?" says the man.

"Yeah."

The man nods. "Stanley Carter," he says, indicating himself with his pistol. "And you are?"

"Francis Blackstone."

"Well Francis, you all found our loot. But we can't have thieves stealing from thieves now, can we? It's in the manual."

"What manual?"

The man looks vaguely put out. "It's a joke, son. There is no manual."

Francis says nothing.

Stanley Carter is probably six foot six and rail-thin with a ten-gallon hat and a mustache that curls at the ends and he wears a slicker coat down to his knees.

"So which one of us are you aiming at, Francis?"

"Both of you."

"Can't be both of us."

"Him then."

"Him? You mean Skidmore?"

"Is that his name?"

"Yeah, that's Skidmore."

"Well Skidmore then."

"All right," says Stanley Carter. "All right. Well let's see how this is going to play out. Now I shoot this fellow here... what's your name?"

"Samuel Blackstone."

"Blackstone. You two brothers?"

"Yes."

"Huh. All right, so I shoot Samuel here. And then you shoot…Skidmore. And then I shoot you. And then figuring your buddy here gets a shot off in the meantime—"

"Now hold on," says Skidmore. "We don't even know how fast he is."

"That's relevant," says Stanley. "That's a relevant question. How fast would you say you are, son?"

"Pretty fast," says Francis.

"Pretty fast. As in medium?"

"Medium to speedy."

"Medium to speedy." Stanley and Skidmore confer with a brief glance, and then Stanley says, "As an example, could you, say, hit two cans—one and then the other, pop, pop —without taking aim? Or would you need to sight the second shot?"

"At what distance are we talking?"

"Normal shooting range distance. Twenty yards."

Francis scratches behind his ear. "Maybe not twenty," he says. "But fifteen. Fifteen for sure. And let's be clear. You're not fifteen yards from me now. I'd say you're more like twelve."

"Or ten," says Ned. "Looks like ten to me."

"Ten?" says Skidmore. "I don't think y'all even know what a yard is."

"And I think you might do with a pair of spectacles," says Ned.

"That boy," says Skidmore, jabbing his finger toward Francis, "is standing fifty feet from me right now. In yards, that is sixteen and change. Do you dispute the math?"

"I do," says Ned. "Hell yes I do."

"Then I am embarrassed for you," says Skidmore. "That's all I got to say. Where'd you go to school? A hole in the ground?"

"Maybe," says Ned. "Are you aware your head is shaped like someone beat on it for a while over the beak of an anvil?"

"Now let's not bicker on this one," says Stanley. "I think we can all agree the distance sits somewhere between ten and twenty yards. We'll split the difference, call it fifteen, but there is still lighting to consider. And frankly speaking, we have the upper —"

Bob Temple slings his pistol and fires twice from the hip and both men buckle and go down with a grunt.

It was so fast Francis can't believe it. It was so fast Francis' eyes aren't even sure what they saw. It was like lightning, just a blur of movement.

Francis didn't even know such a thing could be done.

❧

"Those were heart shots," says Ned, standing with arms loose at his sides. "Both of them. You just aced two men, right through the heart."

Bob Temple says nothing. He's still staring at the fallen.

Samuel too is looking at the dead with something like stunned awe.

Ned says, "That was some fine shooting, Bob. That was something else."

Bob Temple clicks his tongue, essentially breaking the spell, and relaxes his stance and holsters his pistol. He then marches to the fallen with cold efficiency and retrieves their pistols. He hands one each to Samuel and Ned without ceremony and then marches back to Francis, coming to an abrupt halt before him.

"Can I ask you something?"

"Yeah."

"Why did you not shoot?"

Francis says nothing.

A moment passes, and then Samuel snorts and shakes his head.

"Something funny?" says Bob Temple.

"I think there's something you need to know about my brother," says Samuel.

"Oh yeah? What's that?"

"He's never shot a gun in his life."

At that moment the pounding of hooves reverberates from the trail beyond the cave. Temple's eyes rise to the ceiling, as though the sound originates there. He clicks his tongue.

"That'll be thirty-eight others, I suspect," he says. "We better make for it."

"Make for it?" says Ned. "But look at all this treasure."

"Worthless if you're dead," says Temple. "Come on."

❧

They charge their horses up the canyon's west slope. The grade is steep and rocky and mostly exposed with only the odd boulder or juniper tree for cover. The Carter Gang tries to pick them off with rifles from the streambed below. Francis feels like a duckboard at a shooting gallery, going back and forth on the switchbacks while the Carters make a sport of him. He can hear their hoots of enthusiasm each time a bullet sings off the shale above his head. All the while Ned keeps whispering, "Our first shootout. Our first shootout."

Toward the top of the trail they achieve a cluster of twisted pine. Bob Temple drops from his horse and lies flat on his belly, taking shelter behind the spokes of a deadfall. "Go now," he yells, and covers their escape with a fabulous salvo, and then he too is mounted and racing for the canyon's rim, and they crest it together and kick their horses into a standing gallop over a tableland of scrubby mesa extending halfway to the horizon.

A low rise to the east develops into a ridgeline of granite, and before long it towers above them. Temple guides the company up a trail to this higher ground in anticipation of the Carter Gang, who appear on cue beneath them as they top the mesa, a tight grouping of horses running parallel to our heroes, firing at will and yelling insults of the lowest variety.

Bob Temple fires repeatedly as he rides, the boys tossing Temple their own pistols as he shoots empty, reloading the pistols for him and tossing them again, the spent chambers hot in their hands, until Temple makes a glorious shot that knocks the hat off one fellow and onto the head of another. Many will say this is not possible, and so it would seem, which is precisely why its effect is sufficient to bring both parties to a halt.

The Carter Gang mills about at the base of the ridge, esteeming the man with the new hat, the sizable hole within it, the man himself smiling broadly at his good fortune and passing the item about for all to see while the Blackstone Templars regard him from the ridge above.

The fellow presently holds his prize aloft. He looks up at Bob Temple. "I will ask you," he says, "if that was the intended result of your aim, or if you consider it the spooky collaboration of chance and hazard? And if you cannot answer, or will not, I put this second question to you. Can the spectacle be repeated?"

Bob Temple gazes down at them. "You should all go away now," he says.

Answers he of the new hat, "You killed two of our men. We can't go away. Not until we shoot you."

Francis nudges his horse forward. "Shoot us dead, or just shoot us?"

The Carter Gang conducts a brief conference. After this conference, it is the voice of a woman, gruff as it is, that answers on their behalf. "Dead is the preference," she announces. Though she's quick to add they are open to discussion, and can hammer out the details once everyone is within proper pistol-firing distance.

Now the Blackstone Templars circle their horses to likewise confer.

Bob Temple's answer: "We still think you should go away."

"You should come down here," says another man, "and quit all this riding about so that we may shoot you."

"This debate," says Temple, "is going nowhere with a flourish."

"You will not comply with our request?"

"No."

"Then we have no more words for you, sir."

"As you like."

"We could try to shoot one another where we stand," suggests a fourth and not very creative fellow. "That's one way. Just thinking out loud."

"I got an idea," says Ned. "Why don't you go boil your heads!"

Upon this statement, Bob Temple cuts loose with his pistols and the Carter Gang scatters and in the ensuing chaos the Blackstone Templars charge down the far side of the mesa and enjoy a reckless though successful getaway into the Sonoran wilderness.

Dearest girl,

How are you? I am doing well. I am having many
adventures, which I hope to share with you one day.
I think I may have already grown an inch. Are you
taller too? Do you still comb your hair at night?
I hope so. I think of you often and with affection.

I don't know what other sorts of things people
put in their letters, so I'll tell you some of the things
I have seen. This way you can come to know me,
even if we are apart.

Once, when I was a boy, I saw four Indians carry
a dead pony through town. When my father asked
the Indians where they were going they said east.

Another time, I saw a girl in a long wool coat and
a pair of men's boots that were too big for her feet.
She was flying a kite from her horse. It was in an
open field and she was all alone. The girl's kite was
red, and the look on her face said she owned
the world.

Just last week we came upon a logging camp.
It was in the foothills, a little north of Pico Grande.
There were perhaps ten loggers in the camp. They
were gathered about a morning fire, while another
man, presumably dead, lay wrapped in cloth beside
a freshly dug trench.

There had been an accident of some kind. The
loggers gave no details, but as we were preparing our
own coffee among their coals, we were included in a
service of sorts. Words were spoken. A verse or two

was recited, followed by a hymn. And then the goods
of the dead fellow were distributed among the living.
Once again, our chance turnout at their fire made
that our hosts should include us. Their goodwill,
I think, was not grudging but real, as their hospitality
was true in many other ways — but I'll add only this,
because I now understand it as fact:

It is not possible to eat a dead man's chocolates
and not ponder your life, your purpose, if only
a little. The bittersweetness of such a moment is
hard to shoulder. I mention this now, hoping you
can imagine yourself by my side, feeling as I feel.
Thinking as I think.

Our friend Bob Temple was first to leave the
loggers' fire, and he offered no parting thanks or
goodbye. I was not so unaffected, and stayed on
for the morning. I considered this man, this dead
man whom I did not know, and wondered if he was
complete in his life — if he felt complete. Would he
have said so, if he had the chance? Did he have the
chance?

I have the chance. So I'm taking it now, with you,
wishing to be as honest as I am able:

I am not complete. I know that.

I've only just begun to live, to step into my life.
And while the goal is clear — that I should find my
fortune and return to you — the path leading to this
goal is like the wind. I can't see it. At times I can't
feel it. I almost never understand it. But I know it.
I always know it.

I have to stand on this knowing. It's all I have. And though it's very small — sometimes very very small — it's enough. Because knowing, I'm coming to understand, is what I am. What I'm meant to be made of. And the first thing I ever *knew*, was you.

Can you guess when that was? I will tell you.

We were six.

That may surprise you. It means you've lived more than half your life in another person's heart, and you didn't even know it. We met that day, when you visited our schoolhouse. Do you remember? You were only there for one morning, so I understand if you don't recall. They put you in the front row. I sat directly behind.

Miss Dooley had just passed out inkpots. We were told real ink from India was expensive, and we were to make the ink last. She went to the blackboard, and at that moment, you turned around in your seat and faced me for the first time. You were wiggling your front tooth. Your eyes were bright with excitement. You tried to talk but I couldn't understand, as most of your fist was in your mouth. You kept jabbering at me and your tooth was twisted all wrong, and you reached for my hand so I might give it a try — and that is when you knocked over my inkpot.

Ink went everywhere. My lap. The floor. It poured into my satchel and over my books. But when I looked down at the mess, I didn't see black ink spreading everywhere.

I saw the black of night skies. I saw stars and planets and all the rest. Each little puddle—on the desk, on the floorboards—was a peephole to some corner of the zodiac. And reflected in each puddle was you.

You were looking down at your palm where the tooth now lay. It was like a tiny animal curled up to sleep.

Afterward, when I went to Miss Dooley, I asked for a fresh bottle of universe because the last one spilled, and she promptly sent me home with a note and that was that. I didn't even glimpse you again for another year.

From that moment on, my only reason for anything was you. Because I am what I know. And you were the first thing I ever knew.

I believe I'm becoming what I am—in you.

That is what I wanted to tell you,
Francis Blackstone

Magnetizing the Real

Free of pursuit, the Blackstone Templars recommence their journey west, leaving Arizona behind and shearing off the bottom corner of Nevada as they make for the highlands of the central California border. This takes many days. Along the way they have various thoughts, laugh loudly and bicker, ride side-saddle, tell stories, ford treacherous rivers and canyons too, in general aligning themselves with all that is real, all that is good, all that gives colour to life's most vibrantly absurd arc:

Youth.

Oh, how it shines like the pain of champions.

And Out of Nowhere, a Dog.

It comes trotting out of the desert, its shape and movement slowly resolving from the heat sprays until it stands panting before them, tongue lolling to one side, looking up at Samuel, who is parked on his horse.

"It's a dog," says Samuel.

Everyone looks at the dog.

They look out into the desert, the vast inert nothingness of it. They look back at the dog.

Samuel rubs his jaw, still looking at it.

Bob Temple uncorks his waterskin and drinks from it and hangs it on the horse. He leans his forearm on the pommel, glancing around at nothing in particular. He has no special feeling for dogs.

But the dog continues to sit there, demanding in its way, the quiet fortitude of it, that this mystery be acknowledged before moving on.

Ned finally crosses his hands atop the pommel. "Well should we eat it?"

"Shut your mouth," says Samuel. "You don't eat a dog."

"Why not eat it?" says Ned. "We're bad guys now. We have to do these sorts of things."

"We are not bad guys," says Francis. He climbs down from his horse. The dog lies down in the dirt, ears flat against its head.

Francis squats down beside the dog and scratches its heaving side, looking off toward the horizon, scanning it.

"Now where did you come from?"

The dog leads them north. The gang follows.

Bob Temple finds his mind wandering as they ride, his eyes following the dog's legs — something fascinating in their movement, their ease of rhythm and accord — without really seeing the dog at all. Or rather, he is thinking about dogs in general, but not this one before him.

Like everyone else, he's heard it said that man's best friend is a dog. He is doubtful. Mainly because he's seen the so-called evidence for this statement, and any tenderness a loyal, smiling, bright-eyed hound might provoke in him is foreshortened by the knowledge that if Bob Temple fell dead of a coronary, say, on the sunlit floorboards of some cabin in the woods, once all the food was consumed his devoted pal would not hesitate to eat him.

This sours things for Bob. How could it not do so for others?

A mile into their sortie the dog breaks without warning into a dead sprint, disappearing over a low hummock.

"Whoa whoa," says Temple, snapping free of his reverie and raising a hand. "Let's slow it down. Best find out what's on the other side before charging up that hill."

The gang dismounts and tethers the horses and crawls up the hilltop on their bellies. No need for the telescope this time. Directly below them is a small homestead.

The homestead is an unloved, unlovely, dilapidated thing. It has a rusted watertank in the yard and a corncrib and a creaking windtower that is long past operation. There is a small field, fallow. There is also a corral made of fieldstones and what appear to be geese inside, a few chickens pecking about the porch. The dog sits proudly among them.

But there is nothing else around. It's as inhospitable a place as one could imagine. The gang discusses this fact, and none among them can figure the line of reasoning that would prompt a person, no matter how adventurous at heart, to establish anything at all in this particular location.

The four of them lie on their bellies, observing all this.

"They got a cow," says Ned.

Samuel peers at him. "What is with you? Get your head out of your—"

"Why not a cow? It's made of beef. We all eat beef."

"Can you butcher a cow?"

"I can do many things."

"Can you butcher a cow?"

"We are not slaughtering any cows," says Temple. "Besides, they got a gaggle of geese. We get ahold of one of them and we're good to go."

"We haven't heard from Francis yet," says Ned. "You're the voice of reason here, Francis. What's on the menu?"

Francis says nothing for a while. Then he says, "Could do with a drumstick."

Temple sucks his teeth. "Come on," he says. He rises to a crouch and sneaks down the hill. One by one the others follow.

The dog barks when they reach the yard. They take cover behind the corral but the dog keeps barking.

Ned hisses at it. "Come here, boy," he whispers. "Come here."

Upon hearing Ned's voice, the dog tilts its head back and bays.

"Shit. Now or never," says Temple.

They leap over the corral and the geese go wild, scattering in an uproar. Temple lunges for the nearest gander. Instead of fleeing, the gander rears and spreads its voluminous wings. It charges.

"Ho, Jesus," whispers Temple, dancing away in terror. He slips in the mud, landing with a squelch and they are upon him like jackals, pecking fearlessly, ferociously. It is just horrible.

"Got one!" cries Samuel, wrangling it by the neck. He's grabbed the biggest goose and maybe the biggest goose ever, a titan among birds, and it goes straight for the eyes. Samuel tosses the brute and winds up scuttling in the mud beside Temple just as a third goose leaps for Ned's face in a blizzard of wings. He screams and swats.

Francis breaks for the corncrib. He throws the door open. The shelving is stacked chest-high with corn. He stuffs them down the neck of his shirt till he is pregnant with corn, his pockets bulging, and he's loading the crook of one arm when he hears the crash of a shotgun from the porch. Turning, he sees a shirtless, unshaven old man in trousers and suspenders standing upon the steps, yelling obscenities as he ejects the empty from the chamber. He shoves in a fresh load. He aims the shotgun and fires into the corral, spattering mud and goose shit.

"Run!" yells Samuel, hopping the corral.

Temple clambers over, Ned in pursuit. Francis races to catch up, dropping one ear of corn after another.

The Sierras

They ride slowly, side by side in defeat, their faces covered in masks of filth.

Temple holds the reins in one hand, staring straight ahead. "Well that was a wreck of a job."

The plain ahead is charmed with dustdevils. Clouds gather in burning bars of tangerine. The sun descends.

Samuel maintains they were not normal geese back there. They had something in them, and therefore the botch wasn't exclusively on the gang.

Ned too suspects a demon aspect at work, and now recalls a distinct red light coming off the eyes of one goose.

Francis takes an ear of corn from his pocket and shucks it.

"What you got there, Francis?" asks Samuel.

"Bit of corn." Juice squirts from his mouth as he bites into it.

"Got another?"

He reaches into his pocket and tosses an ear to his brother.

"You got a third?" says Ned.

Francis shakes his head, focused on the corn in his hand.

Through the distant haze they can make out the solidity of mountains, just a shapeless smudge on the horizon, vastly purpled by twilight.

"That's the Sierras," says Temple, nodding in their direction. "We probably crossed into California last night."

"You ever been this far west?" asks Francis.

"Hell," says Temple. "I am the west."

After a moment's thought, Ned asks, "You ever been to Tombstone?"

"I have."

"How about San Francisco?"

"On numerous occasions."

"How was it?" asks Ned.

"Just a big hairy town. Probably eat you alive."

Samuel says he heard the restaurants in San Francisco have women that'll sit on your lap and cut your steak while you eat.

"Yeah, well," says Bob Temple. "Maybe that is what I am talking about."

"I'd still like to see it," says Ned.

"Trust me," says Temple, "when I say there is no luck waiting for you there, Ned."

The four ride for a time, their eyes on the mountains.

Ned is struck by a thought. "You know what we should do?" he says. "We should start an avalanche."

"That is a great idea," says Samuel, slowly shaking his head.

"I thank you."

"And what exactly would be the purpose?" says Samuel.

"Are you serious?" says Ned.

"Because it's not clear to me."

"I'm in," declares Francis.

"There you go," says Ned. "That's two of us. Welcome aboard, Francis."

Samuel frowns. "How are you two going to start an avalanche?"

"That is private information," says Ned. "Reserved for those involved. Right, Francis?"

Samuel thinks on this. "All right. Let's hear about it."

"So you're in?"

A spirited discussion ensues. Brilliant ideas are floated. These ideas range from the complex levering of great boulders to firing pistols in unison from atop a snow-covered cornice.

"Not one of you has got the least idea what you're talking about," says Temple. He's remained silent until now, and this is the first they've heard from him on the topic.

"Well, speak your mind," says Ned. "It's an open forum."

"The only way," says Temple, "and I mean the only way to set a proper avalanche is with a stick of dynamite."

Ned glances at the others, and then back at Bob Temple. "Do you have any?"

Temple's eyes remain fixed on the mountains, the path leading to them, as he tugs his hat down tight on his forehead.

"Yes I do."

How to Start an Avalanche

It's next morning when they reach the foothills of the Sierra Nevada range. The foothills are big, even the little ones are big, and the mountains soar ever higher. The base of the range is trees all over, mostly oak and pine, while the upper reaches of the slopes are mantled in an extravagant white glitter.

Their path climbs from the desert floor into the gradual shade of sparse wood, then forest proper. The temperature drops. Blue jays squawk and squirrels fuss. Where shafts of sunlight hit the forest floor, the perfume of pine needles wafts in spicy waves.

The gang enters a small clearing of wild wheat and halts their horses. There is a perfect view of the mountains above where blinding, hysterical light refracts off alpine snow.

While his horse tugs at the meadow, Bob Temple cranes his neck to take in the view. He resets his hat. "I will now direct your attention to the mountain before you."

Everyone follows Temple's gaze to the slope above. "This is important, so listen closely. No one else is going to tell you this stuff. Now you got two kinds," he says. "Two kinds of slides. You got your—"

"How do know about any of this?" asks Samuel.

"Just listen. You got two types. You got your surface type," he continues, "which is dry snow sliding over wetter stuff. Comes about after a heavy storm or an abrupt rise in temperature. Then you got your full-depth slides. More impressive. That's what we're after. Now you see there?"

Temple points to the saddle between two peaks. "What do you see?"

"Which part are you pointing at?" asks Francis.

"Right there."

"That clump of trees?" says Ned.

"No, higher up."

"The sky?"

"No, right there, dummy!"

"I don't know what you're pointing at," says Ned. "Just say it. The snow?"

"Yes, goddammit, the snow!"

"Then just say it. It's a big mountain, and your finger is only, like, this long."

"I couldn't tell a thing," says Samuel.

"I thought you were pointing at that vulture," says Francis. "Because there's one swirling right where—"

"Forget it," says Temple. "Lesson's over." He nudges his horse forward and starts along the trail.

How to Start an Avalanche (Part II)

Within the hour they encounter the first patches of snow, desolate little lobes like dirty white islands melting in the mountain sun. When they reach the treeline they tether the horses and continue on foot. No trail leads higher and the ground is loose with scree and difficult to climb until they reach the snowpack.

From there it's a simple matter of drudgery, one foot before the other.

Before long the horses are small beneath them. The air grows thin and burns in the lungs. A lyrical wind blows steady through the rocks. On a granite outcrop overlooking the Nevada plains they pause for a breather and a canteen goes around. An icy gust turns sweat to hoarfrost, and they quickly resume climbing. The serrated ridge above them grows nearer with each step.

"I was an artist," says Temple between breaths.

"You're what?" says Samuel.

"You asked me how I know about avalanches. Now I'm telling you."

Temple halts and leans on one knee, catching his breath. "There was a time," he says, "when I was passable as an avalanche artist."

"So you've done this before?" says Samuel.

"Was paid to do it."

"Who pays for avalanches?"

"The US government, when you're good enough. I was with the Thirty-Third under Lieutenant General Rossmoor.

Demolitions. Sabotage. Nothing wrecks a supply train like an avalanche."

"Well I guess there's a practical application to near about everything," says Ned.

"I'm just trying to get my head around the fact," says Francis, "that Bob Temple has a past."

"According to legend, I was even a baby once."

Francis asks what makes Bob Temple an artist rather than an expert, and Bob Temple answers that the difference is experts don't know squat. Francis confesses he understands the difference no better than before, and Bob Temple says the difference is in the vision. The foresight, and how it sculpts one's realization from all the little choices along the way.

"Look here," says Ned, "we got a whole new Bob! A whole new different kind of outlaw."

Temple continues, refusing to be rankled now that he's on a topic of genuine interest. "Any demolitions man can measure a priming line, count sticks of dynamite. But it takes an artist to see what's possible when no one else can, to steer the entirety of the project toward the most visually stunning results. The crashpoint, if you will."

"And where would that be, in our case?" asks Samuel.

"So you're ready to listen?"

They nod.

Bob Temple points to a crag of exposed granite on the ridge, above even the snowline.

"That's where we're headed. We have to get above the snow and rope ourselves in, otherwise we'll all come down in a pile. There's a natural chute just below that crag. Once the slide starts it'll fan out from there, following that contour east, eventually picking up that grove of pine trees and carrying it all to the bottom. Our crashpoint. And see where it all ends up? The river."

"Rivers are good?" says Francis.

Bob Temple chortles to himself. "You'll see."

In Defence of Evil

Thirty-eight riders move single file over the candid brown earth, the ramparts of the Sierras barely a mile distant.

At the head of the line, Bursula Carter halts her horse and lifts a hand. The remaining riders come to a halt behind her. She considers the mountains, their snowy vistas shining like rum-drunk angels. She can hear the roar of the river at their base.

She twists in her saddle. "Where's that tracker? Get him up here."

Bursula is the recent widow of Stanley Carter and now undisputed leader of the Carter Gang. She's shaped roughly to the dimensions a name like Bursula would imply. She has bulging, bloodshot eyes and great heaving breasts and biceps like a lowland gorilla. Also, she has no good qualities.

"I said get him up here! Where is that little bitch?"

"Dead!" calls someone from the rear.

"Dead?"

"Afraid so," says Jack Bilworth, tentatively coming alongside her. "If you recall, you placed a bullet in his gut earlier this morning. He didn't do so well after that."

"No?"

"Not at all, actually."

Bursula rubs the stubble about her neck.

"We'll have to get another then," she says. "One that doesn't make that smacking sound with his lips. I'm very sensitive to mouth sounds."

"Will do, Bursy. Next village we come to, we'll round them up and find you a winner."

For the last ten days, the Carter Gang has followed the tracks of four horses across the godless, sun-battered shield of Nevada, and now California too, in order to exact their revenge for the murders of Lester Skidmore Hughes and Stanley Carter. Their tracker was a dud, and yesterday's rain erased all sign of their quarry, but Bursula knows they're close. She can feel it.

"What is that?" she says, peering at Jack Bilworth's coat pocket.

"This? Don't even know. Found him in our camp this morning. I think it's a squirrel. Or maybe a weasel. Mother must have abandoned it."

"Kind of cute, ain't he?"

"He seems to like it right here in my coat."

"Well," she says, returning her attention to the mountains. "Just don't let it stray. Or I might get hungry."

"Duly noted."

She squints at the nearest slope. Her horse spooks and dances to the right.

Jack Bilworth struggles to bring his own horse under rein. "That's an avalanche."

"Toss me that scope."

"That's an avalanche."

She grabs the telescope, but there's no time to even open it. The entire side of the mountain drops, fans out, and rips down the forest in its path before pouring silently into the river below. A great drape of snowsmoke and froth rises in slow motion from the river and then she hears a distant crack, like an explosion, only now reaching her ears, followed by the rumble of snow.

"That was dynamite," she says.

"There's still plenty gold in these mountains."

She thinks on that.

"You want to check it out?" says Jack Bilworth.

"Yes I do," she says.

She flicks open the telescope and peers out at the plain before the river. It takes a moment to understand what she's seeing. She collapses the telescope and tosses it to Bilworth.

"Ride!" she hollers. "Ride for your lives!"

The silent grey spill of the river washes inexorably toward them.

❀

Hoots of pure victory echo in the crisp mountain air. Then the four just sit happily upon the crag, crazed smiles across their faces, gazing down at the glorious destruction below. The explosion, the portentous rumbling at their feet, the unspeakable rapture of the mountain's face sliding away, the eruption of the river and consequent flooding. Everything, every part of it, even more dramatic than Bob Temple had promised. And to top it off, the ghoulish simplicity of it all.

"Hot damn," whispers Francis, unable to wipe the grin from his face.

"I'm next," says Ned.

"There is no next," says Temple.

"I saw in your bag, you got another stick."

"That stick's headed for a strongbox in Chesterville, California," says Temple. "Besides, the first stick already sent all the snow away."

Ned hoots one last time. "That was something else," he says, holding his hat tight in the wind. "Goddamn, that was something else."

"Now hold on," says Francis. "Look down there."

He points.

"That's the flood," says Temple. "You didn't count on that, did you? Call it the artist's touch."

"No, down there. There's riders."

They all look down onto the plain.

Sure enough, they count thirty-eight of them. Thirty-eight riders, staying just ahead of the flood.

Here's How

"And you?" says Temple. "How about you?"

"Telegraphy," says Samuel. "I was a telegraphist. Or telegraphist's apprentice. I got a year to go and then I —"

"How's your shooting?"

"My shooting?"

"Forget it. Ned, what was your profession?"

"Well I like the sound of bank robber."

"And before?"

"Before what?" asks Ned.

"Were you in any line of work that may improve our prospects? Can you shoot?"

"Like a gun?"

"Jesus. All right. Grab your pistols, all three of you. Here's how this will go."

In no rush at all to climb back down the mountain with thirty-eight riders at its foot, they set the targets at twenty paces on the ridge and Bob Temple runs them through the basics.

Here's this, here's that, go like so.

Ned turns out to be a natural, a real crack shot, and is not shy about it. "I believe I love this gun," he declares, admiring its feel in his hand. "If it were a person we'd be, like, finishing each other's sentences."

Samuel is slow and methodical but knocks down targets despite Ned's heckling. Francis finds the Schofield is too large in his hand. It jars his whole arm when he shoots it. "No one ever talks about it hurting," he says, shaking out his arm. "It's like a thunder. I'm numb to the shoulder."

"Let's try this one more time," says Temple, pointing to the stack of stones that has yet to be tilted.

Francis closes one eye and extends his arm and sights the barrel. He fires. He drops his arm and peers at the stack and if anything it stands taller somehow.

Temple stands there a while, looking at the stack. He appears to be thinking.

But actually he's not—his mind just drifted. "All right," he says. "Let's try this one more time again."

CHAPTER FOUR

Around the Smooth Backs of Lanterns

Rather than fall in line with the Carter Gang, sneaking about in their tracks, the Blackstone Templars retrieve their horses and a find a trail heading into the mountains. They ride due west when they can, but a warren of deep valleys requires a roundabout passage. The country is stunning.

It's nearly summer, and glacial melt plunges from alpine heights in twinkling waterfalls; they're everywhere. In the gorges, brown swollen rivers gush with abandon, and bears emerging from long sleep are so hungry for fish, they congregate openly in the rapids — they don't even turn to look at the horses riding by. And the fish are plentiful. The gang can gather all they need in an hour from a trickling brook, and devote the rest of the sunlit hours to hard travel.

"So what is it with your brother," says Bob Temple, gutting a two-pound trout with his jackknife on the shore of a chortling creek.

Samuel is beside him, likewise engaged with a small stack of catch; disembowelling, cleaning, scaling, and then back on the stringer to dangle in the coolness of moving water.

Temple turns to Samuel. "You're smiling. I didn't think it a funny question."

Samuel continues to grin, his hands working the fish. "If you only knew," he says, "how many times that question has been put to me, then you might find some humour in it. It is a funny question. If only because you ask it."

"All right," says Temple. "I will clarify. What is it with this love business. This whole thing about love."

"That part's simple," says Samuel. "Our father is a judge."

"I met a few of them."

"Then you can picture a miserable man. Worn out and bitter. Or just heartbroke, really, at a world he's supposed to fix—but deep down despises. Eventually our mother said enough of that, and went God knows where."

"And Francis?"

"Was the *passionate contrarian*, or so Father liked to say. Father would say, if you want a person to do something your way, tell them they can do it, and do it well. Unless that person is Francis. Then you tell him he can't."

"Makes a little more sense," says Temple, "now you frame it like that. Love as mutiny. As rebellion. I can respect that. Nevertheless, I usually got a line on someone. Five seconds flat. That's all I need."

"You may as well quit on Francis. No one's got a handle there."

"Honestly, five seconds."

"Well," says Samuel, "you won't get a line on me either. That's the Blackstone way. We're enigmas."

"You? You're easiest of all. You're running scared."

Samuel stands, visibly chafed. "I've got nothing to be afraid of."

"While that is a fact," says Temple, "this is reality: You need your brother. More than he needs you. And that has you quaking in your boots. Scared he just might be the bigger sibling in every way but size."

"You're just full of information."

"Imbalance of need will scare any man."

"Like a factory. Just listen to you."

"Balance is everything, my friend. You can carry a twenty-four-foot ladder in one hand if properly positioned. But too much to one side and it all hits the ground."

Samuel splits the fillet under water, letting the current run it clean. Little strings of purple blood cling to the white meat, dancing in the stream.

"Say again?" says Temple.

Samuel shakes his head. He swipes at his cheek.

"Oh dear. I believe I have hit a chord."

"Go to hell."

"It's nothing to be ashamed of. We all come from family."

"You think you know me," says Samuel. "But let me tell you something."

"Okay."

"Maybe you're right. Maybe Francis is all I got."

"All right."

"And you think that makes me weak."

"Your words, but all right."

"Come anywhere near him," says Samuel, "and you will find out just how wrong you are."

"Oh really."

"And I mean wrong. Like you cannot believe."

Sad Pony

By day three in the Sierras, they arrive in a valley of epic proportions. It's hedged on three sides by monolithic cliffs. Over here, a waterfall appears to throw itself down from the heavens — it's the tallest they've seen. Over there, a mountain has been sheared in half by ancient forces, revealing the strata of a prehistoric world. Meadows span the cliffs with a haze of bright flowers and elk herds graze placidly in the grass. The whole valley is a vision from the sparkling depths of unreality.

In later years, a passionate naturalist named John Muir will fall madly in love with this valley and invite the president of the United States, Theodore Roosevelt, to walk with him a while and enjoy the natural glory of this country, to camp with him among the glaciers, to listen to birds at dusk, and after waking utterly invigorated one morning from beneath a light dusting of snow, Roosevelt himself will declare his intention to return ownership of this land back to the federal government for the creation of a national park: Yosemite. It will stand as a beacon of environmental progress, a genuine zeitgeist, spawning similar developments across the globe.

Later still, the Yosemite Valley concessions department will be sold off to international investors and the roadways transformed into a Disneyland of fossil-fuelled ecotourism with bumper-to-bumper jams — therefore erecting a second beacon, this one a dire warning against what a national shrine might become.

For the present, however, our heroes are quite blasted with awe.

The trail T's into a road and before long they find themselves entering an unexpectedly bustling outpost. The town is of decent size, built to supply and entertain the miners and their families who are settling all throughout the valley.

"This will do just fine," says Temple, trotting in with reins loose on one hand.

There is a livery on the left, a saloon beside it, followed by many new and half-built homes. Raw lumber is everywhere. Across the road is a hotel and an armoury, a dry goods store and another with mining supplies. There's a blacksmith's, a hatter's, a laundry, and even a French furniture maker's with a carpet of wood chips out front.

Temple halts his horse outside the saloon. The others stop beside him. They can hear a piano inside. The saloon's name is painted in a garish white font across the front window.

"The Sad Pony," muses Temple, reading the signage aloud. "I could drink something there."

No one replies at first, such is the music pouring onto the street. Then Ned says:

"Someone sure knows how to play a mean piano."

Inside the Sad Pony

There's a row of stools before the bar, a row of people seated upon them. Their faces are swollen like apples. They bellow and sway. They open like caverns and slosh liquid into their heads. Samuel and Ned are nested neatly among them, ensconced, as it were, in the general beerness of the place, merry and shitfaced respectively.

On a stage beneath the second-floor balcony sits the pianoman. He pounds wildly, feverishly at the keys. He's wearing a bright yellow coat with red tasselled trim and cascading split tails. He rocks to and fro. His spectacles perch miraculously from the tip of his nose.

There are also a number of tables arranged about the saloon, and in the corner a sofa with a semi-circle of plush red overstuffed chairs. Bob Temple sits in one of these. He's reading a paper. He has both a wineglass and a shotglass and both are empty. They reside in their emptiness upon the low table before him.

He smacks the open newspaper with the back of his hand.

"Now you see here," he says. "This is what I'm talking about. Experts say the English language is expanding at fourteen point seven words per day and will soon plumb the outer edge of contrived sound. How are we to contend with this?"

"Don't know, Bob."

Francis is standing beside the sofa. He would like very much to share in Temple's dismay but the cast of his soul forbids it. His attention is fixed instead upon the piano and whoever's playing it. He's never heard such music. So this, he thinks, is what a piano is for.

"I'm telling you," says Temple, "modernity will be the end of us. And not just us. All of this," he says, gesturing about the saloon's interior with his hand. "Mark my words. This here, what we call the west — it'll be gone soon. Before you know it even."

Francis sits down in the chair opposite. He puts two fingers in the air and the barkeep nods from the across the room.

❧

"I've been thinking," says Francis.

"Oh yeah?" says Temple, folding his paper over and setting it down.

"You said you can knock out supply trains with dynamite."

"I did."

Temple leans forward to light a cigar over the table and leans back again. He exhales, looking at Francis as he waves out the match. "And have done so. On many occasions."

The pianoman's fingers are now a blur, his whole body leaning sideways, contorted with passion. He stands abruptly and kicks the stool from behind him. It tumbles violently away. He hammers at the keys, nodding in tempo. Whatever it is that keeps a man in check, demands he conceal his true heart, the naked assertions of his soul — it is now banished from the room. The pianoman begins to sing.

"Well I'm thinking we could do the same," says Francis, his gaze locked upon the musician.

"Hit a train?"

"Why not? But forget the avalanches. We can just blow the tracks."

Temple picks up the empty shotglass and ashes his cigar. "Hell. Why not," he says. "Could be a good warm-up for the bank. Get our skills in order."

> *I am he*
> *As you are he*
> *As you are me*
> *And we are all together*

"All right," says Francis. "It's settled." He gets up from the overstuffed chair.

"Where you going?" says Bob Temple.

"I think I'll take a peek at that armoury we saw."

"But what about our drinks? They're bringing them right now."

"They're both for you, Bob."

> *See how they run*
> *Like pigs from a gun*
> *See how they fly*
> *I'm crying…*

Across the Road and into the Armoury Then

"This here's a Cooper Pocket Double-Action Five-Shot Percussion Revolver, designed in 1860, got the walnut wood finish for an ergonomical grip, spur on the hammer, small enough to hide in a gentleman's coat. Finishes in a cool blue."

Francis lifts the pistol from the countertop, inspecting it. He asks what calibre it is.

"What calibre? Well that's a thirty-one calibre. Shoots a nice little ball. About yea big."

Francis tests the weight of the pistol, hefting it up and down. He asks if he could shoot a bear with it.

"What kind of bear did you have in mind?"

"A mean one."

"Now my experience falls shy of bears," confesses the proprietor. "But I am told if you shoot a bear with anything short of forty-five, and he finds out about it, he might get pretty upset. But that Cooper there," the proprietor taps the barrel. "So far as mean men are concerned, it's got the stopping power. It will do the job."

Francis handles the Cooper. He sights it, squinting one eye, and handles it again, running a finger along the octagonal barrel.

"I like the blue."

"Cooper's got a nice touch."

❖

Francis spins the chamber for the smooth hum of it and clacks it shut and sets the pistol on the counter.

"How much?"

The proprietor takes a pen and opens his palm, glances briefly at Francis and then writes a number upon that palm.

"It is not for the faint of heart," he says, and reveals the palm to Francis.

Francis looks at the number and nods. He points to the pen. Upon receiving the pen, he takes the man's palm and crosses out the number and writes another. He circles it. He gives the pen back.

The man looks at this number in his palm, rubbing his jaw with the unnumbered other. He says, "I notice you have a Schofield there on your hip. Would you consider that in partial trade?"

"It's my father's."

"If there's sentiment there I cannot match it from the till. But it must be said your father's pistol is far too large for a young man of your stature. It will throw your arm when you shoot it."

"I confess it does."

"Shall we start again with a new number?"

Francis lays his father's Schofield upon the counter beside the Cooper and takes the pen and starts the process afresh on his own hand this time. They go back and forth. When all is concluded Francis digs into his pocket and retrieves a solitary Double Eagle, the only such coin in his possession, and slides it across the counter to the proprietor.

The Thing about This Coin

The first Double Eagle was minted in 1849, year of the California Gold Rush. It was comprised of ninety percent gold and ten percent copper alloy for a total weight of 1.0750 troy ounces, making it a twenty-dollar piece.

Francis Blackstone's uncle Bert had acquired two of these coins during his adventures west. He gave one each to Francis and Samuel for their fifth birthdays. They were instructed to hold on to them.

But somewhere in the universe there exists a hungry, enigmatic vault housing so many items from our youth, and Francis' treasured coin slipped beyond the veil of his quite limited powers of organization and soon found its way there. When precisely it departed Francis could not say. He was a kid and it disappeared and that was that.

Some years later, at the age of twelve, Francis made a trip to Santa Fe. He did not alert his family beforehand. He made these journeys frequently—not just Santa Fe, but anywhere—leaving without word and returning without explanation, sending his brother into genuine fits of concern.

This particular journey was five days round trip. He had accomplished nothing in Santa Fe. He simply rode there, and was now riding back. It was evening. He was very tired and truth be told was even questioning the merit of these escapades, whether they should go on or cease, when the trail entered a broad gulch and he became aware of a thing in his boot. He felt it shifting directly below his right heel. He wiggled his foot within the stirrup, working the item forward until it halted beneath the pad of his big toe.

It was a coin. Its flat roundness was unmistakable.

He probed it with his toes, and while considering the situation on the whole — the strange introduction of a coin he should have felt there long ago — he concluded that given the limited information at his disposal he would draw no conclusions. Nor would he remove his boot and disclose the mystery. Rather he would savour it.

Francis rode deep into the night, his thoughts frequently returning to the coin in his boot, toying with the anticipation of its discovery, all the while sensing at the margin of his heart that he already knew precisely what he would find there.

When at last he parked and made camp for the night he took his time with the horse and with the preparation of the fire. With every step, the coin moved beneath his foot, demanding his attention.

Only when all was in order, and there was not one thing left he could possibly attend to, Francis Blackstone sat down in the dirt beside the popping red flames and pried off his boot. He removed his sock. He tipped it upside down and worked the item free. A Double Eagle dropped into his palm.

Was it the same coin? No way to tell. But Francis held on to this one, intuiting the existence of some other order which had placed it in his care, and also the eerie implications of misplacing it twice.

Ever since, whenever Francis thought upon the coin, it provoked a soft whisper of sensation. Like a warm tickling breeze.

He felt it here. And here. And here.

One Such Moment

"I believe you will be happy with this purchase," says the proprietor.

"I believe I will," says Francis.

"Shall I box it up, or will the empty holster suffice?"

"I think the holster is begging for it."

Francis slips the Cooper home and it's a perfect fit; every joint, every bone in his body, all of it now in proper arrangement.

"If I may be so bold," says the proprietor.

"You may," says Francis, retrieving the Cooper from its holster and gazing at it in unabashed admiration. That tickling breeze goes all through his body like never before.

"Then I will speak my mind," says the proprietor, "the contents of which arise first from my heart. You are a young man. You are daring. You are looking to make your mark and your fortune."

"Make a girl, actually. But my fortune's a key step along the way."

"Well then, many a gentleman has made his fortune on a Cooper. You are now well positioned, shall we say?"

"All right. Your point?"

"It is this. Being young, it may be some years before you realize the windows of fortune do not open or close upon a man's life according to his desires but something larger."

"All right."

"Only in ignorance does man draw this conclusion or that, reducing what's larger to the designs of personal fancy.

Which is to say everything happens for a reason, yes, but only a fool supposes the cause."

"I've learned that one."

"Then you're further along than I surmised. I'll add only this. All moments are not equal. Some are cut from different cloth altogether and have the strength to define a gentleman and his fortune and I believe, young sir, this before us is one such moment."

"I believe you are right."

"I feel it in my spine."

"I do as well."

"I'll ask you to remember this shop. My name is Von Stedt. When they ask you later you tell them it was here. It was Von Stedt who sold you the Cooper."

Francis says he will.

But Before Francis Leaves

"How much for a couple boxes of those percussion caps up there? Other shelf. Nope. Keep going. Beside the stuffed wolverine or whatever that is. Right there, that's the one. I like the picture on it. What is that?"

The proprietor retrieves the box and turns the box around, studying the side-flap. "I believe it's an illustration of a genie, as that is the brand's name as well."

"What's a genie?"

"A creature of great power. From the fairytales of the Far East."

"Perfect. I'll take a pocketful of those."

"These ones are loud. Just so you know."

"That's fine. I've always liked things that go pow."

Bob Temple Goes for a Ride
to Clear His Head

Upon leaving the saloon Temple mounts his horse and follows the road out of town. It's a beautiful afternoon, not too hot, the sky is clear, and he wants to enjoy it but finds himself pestered by a strange federation of ghostly concerns. Chief among them: Who is Bob Temple? Who is he, really? And who is anyone, for that matter?

It's a question he can't get at, no matter what angle he takes. What's more, Temple blames Francis. Not for any logical reason. But ever since he met Francis, it's like the line of his thinking has changed. He finds this vaguely irksome. Discourteous even.

Unlike Francis, Temple can readily accept he's got more years behind him than ahead. It's just a fact. No way around it. He can even accept that people might come to nothing, might never change or advance without the hot clean irreverence of youth. But that doesn't mean he has to like it. Or want it ordering his drinks.

The road crosses a stream and Temple pauses midstream to watch clear water slip over pewter-smooth stones. In the sky above, three ravens harry some bird of prey, something majestic, an eagle perhaps. Temple doesn't know what he's doing out here, wandering about. It all feels so purposeless. Everything. On impulse he wheels the horse about and heads back toward town. The horse clomps along.

Actually he does know what he's doing out here.

He is looking for something that counts for something in a life that, when it comes down to it, amounts to very little.

What has he actually accomplished? He is forty-six years old. He's nearly over the hill.

Riding down it, other side, the town comes into view, significant with life. He notices the lamplighter going lamp to lamp out front of the shops. Townsfolk on the sidewalk, the spectrum of their aliveness in the colourful coats and bonnets, the boisterous children in black boots, faces round as doorknobs.

Temple slows the horse from a trot to a walk.

He can still feel the residue of his ponderings in the tightness of his neck, his shoulders, but he knows if he leans his head in just the right way he'll get that luscious pop, that release of tension that will make everything all right.

It doesn't come. So he swings his head in a slow circle, chin to chest, rolling his eyes to keep view of the road. When he levels his gaze he's approaching the town's public well. It's just beside the road. There's something about the old Negress standing there beside the pump; long wool dress, two tin buckets, a silvering ponytail.

As Temple draws near he realizes what it is. She's staring him dead in the eye, like she's been waiting.

She shakes her head slowly as he rides past.

A Decent Fellow

The gang regroups at the hotel around suppertime. They appear to be the only guests, and they eat in the kitchen with the hotel's owner and his matronly wife. She has an efficient, sharp, lively energy, quick to laugh, quick to scold. Her name is Matilda. The owner, by contrast, is a taciturn man, remote and distracted, with bushy black eyebrows and a scholarly nose. He rarely looks up from his plate of meatloaf and peas.

He's a decent man though, perhaps modest to a fault, introducing himself simply as R.

"Call me R."

The Thing about R

People think he stays awake all night but the truth is he can read in his sleep. Lantern on, hunched at the desk, flipping page after page—it really is amazing. He is unexceptional in every other way.

does all the talking, bustling here and there about the kitchen.

"Where you all coming from?" she asks.

"We're coming out of Nowhere," offers Francis.

She says aren't we all and spoons more peas onto their plates, skipping over R despite his raising the plate. She says, "Are you all staying here in the valley or moving on?"

"We're off to rob a bank," says Ned. "Or actually, we're starting off with a train now, just to get up to speed and all, get our feet wet, and depending on how that goes we'll hit the Manhattan Company branch out of Chesterville."

Matilda says starting off with the train makes good sense in her mind. It shows a quantity of wisdom on their part as emerging outlaws because there will likely be some quirks to work out in their general manner as they discover how best to work together, and they'll want to be solid as a panel before trying anything big as a Manhattan Company.

"That's good to hear," says Temple, wiping his mouth on a napkin, "as I was thinking something along those lines myself. But you worded it just right."

She says the success of such a venture can be multiplied by the number of collaborators when there's a unified vision in place, and also a disciplined partition of roles. But without said vision, the equation works in reverse with chaos, entropy, and displeasure the inevitable outcome. Such is the nature of collaboration. Goes both ways.

"Boy, you really know how put it," says Temple. "That's it exactly."

"More meatloaf?" says Matilda.

"Right here," says Samuel, sliding his plate toward her.

Francis mentions that after today's purchase of the Cooper, his life savings adds up to zero. Samuel offers to cover some of Francis' travel expenses but it's clear no one has a lot of money.

"Stay on for tomorrow," offers Matilda with a brightening glance. "We could use some help with spring repairs, and you'll earn a few dollars. Isn't that right, R?"

Her husband glances up briefly with the tiniest of nods and then returns his gaze to the remnants of his meal, arranged just so upon his plate.

Life Choices

Bob Temple climbs the stairs to his quarters and takes a long hot bath in the clawfoot tub. He stretches out and smokes a cigar. He opens the window and blows smoke out the window, ashing into the bowl of his hat, which floats upside down before him. He is thinking about the day. About the happenings of the day.

And then, without warning, he is thinking about *thoughts*. Just like that. As though the very kinetics of his boredom has flipped some lens in his head, and now it's all pointed the wrong way around. Lying there in the tub, cigar held high, he wonders, for the first time in his life, what exactly thoughts are made of.

What...is a thought...made of.

He ashes his cigar. Staring at the ceiling.

What is a thought...*made of.*

These examinations stir something in Bob, a vague sense of the unknown, of something bigger than himself. Of a realm, or many realms, he has no understanding of.

And he doesn't like it.

Bob Temple rises from the bath and dries himself off. He stands before the washstand and shaves meticulously with a bone-handle razor. He focuses on the task, steering all thoughts to it. He trims his mustache. His sideburns. He combs his hair. He locates his trousers from the pile and steps smoothly into them. Belt comes next, followed by socks. Boots, laces. Finally his shirt — an odd ordering perhaps, but it has always been thus — buttoning it right to the top before he tucks it all in, doot, doot, doot. And there we are. He takes a deep breath, feeling subtly refreshed and invigorated.

Then he just stands there a while, uncertain what to do with the rest of his life.

Therefore

Bob Temple spends the evening drinking bottles empty and heaving the empties off the third floor of the hotel balcony into the street for the sound it makes. He is pretty happy with the results. It feels good to accomplish something.

Maybe Love Is a Piano Unleashed

Francis, meanwhile, falls fast asleep with his new pistol beside him on the pillow. Does he dream of this pistol?

He dreams of pianos.

There are four of them, and they are zipping through space.

They are burning like comets.

They are hot with speed and perfectly tuned, approaching the ineffable as only burning pianos can, dragging behind them, each, over the humped back of stars, the songs of happily escaped machines.

In this dream Francis is riding one, the lead piano. It's like riding upon love itself, the thrill of love, steering it this way and that—wind in his hair, Earth far below. Fingers dancing across ivory keys.

And now he is soaring through the Big Dipper. No longer looking at it, but from within it, the stars of the Big Dipper don't form a giant ladle anymore. They're shaped more like a pistol. And as Francis thinks this thought, the distinct outline of his Cooper takes shape, glowing blue in the night sky.

A new and wondrous zodiac. A sign for all to see.

A Tale of Four Men

Next day, Francis is first down for breakfast. R is sitting alone in the kitchen, pensively picking candle drippings from the table and brushing them into a small mound beside his coffee mug.

It takes some time for R to realize Francis has joined the table but then he recalls himself and his role within the service industry, though there remains an atmosphere of reluctance about him.

"Coffee?" says R.

"Sure."

He lifts a kettle. "You want that in a cup, or..."

"Yeah. Cup would be nice."

"I'll get you a clean one."

"Thanks."

They drink their coffee in silence.

This is a sad man, thinks Francis. A sad man.

Francis glances casually about the kitchen. He drinks his coffee. A thought occurs to him. It comes out of nowhere, this thought. Or rather, the notion has been there all along but never with such thrust. Such conviction.

The thought is: Coffee is good.

"What's in this stuff?" asks Francis, staring into the pitch-coloured contents of his mug. It's as though he has never had coffee before. As though the harmless, unremarkable beverage of so many mornings past is now a four-hundred-pound gorilla hammering a railroad spike into his adrenals with the black meat of its fists.

"Coffee all right?" asks R.

"Very," says Francis, standing to pour himself another. "You know I was just thinking." He returns with the kettle. "With a pot of this and a large army I could probably take over the world."

When R makes no comment Francis takes his seat at the table. He sets down the kettle. He openly observes R, who in turn pays Francis no notice.

"Would you like to see something pretty?" says Francis, considering the lamp in his satchel.

R takes a deep breath, appearing to think on this. After a time he replies that he would not care to. No.

"You sure? I got it right here."

The man shakes his head. He says it would have no effect. He says too many pretty things have come and gone in his life and look where it's got him. Just another lonely man with a pile of wax, waiting for the world to care. He says what we actually see and do in this world is of the least importance — is only remotely linked to any outcome.

"You think?"

The man says he does indeed. He says somewhere sits an idler in the murk of his own boredom, toying with a scrap of wire. Half an hour later he holds the first paperclip and a millionaire is born. Another man, a genius we'll say, sweats a pound a day to put supper on the table and dies of blacklung in a coalmine. And then a third man regards the first two and concludes there is little elegance in this world and next to no meaning. Rather, he believes the guiding principle of our universe is whimsy. Omniscient, unfathomable whimsy.

"Now look at me. Look at my eyes. Which man do you suppose I am?"

Francis says nothing.

"I am all of them," he says. "I am each. Worse still, I am a fourth man too. The credulous buffoon! And it is because of this fourth man I deserve no mercy, for in spite of everything I still believe in God. I do. I really do. I just don't know what scares me most. That he might not know what he is doing, or that he does."

Francis looks at the man.

He thinks, There are many ways to lead a life.

Why Is Francis Blackstone Like Himself and Not Some Other?

For as long as Francis can remember, right up to his leaving home, he and Samuel assisted their father with the weekly purchases every Friday evening at five-thirty sharp. Their father had a list. They went down the list in order. If an item they searched for proved to be unavailable for any reason, their father would halt as though suckerpunched right there in the aisle of the bakery or the butcher or wherever. He would then glare at the void where the item in question should exist, pinch the bridge of his nose — *the imbeciles!* — and finally shut his eyes to conduct a private examination of the injury.

This happened every week. His father's unsuspecting astonishment never failed to astonish Francis, who grew to feel these outings were highly instructive. For in the midst of his father's pompously solemn displays, Francis was forming the first parameters of who he would, and would not, allow himself to become.

Upon returning home, Mr. Blackstone stood straight as a flagpole beside the kitchen stove. He removed the purchases one at a time from the crate and handed them to Francis and Samuel to check off against the bill of sale. If it was discovered they'd overpaid for an item, they returned, the three of them together, Saturday morning at eight o'clock, for the reckoning. If they underpaid for an item, they returned at the same hour to pay their debt. It didn't matter if it was only a penny. It was never about the penny.

Perhaps this helps you to understand.

A Special Visit

The others soon join Francis and R in the kitchen. Matilda comes down, looking spruce and coiffured, and cooks ham and eggs and after a pleasant breakfast she announces there is plenty to do. She says let's work together on this and it will be done in a moment. She says teamwork is her motto. It's how things get done around here.

Francis quickly comes to understand that teamwork is Matilda's word for drawing up a list of tasks for others to complete. He and Samuel are given paint detail and chip and slather at the hotel's pine siding while Temple works the roof, and Ned digs a fresh hole for the summer outhouse. Matilda follows them around, calling out encouragements, directing, directing, while R shuffles about within the unlit confines of the hotel.

Later that night, while preparing for bed in his private quarters, Francis hears a knock at his door.

"Yup."

Matilda opens the door, standing there in her nightgown. "Just checking in. Got everything you need?"

"Yes ma'am."

"You sure?"

"I'm happy with things, thank you."

"Okay, well that's good."

She stands there a moment.

"But look at that," she says, stepping into the room. "Please tell me you don't always wear your pistol to bed."

"No ma'am, it's a new item. I'm just extra fond of it right now."

She continues to stand. Looking around. And then: "May I sit down?"

"Help yourself."

She sits down beside him on the bed. Francis tries to have a thought about that but she's already turning toward him, a cloud of perfume sinking its pink teeth into his awareness.

"You know, you are an extraordinarily handsome young man. Anyone ever tell you that?"

"Just my mother, ma'am. Which I never took to mean much."

"Well you are."

"Thank you, ma'am."

"And you have an interesting demeanour."

"I don't even know what that is, ma'am."

She smiles, tossing her hair. "And please, stop calling me ma'am."

"All right."

"Makes me feel old. I'm not that old, am I?"

"To tell the truth, I'm not sure of your age."

Matilda bursts into laughter as though Francis has said something clever. Then she stops. "Would you mind it much if I touched you?"

"Well, the thing is, I already got love in my heart."

"You got a girl?"

"Yes ma'am. A very special girl."

"How special?" Matilda shifts her posture in such a way that her bosom now dominates his view.

"Well ma'am, she's got the better part of a whole galaxy in her blouse."

Matilda sniffs and straightens, clearly outmatched, and inquires who's quartered in the next room over.

"That would be Ned Runkle."

"The big one with dark freckles?"

"No, that's my brother. Ned's the skinny one with the toothbrush grin."

"Does he have love in his heart too?"

"No ma'am. I'm not aware he keeps much of anything in there."

"Perhaps I'll pay him a visit then."

"Yes ma'am. I believe he'd welcome that."

Dearest girl,

I hope you are in good health. I am doing well.
I think of you often, and also the promise I made.
I wonder, do you think of me too? It may be some
time before I return but I want you to know I am
coming. Every part of me says this is so. It is my
deepest hope that you believe me, and will continue
to wait.

Now I will tell you something else I have seen.

Do you know the garden behind the church-
house? Do you know the old apple tree there? Just
last year I discovered something in that garden.
The tree grows two kinds of apples. Don't ask me
how. My father tried to explain it. In autumn that
tree gets so full and round it looks like an upturned
bowl. And once, when I was sitting on the bench
beneath it, a whole flock of goldfinches came to
roost. The tree's limbs actually creaked beneath their
weight, while the little birds themselves were mute as
ornaments.

I watched them for a while. I wondered at their
silence. They didn't make a peep. There were many
apples on the ground and I chose one from between
my feet. I bit into the apple with a loud crunch and
the birds sang out all at once, not one before the
other like you'd think, but like each bird was struck
by the same peculiar thought: If I sing now I will
be first, and those that follow will be second and
third and so on, and so each bird was mistaken, and

in their mistakenness came together as one tuneful outburst like an explosion of something. Like an explosion of gladness or something. Or even the shape of gladness itself carving its reflection on the air.

I often think back on those birds. I think about the suddenness of their song. It's another of those things that's stayed with me. Do you want to know something else?

That was the day I first watched you through your window.

It was later that same night. I finally figured out how to climb your roof. When I stood at your sill you were already sitting on the edge of your bed. It was mostly dark in your room. You weren't doing anything, just sitting there on the bed. I watched you for the longest time. You wore a faraway look on your face. Like you were somewhere else in your mind. At one point you stared out the window and I swear you were looking straight at me, though I know you couldn't see me for the darkness outside. And then you untied the ribbon from your hair. You coiled it nicely in your lap. You reached down and took off your stockings. First one, and then the other. You laid each stocking neatly on the bed beside you.

Then you just looked at your toes a while, wiggling them.

That is when I knew I loved you.

Wildlife

Next morning Bob Temple wakes to find a giant cockroach drinking from his eye. The heft of it, the actual weight and contour of this beast as he tugs it from his face, is like a bar of soap. Temple makes an involuntary sound, a grunt or a groan. He hurls the animal against the wall where it thumps horribly and drops to the floor and scuttles away.

Temple yanks his legs beneath him, middle of the bed. He stares at the floor with revulsion and contemplates his escape.

His clothing lies in a haphazard pile beneath the wash-stand. It's perhaps six feet away. Bob Temple crawls on hands and knees to the edge of the bed and peers over, then under. He climbs to his feet. For many moments he stands there upon the mattress, underwear hanging from his rear like a neglected diaper, while he considers the enemy floorspace between himself and said clothing.

He's not crazy about his options. He's concerned that firstly, he will come into contact with another cockroach. Second, that someone will see him standing on the mattress, trying not to come into contact with a cockroach.

As he ponders this Dilemma of the Cockroach, and by extension the animal kingdom as a whole, Bob Temple runs through a list of animals in his head. He's trying to think of an animal that eats cockroaches. Something that can rescue him. A snake perhaps?

No, he thinks. Snakes are worse. Plus you can't call them. A cat then? He's seen a cat around. But cats are mysterious and malevolent, bringing to mind every woman who's ever vexed him.

Bob Temple has no idea what lizards eat.

In the end there's nothing for it. Bob leaps. His landing is brash and indecorous, vulgar even, depending on the angle, and he is a little embarrassed but also relieved, for which he laughs, a nervously elatedly victorious laugh, because he is now arrived before the washstand, and therefore his clothing, without undue touching of the floor.

Then he shrinks in horror as countless black legs go scuttling about the sink. He bites his fist and reflexively empties a bottle of aftershave over their abhorrent shiny backs. Take that you little fuckers. They go still on the instant. For a moment Temple thinks he's devised a new and wholly satisfying death for all vermin and then bends closer to the sink, one ear cocked, only to realize they are drinking. He can hear them drinking.

Pleasantries

Francis rises early that same morning and pulls back the curtains. The sun is a glass ovary on the crest of the mountains. The last of the stars recoil from its light and all along the street windows go bourbon-coloured in the new brightness of day. Francis watches through the window. Nothing of particular interest takes place but he's interested all the same. In time he dresses and sits down on the bed and pulls on his boots. He exits the room at precisely the same moment as Ned, the two bumping shoulders in the hall.

"Ned, how was your night?"

"The room was smaller than the bed," he complains. "But otherwise peaceful."

"Peaceful, huh? Well that's good, Ned. That's real good."

Ned stares back. "Shut your mouth, Francis."

Francis cracks a grin. "I didn't say anything. Just inquiring how your night went. If the pillows were soft, if you had enough bedding. See if your thoughts on teamwork had evolved any. You know it's how things get done around here."

"You little bastard," says Ned, throwing an arm around Francis' shoulders and pulling him tight. "You think you're so smart."

"Smarter than you, you pigeon-toed oaf."

"That's what scares me."

From the nearest room comes a genderless shriek. A moment later a door flies open and Bob Temple stands there in his underwear, panting, a bundle of clothing under one arm and a hunted look in his eye.

Ned and Francis share an inquiring glance. "Morning there, Bob."

"Fuck your morning."

Breakfast is once again a quiet affair, with no Matilda this time, and coffee and toast but not much else.

Next Stop, the Mining Supply House

Before leaving town, the gang has one more item to pick up.

"How much for your dynamite?" says Temple to the proprietor.

"We got local made, and we got De Beers. Which is the best. Comes out of South Africa, so costs a little more."

"Well then De Beers, of course."

"Good choice."

The proprietor is crusty and greasy like something crawled out of a toolbox, and the empty sleeve of his right arm is tied in a knot. He has a tooth.

Temple repeats his query about the price of dynamite and Ned raises a hand, reminding all present that he publicly called dibs on the mountain, and by all rights is next in line for the use of explosives and will be happily purchasing today's dynamite to maintain his position. He reaches into his pocket.

"How much for a stick of the good stuff?" says Ned to the proprietor.

"A stick?" says the man. "Well dyno don't sell as sticks. Goes by the pound at thirty-six cents."

"You're kidding," says Ned. "Well give us five pounds then. No, make it ten."

"Hold up there Geronimo," says Temple. "We got to carry this stuff."

"That's what horses are for," says Ned.

"Ever heard the phrase 'stable as nitroglycerine?'"

"Sure."

"What do you suppose dynamite is made of?"

"Hell if I know."

"We'll take a pound," says Temple to the proprietor. "And this crazy goon is paying."

"You want blasting caps with that?" asks the man.

"Yeah. Make it a pound plus caps," says Temple.

"Caps come individual and packs of five."

"Yeah, couple packs, and let's see . . . some fuses. Say twenty fuses, and a roll of det cord."

"How about a plunger?" asks the proprietor.

"To detonate?" says Temple.

"Of course."

"Would you use a plunger?"

"Never trusted them myself," says the man.

"Me neither. So let's play it straight."

"You got it. How about a set of pans then? Most the fellas are doing good with pans this season."

"Nah. We'll stick with the dynamite," says Temple.

"These rivers are still glittering as they say."

"Yeah well, there's more than one way to get gold. We'll stick with the dynamite."

"I'll tell you what I tell everyone," says the proprietor, carefully laying the dynamite, one stick at a time, into a box of sawdust.

"What's that?" says Temple.

"Keep your distance from the Ahwahnechee. You see even one of them, you keep your distance."

"And where do they abide?"

"All over. It's their land. This whole valley. Not to scare you off, but just keep it in mind."

"You're saying they're hostile?"

"Hostile? Well, in a matter of speaking, yes. But then I suppose anyone would be after State Militia moved in— started burning their villages. Stealing their food. And chief wasn't too happy about them killing his sons. So just watch your back. That's all I'm saying."

"Will do," says Temple. "Pay the man, Ned."

Ned counts out change on the counter, pushing coins forward one at a time. "Eighty-two. Eighty-three. And a nickel makes eighty-eight. There you are. Is that what happened to your arm? The Indians got you?"

"Nope," says the man, using his one hand to slide the change off the counter and into his apron pocket. "This here was a beaver. I suggest you not toy with them either."

Out on the street, Ned ropes the box of dynamite to his horse. Francis presumes they'll all head back to the hotel to gather their things. He suggests as much.

"I'm all packed up," says Ned. "Got all my stuff right here."

Francis smirks at him. "A little too much woman for you?"

"It's not the woman," says Ned, "but the man I can't bear to see. It's those eyes. He is perhaps the saddest creature on earth."

"Like a little lost kitten," says Temple with a thoughtful air, and Francis notices Temple's kit is fully packed as well.

Francis turns to his brother, and sure enough his kit is snug and secure against the horse's rump. "Not you too," says Francis.

Samuel shrugs, his face going red, even his neck. "She

did the rounds, Francis. Up and down that hall, knocking on doors all night. What could we do?"

Francis shakes his head and says he'll be back in a minute.

Once at the hotel he goes straight for his room on the second floor. He's packing his saddlebags when he hears something scratch his door, twice. He stops, waiting for more.

But there is no more. He goes to the door and opens it and looks left and right but the hall is empty. By chance Francis glances at the door itself and notices a small X has been etched into the white panelling beside the doorknob. Was that there before?

Francis goes to the window and glances down at the road just as a man jumps his horse and gallops east out of town.

Francis stands there, thinking about that.

He goes back into the hall and opens his jackknife. He quickly scratches an X into every door on the second floor. Returning to his room he stuffs his baggage and as he's finishing he hears a commotion in the road. He goes to the window and down there in the road, lining up at the hitching rail, are many horsemen and their horses. Francis doesn't count. He knows exactly how many there will be.

Francis slings his saddlebag over his shoulder and closes the door behind him and hurries down the hall. He halts atop the stairwell, listening to the clatter of the front door, followed by many voices and many boots on the hardwood floor. Francis runs to the other end of the hall and charges up the stairs to the third floor. He hears men climbing the stairs below, kicking open doors on the second floor, one after another, flipping beds, cursing.

Francis goes straight to the hall window. He works the latch and slides the window open and hangs one leg over the edge, and then repositions the saddlebag over his shoulder and reaches for the iron drainpipe with one hand, and then both hands, and straddles the pipe and slides to the ground and drops to a crouch. He sneaks and weaves among their horses until he comes to his own horse and hastily heaves the saddlebags over the horse's rump without even securing them and puts one foot in the stirrup, ready to jump aboard, when he pauses, looking back at all thirty-eight horses at the rail, their riders still crashing about, flipping beds inside the hotel.

❊

Temple, Ned, and Samuel stand in the road outside the mining supply house, kicking pebbles, waiting for Francis' return.

They hear him before they see him. The gallop of a horse through a small town is unmistakable. Francis comes around the bend and into plain sight but doesn't slow as he draws near. He's leaning into the horse's withers, whacking its flank with his hat. With one hand he points back behind him, to the place whence he came. Then he points forward, to the road ahead.

He flies by, staring straight ahead.

"What in hell," says Temple.

The three share a quick look of confusion. Before any one of them can speak, they turn to the thunder of hooves as thirty-eight horses come pounding into view, heading straight for them.

Temple, Ned, and Samuel jump saddle and they're off.

Devil Take the Hindmost

The road winds through an oak grove, dappled with sun, the light clicking on and off as Francis races beneath the trees. When he breaks free of the forest and reaches the meadowland at the mouth of the valley, Francis glances over his shoulder and sees Samuel, Ned, and Temple right behind, and the Carter Gang not much further behind them.

Francis whacks the mare's flank, trying to bring her to a lather. Riding this hard beneath the heat of the morning sun, it shouldn't take long before his horse, and consequently the other horses too, break a sweat.

Francis reaches down and feels the side of the horse's neck, the muscles pumping rhythmically beneath his touch. The flesh is hot and moist. The black pelt grows slick. And then he hears the first whinny behind him.

He turns over his shoulder and sees within the throbbing anonymity of the Carter herd a single animal rear back on its haunches and throw its rider and roll madly in the dust of the road. Before Francis faces forward, a second horse enters a similar state of derangement, and then two more on the instant.

Francis rides on, slowing just enough for his brother to catch up.

"What's going on?" yells Samuel.

Behind them, the Carter Gang is in chaos, their horses squealing like train-brakes and writhing in the dirt.

Francis reaches back and retrieves something from his saddlebag. He holds it up for Samuel to see. It's a solitary red pepper, glistening with oil. Just like the ones he placed beneath the saddles.

Francis and the Cooper

With the Carter Gang far behind, horseless and disabled, the Blackstone Templars ride through the morning, across meadows, over streams. They pass like dusted wraiths over the blackened turf of a pine field recently demoralized by lightning fire, and then into meadow again where sunrain materializes from an azure sky and dampens their brow and cools their horses. There is a wind, which means weather in these mountains is on a conveyor belt. You can see storms glowering on the peaks, and the blue between storms, and the storms lining up just behind. The gang moves northwest.

Bob Temple says the Central Pacific Railroad goes direct through Sacramento, and Modesto too, which they could reach in a week. From there to Chesterville is anyone's guess as the town somehow jumps about on a map, appearing both here and there depending on who's looking.

"Let's stop a moment," says Francis. "I want to try this thing."

They pause on the banks of the Merced. The river pours through the bowl of the valley, an icy blue with yellow flowers clustering about the trail.

Francis lifts the Cooper from its holster and loads all five balls into their chambers and tamps each in place and then loads the percussion caps onto their pins, just like he was shown.

"First time?" says Ned.

"Yup," says Francis, lifting the pistol and pinching one eye.

"What are you aiming at?" says Samuel.

"Just that tree."

"Wait. Let's set it up proper."

Samuel jumps down from his horse and gathers a handful of riverstones and stacks them on a nearby log.

Bob Temple lights a cigar, observing the weather, and Ned just watches all.

"All right," says Samuel, stepping back from the log. "Let's see what you can do."

Still sitting horseback, Francis cocks the pistol and then jerks the pistol level and fires.

The gun booms in his hand, shattering the diamond of stillness they did not even know existed until the whole thing flies apart on a sound. When the world again takes shape the target is gone.

Bob Temple's heart skips a beat.

"Nice shot!" yells Samuel.

Ned slow-claps three times and glances over at Temple, whose cigar lies smoking in the dirt. "You all right there, Bob?"

"Of course," he says. "Yeah, of course. Good shot, Francis."

Except Bob Temple didn't even hear the shot. He doesn't know what he heard. Temple twists about in his saddle, as though searching for its source.

"What's up, Bob?"

"It's nothing." He shakes his head dismissively.

"You sure?" says Ned.

"Yeah, we're good." says Temple, glancing back at the mountains again, the ridgelines and peaks. "You didn't hear nothing though?"

"Like what?"

"You didn't hear any bells or . . . you didn't hear any bells?"

"Bells?"

"Forget it," says Temple.

"What kind of bells?"

"Forget it. Let's keep moving."

Bells or no bells, thinks Temple, it came from far, far away.

CHAPTER FIVE
Whispering Hush, Dear Child, Sweet Vivid Child

It takes all of midday to climb Tioga Pass. The path is an endless series of switchbacks through stunted pine and there is still snow at the top and jaw-cracking views of the next valley over, an hourglass lake in the vale, same blue as the sky.

"Beautiful country," says Temple.

They sit their horses in silence, gazing down into the valley.

Ned says, "Is it true what they say? About you scalping an angel?"

Bob Temple doesn't reply immediately. He continues to take in the view. "You know, Ned," says Temple, adjusting his hat. "I have often wondered at your jackasstic nonsense. Asked myself if it might not be an act. A way to draw laughter from friends. But no, I believe I now see the light, or its lack thereof, and so comprehend the full scope and sincerity of your stupiddom. It is a thing of marvel really. Now that I ponder it."

"I'm not saying I believe it. I just wanted to hear what —"

"Shut your mouth, Ned," says Temple, tugging on the reins and leading his horse down the pass. "Just shut it."

Their descent is steep, and before long they reach the floor of the valley. A sprawling expanse of meadow opens before them, severed by a brook, the delicate tinkling music of which is a perfect match to the cadence of light that flickers like sequins across the water's rippling surface, and they ride its grassy banks, the grass itself running with the wind on long pulsing waves.

Samuel pulls alongside Ned. "You don't have to aggravate him."

"I wasn't even trying to," says Ned.

"He's having it rough," says Samuel. "I think he's feeling his age, being around us. Maybe go easy on him."

"Since when are you the sage? Isn't that your brother's job?"

"Maybe we're not so different."

Ned snorts in response and Samuel's back goes straight. "Just saying Temple's a person too," says Samuel. "And touchy with a pistol."

In the distance two riders approach on horseback. They don't appear to be in any hurry. They ride side by side, two inkblots shimmering on the distant grassland.

"Ahwahnechee," says Samuel.

"How you know from here?"

"Size of their ponies. And the way they sit them. They're riding bareback."

But the truth is, even at this distance there is something of the legendary shrouding their approach, some cool aura that Samuel cannot identify except for its otherness and that's enough.

As the Ahwahnechee draw near, the gang get their first view of the Yosemite Indians. The two braves are shirtless with chests and faces painted in broad white stripes, and they wear many necklaces and their black hair is pulled back into plaits. Their limbs are long and athletic, their gaze direct. Altogether their appearance is irrevocably masculine, like men of another order—or painted deities even, on errand from a myth.

When the Ahwahnechee are roughly ten yards away it becomes clear they will take the centre path down the trail, forcing the gang to either side, and perhaps it is the boldness of two men riding directly through four that makes the Indians twice as intimidating.

The Ahwahnechee glance coolly, intrusively into each of the faces they pass and ride on and speak not a word and when they have passed Francis turns over his shoulder to watch the riders recede into the distance.

"That's it?" says Francis.

"We'll see," says Temple.

Peace and Other Torments

They pitch camp later that afternoon in a copse of willow for the cover it offers but the trees block the wind and the mosquitoes are wretched. Between the wrist and elbow of one arm Francis counts eight. He watches with fascination as they suck greedily at his flesh, their little bloodsockets swelling like berries until one by one they buzz fatly away.

But where to? To what other purpose?

Does anyone know?

Over the pulse of coals, the Templars cook beans and bacon, and mosquitoes add themselves to the mix. No one bothers to pick them out. Every thing broken down to its mineral constituents must have some nutritive value. At the very least, thinks Francis, he recovers some little bit of himself with each mosquito he eats.

After supper he and Samuel wash pots in the brook. They squat on the grassy banks with the stack of pots between them, scouring out the burnt beans with green stalks of horserush and sand and rinsing the pots in clear cold water that scalds their fingers red. They don't speak, though their movements commune and accord as will happen among brothers. It's almost like the old days, before their mother left and things went raw.

While Francis and Samuel Wash Pots

Bob Temple goes for a stroll.

The sun is still up, not very high, but warm and bright, and Temple wanders the deer trail out of camp and squelches down to a peat bog at the terminus of the valley. He sits down on a log. There are little slicks of oil, tiny chemical rainbows on the surface of the peatpuddles. Temple looks at that. He looks up at the mountains, studying their ridgelines.

Sometimes Temple believes the nature of his past has placed some voodoo upon the present, as well as any mercy or solace that may enter into it. If that is the case, he wonders, how is a man to move forward? And what if he can't?

Temple closes his eyes for a time. He listens to a creek somewhere behind him, further up the vale. A gentle wind brushes his cheek and then all the aspen come alive, their leaves shivering in the breeze. It's the kind of sound that makes your whole body go quiet. Even your skin starts to listen. You open your eyes, and the grass and the rocks and the lichens on the rocks—everything is new.

Temple tips his face to the sky, his cheeks drawing like embers. When it's warm like this, the sun like a god, in light like this a person can forgive himself anything. Nearly anything.

Bob the Barber

"How long does it take to cut one person's hair?" asks Ned.

"Long as it takes to do it right," says Bob Temple. He stands behind Francis with a pair of tin shears, snipping clumps of raven-black hair in the firelight of their camp.

"You're just a bit of everything," says Ned. "Full of surprises, cutting hair. Where'd you even learn it?"

"Same man who taught me dynamite."

"That will do," says Francis, preparing to stand.

Temple presses Francis back down. "His name was Hun Chow," he says. "Old guy. A miner. He could do anything with dynamite. Could probably carve a rocking chair out of the stuff."

Temple takes up a handful of wavy black bangs, cuts a straightish line. "It was actually Chow's map that started all this. His map to the coalmine. Which reminds me, Francis. You still have that thing?"

"God no. It stunk to high heaven."

"So you tossed it?"

"I tossed it, Bob. It was that or feed it to the vultures."

Temple is about to complain but chances are he would've done the same. The map was a human hand. A petrified fist, once belonging to Chow's long-dead brother. It looked like a shrivelled claw. It had creepy little markings inscribed into the leathery grey palm. You had to pry back the fingers just to read it.

"Well," says Temple, still snipping away. "I suppose Chow isn't around to argue."

It's perhaps because of this fact that Temple feels comfortable confessing his long-held admiration for the old man.

"It's like Chow . . . it's like he had this, this very particular kind of intelligence," Temple expounds for the youth. "Call it oriental, what have you. Clever with his hands. Headstrong. Never let you see his real thinking. I always said Chow would make a stupendous cardsharp."

Bob Temple taps the back of Francis' head and then tilts it forward. And then a little to the side.

"Plus he had this bulging mole on his forehead. Had three black hairs coming out. It's like you could just stare and stare and it never got less interesting."

Temple quietly recalls how he'd once, in a fitful moment of abandon, reached across a table in attempt to touch the mole and the old man had slapped his hand away. They never spoke of the incident. They'd simply looked away from each other, like it never happened.

"Now you see here," says Temple, crouching down as he works the hairline above Francis' ears. "This is how I finish up. I start by naturalizing the sides."

"Is that a word?"

"It's what I call my technique. Barbering's got all kinds of techniques. And there you are, Francis. Good to go."

Francis stands up and brushes the hairs from his chest. "How does it look?"

"You're really asking?" says Samuel. "A known felon just chopped your hair with a bolt-cutter. It looks like you'd expect."

Francis grins and tips his head forward and rubs it vigorously to rid himself of loose strands and he hears a faint zipping sound overhead. He straightens, confused, and turns around to see the feathered shaft of an arrow protruding from the tree directly behind him.

A war cry erupts from the trees and the first Ahwahnechee sprints into the firelight, heading straight for Francis with tomahawk upraised. Just before the blade splits his skull, Samuel swings a campshovel with all his considerable strength and clotheslines the man in the face—a blow that lifts the man clear of the ground before laying him flat upon it.

A tense moment follows, each person turning in place, pistols drawn, awaiting the next wave of assault. But nothing comes.

"Is it over?" says Ned. The Ahwahnechee man still lies out cold on the ground. He's breathing but otherwise dead to the world. It's one of the two fellows from earlier that day.

"Holy hot damn, man," says Ned, turning to Samuel. "You just levelled him! Were you swinging for the stars or what?"

"We should scout about," says Bob Temple. "There were two before, and I doubt—"

"Ah, bitch!" yells Ned, hopping on one leg. He has an arrow sticking out of his right flank. Still hopping about, he levels his pistol and opens fire into the darkness surrounding their camp, and then everyone is firing, blindly firing into the night, and then just the clicks of their empty chambers going around and the pistol smoke hazing their camp.

"I'm out. You?"

"I'm out."

"Reloading now," says Temple.

"I can't see a thing. You got spares?"

The haze clears just enough for the gang to identify a second Ahwahnechee marching into their camp. The man is huge, purposeful in his stride. He goes straight for Ned and shoves him hard to the ground. Ned turns just enough to avoid landing on the arrow and the Ahwahnechee is upon him in an instant. He stamps one foot upon Ned's buttocks, pinning him to the earth, and grabs hold of the arrow and yanks it free in a single swift movement. Ned yells in fury.

The Ahwahnechee points the arrow at Samuel, yelling what must be accusations or curses in his native tongue. He points the arrow at Temple and again yells his complaint, his eyes fuming in the firelight. The Ahwahnechee returns the arrow to his quiver and grabs his unconscious companion by the wrists and drags him out into the night.

Ned climbs to his feet and brushes himself off. The others stare off into the darkness where the Indians departed.

"I'm bleeding like a stuck pig," says Ned. "Next time, we make sure—"

A bright flash and a bang, and they turn to find Bob Temple standing there with arm outstretched, pistol in hand. Apart from re-cocking his pistol, he doesn't move an inch.

Samuel watches Bob a moment. "Did you get him?"

Bob Temple doesn't respond. He continues to stand there, his stance unchanged. Upon some unseen cue he drops his arm and marches into the dark. A moment later they hear another shot, and then two more.

Francis and Samuel look at one another but say nothing.

Another shot rings out, the last one.

Bob Temple doesn't return immediately. What takes place in this interval remains a mystery. When he emerges from the darkness the light smouldering in his eyes is such that no one dares acknowledge him. It's like a different Bob Temple. Yet another side of him no one cares to meet.

Temple's arms are slicked to the elbow with gore. He sits with a grunt beside the fire, staring into it, trance-like, blood dripping from the longest finger of each hand.

Temple clears his throat, still gazing at the fire.

"Like I was saying," he says. "Lots of techniques."

Why Is Bob Temple Like Himself and Not Some Other?

It's mainly because of his dream. The same dream he's always had.

He is in the saddle. He is tired and confused. He has ridden all day and is still far from the sun.

Why must he reach it? This question is never answered actually.

On the high desert road he discovers he is not alone but in fact travelling with a companion and has been all along. Central to the dream is a finger, solitary in its pointing. Also the scorching orange kiss of the sun at his back.

You said it was in the east, complains his companion.

So it had seemed from the west, where the sun now resides, pouring its lovely golden self upon the place whence they came.

Except Temple is not there. He is here instead, and there is a brokenness. It's like the ringing of bells. No matter which way he goes, it comes from far, far away.

Return to Trail

Ned rides his horse with both feet before him on the pommel, basically resting upon the horse's neck, as it's the only comfortable position for his wound.

"Shot with an arrow by the Ahwahnechee," he says aloud.

He's said this perhaps ten times already. It apparently has some ring to it. Some nuance that appeals to himself and no one else.

Or maybe it's because when we're young, we don't yet understand most of life is lived in the small moments. So we have to get shot with arrows. We have to jump too high and fall too far. This way we can relax and know we're not dead.

"Ned Runkle," says Ned, as though reading headlines in the sky. "Shot by Indians in the mountains of California..."

"You sing that one more time," says Samuel, "and you'll be singing a different tune."

"You're just jealous. Admit it."

"That you got shot, and I didn't?"

"You know this makes me a genuine baddie now," says Ned. "Don't pretend otherwise."

"How precisely does a second hole in your butt make you superior? That's what I'd like to know."

"Oh, you know."

"You better tell me then, because I plain don't."

"The women," says Ned.

"Ah."

"They love the scars."

"Of course."

Ned turns to Francis. "Hey, Francis, you decide for us... do women love scars?"

"More than anything, Ned. It's their favourite."

"There you have it."

"Why don't you ask him about his woman," says Samuel.

"What's her name again?" says Ned.

"Still working on that," says Francis.

"He doesn't know it," says Temple.

"You don't know her name?" says Ned.

Francis just grins.

"But what if it's, I don't know... Honeypie," says Ned. "Or Iguana. What if her name's Iguana?"

"It won't be."

"But what if it is?"

Francis shrugs. "Doesn't matter. She has other qualities."

"Or what about—"

"I'm telling you. It doesn't make the least difference to me."

"You are a minor wonder, Francis Blackstone. You know that?"

Francis grins, touching his hat. "And I'll tell you something else," he says.

"Oh yeah?"

"I don't give a damn what you think. Because we are in love."

Why Is Francis Blackstone Like Himself and Not Some Other? (Part II)

When Francis is six his father takes him to Winless, Arizona, to visit his grandmother. She is very old. The oldest person Francis has ever personally known. She is a mummy, and Francis refuses to touch her.

His father scolds him, insisting Francis should show respect for his elders. Francis is advised to pay attention to any wisdom she might impart.

But Francis can't see beyond the hideous bald patches on her scalp and the bags swinging from her eyes. It is literally his worst nightmare. His little heart races like a rabbit. He somehow evades her raspy kisses and brittle embrace, but most terrifying to Francis is her home, which he cannot escape. It's a museum of seclusion and decay, cramped with fusty memories, souring old trunks. Everything inside him recoils from the glass cases filled with china, and the shadowy knickknacks on the bureau. Every item he looks upon—every Delft teapot, every demented angel—is scary and pulsating with loneliness.

Francis sits on the sofa and listens to the solemn tocking of the clock. He eats stale peanuts from a glass dish on the coffee table. All the while his father whispers vehemently with his grandmother in the kitchen. Francis' grandmother is too old to be living alone. She should move back with them. She needs help.

After an infinity of boredom, nearly lethal in its span, Francis' father emerges from the kitchen and takes young

Francis by the arm. "It's time to leave. Say goodbye to your grandmother."

Francis looks down into his lap and realizes he's eaten all the peanuts from the dish. He apologizes.

"We'll buy her more," says his father. "Come on."

"Oh, don't bother," calls his grandmother from the kitchen. "The doctor says peanuts aren't good for me anyhow. I just suck the chocolate off."

Francis is hustled from the room and handed his coat and he puts it on. His father gives him his hat and he puts that on too. They walk out the door. Francis doesn't know it yet, but those will be his grandmother's last words to him.

Is it any wonder, really, he's never sought any counsel but his own?

As for Food Specifically and Luck in General

On a hot blue morning, between the towns of Slokum and Tyne Lake, Francis takes down a rabbit with his Cooper. One shot, one rabbit. Even before he pulls the trigger, staring down the barrel at that doomed round bunny, Francis already knows how it'll go. It's like that. The Cooper aiming itself.

❀

Twenty miles outside Modesto, in the heart of Stanislaus County, they spend the entire day working a walnut grove. They eat nuts all the while and still get paid.

❀

In Modesto proper they happen upon a church supper before they've even found lodging for the night. Sawhorse tables on the lawn and half a dozen grills. No one asks their names. No one cares where they came from. They eat so many chickens their hands hurt.

❀

And after the picnic the pastor takes them aside. The man is ill in some fashion. His body is no longer in accord with itself. It moves all wrong, every joint, every organ out of sync with the rest. Whatever the agent of distress, it has obliterated regions of his mind as well, leaving behind a shell of predatory goodwill.

Smiling beatifically, the pastor instructs them to stand in a line and put out their hands like so. He carefully places communion wafers into their outstretched palms. He pats them each on the head, even Temple.

"Now be good little boys and eat your Jesus."

The wafers are soaked in laudanum. He's that kind of fellow. It's that kind of church.

Like Francis' aim with the Cooper, it appears the gang's luck has gone magical and true.

And then the smooth straight line curves round.

CHAPTER SIX
If the Sun Is Too Far,
Lying Cold in Its Chamber

Francis Blackstone turns fifteen years old in a redbrick hotel in Modesto, California, and his brother Samuel pays for his first shave and a bath for seventy-five cents with lilac oil included. Francis comes out smelling like a dandy.

He and Samuel stand abreast in the road, taking it all in.

It's that time of year when people rise in the morning, go about their day, mark their calendars, and so forth. The rich tone of it lies thick as nostalgia on the air.

"I got a feeling," says Francis, picking his teeth with a toothpick.

"Who knows," says Samuel, doing the same. "Maybe one is enough."

A passenger buggy approaches and Samuel raises two fingers for a ride. The driver doesn't notice however and rolls directly past. Samuel says to Francis, "What do you suppose Father's doing right now?"

"Reading something."

Samuel chortles. "Probably right."

"He's probably in the den right now, reading that book."

"Which one?"

"I don't know," says Francis. "Whichever book he's always reading."

They stand for a time. Two brothers watching the road. Samuel begins to fidget.

Francis turns away and flicks his toothpick. "Why don't you say what's really on your mind."

Samuel hesitates. He considers the question that's been growing on him. "Do you think she's with someone?"

"Mother?"

Samuel nods and Francis falls quiet. He says, "I don't know. I've tried not to think about it." After a moment he says, "I suppose I hope so."

"Me too," says Samuel, nodding. "And I hope I never meet him."

Another wagon comes clattering up the road, this time from the other direction. Samuel steps forward. He again raises his hand and again the wagon rattles by. Samuel spits in the road. He toes at a pebble.

Their mother is the clattering tailgate on a wagon that doesn't stop. Their father is the rutted track it leaves behind.

Francis says, "I thank you by the way."

"For what?"

"That Indian, back in the valley. He had me cold and you know it."

"You're my brother," says Samuel. "What could I do?"

But Francis knows Samuel could have done any number of things. Somehow he chose the one that made them both not dead.

"Well," says Francis. "That was some swing. You really put your back into it."

Samuel smiles. And then, because their manner is running perilously close to sentiment, its soft ugly head rearing like a velveteen Cyclops, Samuel rescues them both by placing Francis in a headlock and tweaking his nose. A generosity for which Francis is grateful.

Left to Wonder

In a small room above the saddler on Nickel Street, they take Ned in for a doctor's visit. The doctor says little, scrubbing the wound with iodine and packing it with a clean cloth. After departing the man's office, Bob Temple sneaks back upstairs on his own.

"I have some concerns," he begins.

The doctor sits in an upholstered chair behind a mahogany desk while Temple describes his condition in great detail from a wooden stool opposite. He describes the bells. He describes the accompanying feeling, or presentiment, that he is being called from a great distance. Also the inkling of doom that sits like a mist on his eye.

The doctor listens patiently. He nods. He squints at key junctures in the monologue to demonstrate his attention. When Temple is done speaking the doctor leans forward on his desk and steeples his palms in thought. He rubs his nose with that steeple. He says, "Tinnitus."

"You sure?"

"Absolutely."

Bob Temple scratches his neck. "What can I do about it?"

The doctor leans back in his seat. "You are in which line of work?"

"It varies."

"I see."

The doctor again steeples his palms. They again go to the nose. "In that case," he says, "I advise less drink, and never from a pewter mug. And do you plug your ears when you shoot? No? Well consider it."

"Will that stop the bells?"

The doctor nods in such a way as to make Temple feel the answer is no, not really. But it's good counsel all the same.

Temple rubs his jaw.

He says he forgot to mention he gets this strange feeling of unreality. About everything. Like maybe his whole life was hallucinated by a school of pulsating jellyfish. Or like people can hear his thoughts. But they pretend like they don't.

"Do you see what I'm getting at? Have you heard of this sort of thing before?"

The doctor looks at him. "I will be honest with you."

"All right."

"I'd say you're suffering from what we call an existential crisis. The tinnitus is a symptom. Not the malady itself. More an indicator."

"All right. What can you give me for it?"

The doctor supposes aloud that Bob Temple has done something sufficiently bad in his past that he is now divided in himself, at once seeking to bury this deed and to also parade it, such that he can be properly remorseful and penitent and absolved.

"Cut it," says Temple. "I didn't ask for a scolding. Your armchair voodoo. I'm asking what you can do about it."

The doctor thrums his fingers on the desk. He gets up from his chair and goes to the bookcase by the window. He stands there a moment, nodding at the shelves. He selects a book and returns to the desk but not his chair, instead going down on one knee beside Temple. He places the book into

Temple's hands. It's a King James with gilt writing down the spine.

"Pray with me," says the doctor.

These Crooked-Tooth Streets,
No One Knows Where They Go

They encounter the train tracks on the way back to their hotel. It's Samuel who first spots them. "Well there it is," he says, pointing out the parallel stripes of iron running the gravel bed beside the road. "You suppose this is a passenger line?"

This sidebranch of the Central Pacific runs the ninety-five miles between Modesto and Fresno. Temple isn't actually sure what kind of train it is, what it carries.

Francis stares down the tracks at the point where they go from parallel to pinched.

"We should take a crack at it."

"It may not even be a passenger train," says Temple. "The Sacramento line, sure, but this could be a goods train. Lumber or cows, or who knows what."

"And it could be passengers."

Temple thinks on this. "We'll intercept it twenty miles down the line. Middle of nowhere. Good practice either way, and by the time we reach the Central Pacific proper we'll have our ducks in a row."

The gang is in agreement. They are excited to begin.

"But first," says Temple, "I'd like a twist at the tiger's tail. Who's in?"

Modesto, California, has more gambling houses than any other kind of establishment. Temple has the itch, and a pocketful of change. Overcome by a sudden, inexplicable goodwill, Bob Temple announces the first card is on him.

"Who's coming? Ned?"

"I think I'll lay low," says Ned. "Give the old caboose a rest before we saddle up again."

"Me too," says Samuel. "I'll see you back at the hotel."

"Francis?" says Temple. "Come on. You aren't curious to know what goes on in a den of vice?"

"All right."

"Good man."

Temple leads the way. The streets of Modesto are boisterous and brassy. On the nearest corner, three mariachis in red velvet suits blow trumpets at the sky. Directly opposite, a pair of prostitutes lingers on a bench, legs crossed, sipping tea and addressing passersby. Bob Temple is enthralled.

"It's like something straight out of a Dickens novel!" he exclaims. Bob Temple sometimes likes to compare things to said novels. Especially when in a good mood. "All these crazy little streets, everybody out and about…"

Like most people, Bob Temple has never read a Charles Dickens novel. He has a sense of them though. And this place here, it's like an exact replica of the imaginary book in his head. He nods to himself, looking agreeably about: shoeless children, skinny dogs, cowboys, reprobates, Mexican saints. They got it just right.

Francis, on the other hand, is absorbed in the actual noise of it all, the chaos of voices as he and Temple pass idlers on the street. Francis picks up bits of conversation as they go, but only the bits: a friendly argument here, a discussion on wheat prices there. It's as though Francis has arrived at some mythical location where words are discarded after being stolen by the wind, all the fragments of dialogue cut short in a breeze.

Temple leads Francis into the first place with a tiger emblazoned on a placard in the window. It's a public house. There's a long mirror behind the bar, a pair of couches and a low chandelier hanging over a solitary card table. Six men stand around the table, hunched and speculative in a mystic cloud of cigar smoke.

"You ever play before?" says Temple.

"Is this faro?"

"The one and only," says Temple.

"Is it hard?"

"Well. Depends on whether you're aiming to win or lose. We'll call it a matter of perspective."

Francis is literally down to his last dime. This seems an efficient way to blow it.

Overlaying the table is a felted board upon which each man has laid a single card and his wager. Temple and Francis squeeze in.

Temple explains into his ear, "Now this man here, end of the table, he's what you call the banker. He flips two cards from the deck. There and there. If that first one matches your card, you lose. If the second one matches, you win. Plus there's side bets."

"Sounds simple enough."

A barmaid appears at Francis' shoulder. "Something to drink?"

Temple leans past him. "Whiskey and a wine. Mixed." His voice returns to a whisper. "Now just forget everything I told you. Faro is perhaps the only game on earth that has nothing to do with the rules. It's a cheater's game. It's about who cheats best."

"Does the banker know?"

"He's best of them all. That's why he's the banker. Now watch and learn."

Temple raises a finger and receives a card. He places it on the board. It's a jack of hearts. He sets a dime upon the upper left corner of the card. He lights a cigar. He glances at the men left and right of him. The banker pulls a card from the deck and turns it over. Six of spades. He turns a second card. Four of clubs.

Francis notices the moment the second card is overturned, there is a bustling about the table, a twinkling of subtle movements and gesturing. Among them Francis notices one player shift slightly to his left and by some arcane force the coin sitting atop his card slides free and disappears into his hand.

"Horsehair!" yells the man beside him at the table. "He's got a horsehair attached to his dollar! Just took it back!"

"I did no such thing," argues the accused.

The accuser steps back and punches the other fellow in the nose.

"So that's faro," says Temple.

The barmaid appears and Temple lifts the glass from the tray and drains it in a series of hectic, audible gulps, returns the empty to the tray and nods at the barmaid to indicate another. "Ready to give it a try?"

"Why not," says Francis.

❖

Francis and Temple sit down on the couch with more drinks, just watching the activity at the table. They don't speak.

Francis tripled his dime and then lost it all. He's fine with that. Temple managed to come out ahead on his wagers but despite his winnings a dangerous mood has overtaken him. He feels the self-destructive urge to express himself honestly. This has never gone well.

"I'm feeling old," says Temple to his wine, avoiding Francis' gaze. "That or losing my mind. I don't know which. It's the damnedest. Hearing bells and such."

Temple cannot conceive why he should bare his soul to Francis, the one person most likely to put a bullet in it, but it's like a landslide now and he cannot halt the words.

"There comes a time," says Temple, still speaking to the glass in his hand, "when you realize your thoughts have all turned to the past. It used to be the future, but now it's the past. And that, my friend, is how you know you're getting on. It is the grand turning from which there is no return. And I know you don't know what I'm talking about, because I was you once, Francis, long ago, I was there, I was young and brimming with vigour and understanding nothing at all about what lies ahead, so I sure don't know why I'm telling you of all people, but there you have it."

Temple sniffs and touches his nose.

"Feeling old, I guess. Like it's all catching up," he says. "And there's no way to go back and fix it. Any of it."

Following this confession, it takes Temple a moment, and considerable strength of will, to bring himself to even look at Francis but when he does Francis is not there and Temple is alone on the couch with his wineglass and what remains within it. His vision stings and blurs for the tiniest of instants.

❋

Temple swipes his eyes and lifts his glass and then pauses, noticing Francis' empty glass is gone too. He was sure Francis drank something—didn't he? Temple glances briefly about for some residue of Francis, or rather some evidence that Temple has not been sitting here on this sofa talking to himself all along but he finds nothing to confirm this, one way or the other, until he stares at his left hand and then places the right hand atop it to quell the shaking.

But this just sends the shaking to his elbow.

Awakening

Bob Temple is still sitting on the couch, coming to grips with his ninth or possibly tenth glass of wine when another man enters the public house. The man wears a hat and a vest and maybe a mustache, maybe not, by which to say he is any man. Any number of men.

To Temple this is — by virtue of some bleary logic that nevertheless shimmers like an apocalyptic rainbow — a distinguishing moment. Whatever this man's appearance, Temple realizes, it will change. All of it, gone. Vanished. Of no consequence whatsoever, because no man is who he appears to be on the outside. He is something else.

How has Temple failed to understand this before?

Perhaps, thinks Temple, this is why the author has not bothered to describe Temple's own appearance in any meaningful way. And upon that thought Temple sees himself, for the first time, as inhabiting two worlds: the one self-initiated and organized, a shuddering nautilus of private whims. The other world too terrifyingly huge to contemplate. For it is linked to fate, and also to Temple feeling like a mere whisper in a grander, grittier pronouncement. One that has the ability to quite literally erase him from existence.

But then, thinks Bob Temple, perhaps this concern is merely a projection of the author's — for the author too has a life, and an author larger than he, and after all, Temple's life and the author's can't be so different. In fact Temple has the advantage of having originated in the author's mind and therefore been granted unique privileges, unique access, shall we say, to regions of the author's life he would certainly not like made public. Oh, the stories Temple could tell.

You can't stumble about inside someone's noggin without learning a secret or two. For example —

And the author cuts him off there. Because he can do that. And Temple nods quietly to himself, grasping something he has not grasped before.

Temple stands abruptly and walks directly to the newcomer at the faro table and taps him on the shoulder. The man turns about, appearing faintly repulsed at having been touched by this swaying languisher, though the philosophical glow clinging to Temple's person is unmistakable.

"Can I help you?" says the man.

"I want you to know," slurs Temple, "your face is meaningless. Means nothing. And that's final." Temple makes a horizontal slashing gesture with his palm, the momentum of which nearly sends him tumbling. The newcomer twists away, unimpressed, returning his attention to the table.

"Don't you turn away from me!"

Temple spins the newcomer about and punches him in the jaw, only to discover it is not the newcomer he has punched, but the man beside the newcomer, Temple having selected inaccurately, and this other man, the actual recipient of the punch, is also the recipient of eleven boxing titles between here and Tacoma, and he returns to Temple the initial violence done to himself as though eager to reshape the structure of Temple's personality by way of his face, which in the strangest fashion is esoterically satisfying to Temple. As though some previously reached understanding about the mutable appearance of all things were now physically confirmed.

Lying on his back on the floor, Temple gurgles a sigh of relief.

A Thing Is Discussed

"Since when do you smoke?" says Francis.

Returning to the hotel, he has found Samuel sitting alone on the front steps with one of Bob Temple's cigars in hand. Samuel rakes a match against the steps and lights the cigar, puffing it alive.

"Since right...now," he says, blowing the first cone of smoke. "I'm making some changes, Francis."

"Oh yeah?"

"I've been doing some thinking."

Francis sits down beside him. "Well I'm happy to hear it."

Francis doesn't inquire any further about said changes. He already has a sense of them. He points back at the hotel with his thumb. "How's Ned doing?"

"Ned? Oh, he's fine. Just resting inside. Ned's always fine, you know that."

"Yeah."

Samuel checks his shoulder and then turns back around. He considers the cigar in his hand. "Did I ever tell you," he says, "I once saw Ned knock himself out with a sneeze?"

Francis smiles. "I've seen him do that too."

"No!"

Francis nods. "You know that little scar he's got above his eyebrow?"

"He told me that was a fish hook!" says Samuel.

"He was just opening the cabinet, and kerchoo. Kerblam. Flat on the floor."

"Damn," says Samuel, puffing meditatively upon the cigar. "And he had this whole story about the fish hook."

"I guess there's no need to mention it," says Francis. "Would just embarrass him."

"Oh, Ned wouldn't care if I knew. It's you he wants to impress."

"Me?"

Samuel gives him a look.

"Why me?"

"Come on, Francis. You know he thinks you're some kind of hero or something. Some kind of sage."

"Well. I guess that says more about Ned than me."

"I tried to tell him."

"Ned's a good guy. He's got a good heart," says Francis.

Samuel pulls the cigar from his mouth. He studies it a moment, perhaps questioning if it might not be the idea of the cigar rather than the cigar itself he is drawn to.

"You want to know something else?" says Samuel. "I have never once in all my life seen Ned scared. I was just thinking that. Not once."

"I guess I haven't either."

"Temple likes to razzle him. We all do. But there's more to Ned. I'm just really realizing that."

"Yeah," says Francis. "There's probably more to everyone."

Samuel strikes another match, this one just to look at. "Nah. Not everyone."

❧

Francis takes a puff on the cigar and then after a long bout of coughing vows to never do so again.

"Can I ask you something?" he says, pushing the tears from his cheeks. "What are you even doing out here?"

"Smoking a cigar, brother."

"No, I mean out here. Riding about." He gestures broadly with his hand. "You and Ned—you two were never the hellraisers."

"Ned's out here to get rich," says Samuel. "I thought that was obvious. Get rich and maybe see his name in writing somewhere. Written across some marquee."

"And you?"

Samuel looks straight ahead. "I think you know."

"Not really," says Francis. "Is it because of Mother? I know you never cared for home much after she left."

Samuel shakes his head. "No. It's not like that."

They sit for a while. Samuel strikes another match. When it burns down to his fingertips he hisses and tosses it away. "I'm not like you, Francis. No one here is."

"Oh, don't start with that."

"You asked. I don't like talking about it either."

Francis goes quiet.

"You remember," says Samuel, "you remember in Sunday School, when they told us to recite the Lord's Prayer, and that one time you changed all the words?"

"I remember they striped me for it. And made me copy out six pages of verse."

"You told them," says Samuel, "you did it because you had a star in your heart. And your heart was in your head."

"I don't recall that bit."

"It's what you said."

"Well anyhow."

"And after they knocked you about with the switch, and you came back bruised all over, your whole back just swollen like a plum, they asked you to recite the Lord's Prayer again. To do it properly."

"Yeah."

"And do you remember what you did?"

"I do."

"Well that's why, Francis. That's why I'm out here. Why I go where you go."

Francis just sits for a while.

"It's hard for you to hear, isn't it," says Samuel.

Francis nods.

"Imagine being the one having to say it."

Francis smiles.

They sit for a while.

When the last trace of awkwardness has been buttoned up and tucked away Francis says, "But guess what."

"What."

"Bob Temple's in jail."

"For what?" says Samuel, flicking a lit match into the street and striking another.

"Stopping a fist with his jaw back at the gambling house, and then getting carted off in a wagon only to have his face recognized on a wanted poster. Did you know Mr. Robert Laramie Temple's got five hundred dollars on his head?"

"No," says Samuel. Then: "Should we do anything about it?"

"He's already turned in. The reward's probably collected."

"No, I mean about busting him out."

"I didn't realize you cared so much."

"Yeah," smiles Samuel. "He's a bit of a puffed shirt. A disappointment all around. But he's growing on me."

"Me too I guess. You got a plan?"

"I thought we do it your style. No plan at all."

"You just keep getting better."

Outside the Jailhouse

It's nighttime, and there's hardly any activity on the street. The nearest lantern flickers inside the sheriff's quarters, other side of the jailhouse. The three boys hunch in the shadows of the brick wall separating Bob Temple from the extant world.

"How much do we use?" says Samuel.

On the ground before them sits the open box of dynamite. Francis rubs his jaw. Ned is holding the reins of their horses. He glances up at the barred window outside Bob Temple's cell.

"I say all of it," says Ned.

"You understand Bob is just other side of this wall, right?" says Samuel.

"Okay, half then."

"That's still a lot of dynamite to blow out the bars on one window."

Ned throws his hands in the air. "What do you suggest?"

There are actually equations to determine how much explosive to use in any given situation but they don't know about these. They resort to a complex system of coin tosses, and by their lights calculate an exciting variable that ranges between one and seven sticks of pure nitroglycerine dynamite.

"Hold still," says Francis, climbing his brother's shoulders. Ned grumbles that it's his dynamite, he paid for it, and laments the present debility that disallows his climbing the window.

"You get the next one," Francis assures him. "Now pass me up a wad of that paraffin."

Ned passes him the paraffin. Balanced atop his brother, Francis moulds it between his hands and reaches up to the barred window and slaps a thick band of paraffin along the bottom edge of the sill. He presses in a single stick of dynamite and slowly lifts his hands away. The dynamite stays put.

"Give me another," says Francis.

"You sure?" says Samuel.

"Hell no. Give me another."

❧

Meanwhile Temple is lying on a cot in his cell, touching at the alien puffiness of his face. It doesn't even feel like his face. It feels like a haunch of meat with nerve endings going haywire beneath the calloused pads of his fingers.

He scrapes a bit of dried blood from his lower lip and is inspecting the black flake between his fingertips when he hears something outside the window and sits up on his cot.

Francis' face appears briefly through the bars of the window. "Get back."

"What? Francis? Is that you?"

But Francis has already dropped from sight.

Temple has perhaps two, maybe three instants to consider the meaning of this visitation before he hears a familiar hiss outside his window.

"You sonuva—"

Temple throws himself to the floor and rolls the cot over his backside. The explosion atomizes the exterior wall and blows the bars opposite from their footing, throwing Temple clear of the jail cell and into the administrative lounge. He wakes half-deaf and bedazzled with a giant Samuel Blackstone gripping his wrists and hauling him up from the ringing rubble. Bob Temple is shoved about until he finds himself straddling a horse and holding on for dear life as they gallop out of Modesto and into the jangled, preposterous night.

Dearest girl,

I haven't yet told you about my father. He is
supposedly a very smart man. He wears a suit
each day. Even Sundays, when he doesn't leave the
house. My grandparents were missionaries. When
my father was a boy they took him to South America
by steamer and he caught malaria. Now he has a scar
on his chest where they bled him. Here is what my
father believes.

He believes eating after sundown is unhealthy.

He believes talking too much is unhealthy. It
weakens the heart.

He believes air baths are healthy. Each afternoon
he opens all the windows and doors in his den and
takes off his clothes. He sits at his desk for fifteen
minutes with eyes closed. And then he is done.

Music is healthy, but not all music. Wagner is
healthy. Schubert is healthy. Chopin, not at all. We
own a phonograph. He can listen to Brahms all day
but who can say what he hears?

My father has many opinions but I don't know
what they do for him. He also has about a thousand
books and he says he read to me as a child — but if
this event ever happened I no longer recall it.

Do you ever wonder about that, how memory
paints a different picture? I do. My oldest memory
is more like a vision. I can see my hand outstretched.
The dense pelt of a cat moves beneath, a very big cat.

I grip the scruff of its neck and then I am straddling its back, bounding through woods, wind, meadows, stars. I don't know when this could have happened, or even how, which makes me always wonder if it was a dream. All I can say is: I remember.

My mother is harder to describe. We would often find her standing alone in a room, peering at some wall like it held back the sea. When she came out of these moods she would say incredible things: She had kissed the devil in her youth, curly horns and all. If she disappeared for a day it only meant she had died. The secret to real courage was wonder. A good pair of boots and wonder.

The truth is she was a champion without a fight. I think those walls she stared at reminded her of another life. One she was promised before the world took hold and burned her down to a nub. But she kept her feelings hid well. Maybe too well. You only ever saw them in the tiniest things.

Like once, back when Landry's had that old slot machine against the back wall—do you remember? We would have been about eight at the time—I found a penny lying on the floor while my mother was making purchases. Without much thought, I shoved the penny into the slot and yanked back on the lever. Before I knew what was happening, coins were pumping out onto the floor. Old man Landry broke into a sweat and rushed in there with an empty sack. He started scooping up the coins.

He said that slot machine was a display only, never meant for use.

My mother didn't say a word. She just went about her business. If you saw her that day, picking out borax and purple thread, you'd have never known she was bothered. But before leaving the store, she did one thing.

She went right up to Landry with his sack of coins on the counter, and she pinched a single penny from the pile. She held it up so Landry could see.

This one, she said, was already his. Then she put the penny in my hand before we walked out the door.

She became my hero that day.

Much later, when she walked out the door for real, it was like we'd rehearsed it already. Because really, it was just that penny business all over again: her staying quiet and quiet and then finding her voice all at once.

Besides, in her own way, she had prepared us all along for what she was about to do. She read it to us—or recited it, really—every night before bed. A poem she called "With Wings Like These."

I can't say I ever understood the poem, not entirely. When I'd ask her anything about it she'd say, Just listen. You must listen. And then she'd recite it again. It began "When black night and its genie," and then went on to tell the story of a sun that was cold, and too far away. But the part I got was at the end, where she just flies out the window to meet the sun in the sky, like nothing else mattered, and it's the most beautiful thing you can imagine.

I've often wondered where my mother learned that poem. A governess? A book of fairytales? Maybe she made it up. I used to imagine her with wings on her back, floating high in the sky. And then one night she just disappeared.

My mother read to us too. She read from huge, clothbound books that covered her whole lap. She liked the weight of them because a book, she said, holds so much more than its pages. She said books were the only kind of art she knows about that's made completely in code. Two folks look at a page full of writing: one sees squiggles, the other, a world.

So one evening we were on the steps of the porch, Samuel on one side, me on the other, with Mother reading *Alice's Adventures* by lamplight in between. My mother did all the voices. She did the Duchess. She did the Dormouse. She even sang the "Lobster Quadrille" as though it were a song instead of a poem.

She was reading that passage where Alice is called up as a witness and accidentally knocks over the jury box with all the animals inside, when Samuel pointed to the page beneath our mother's hand.

Look, he said.

A firefly had landed there. Together we watched the thin panel of light, furthest from the firefly's head, as it blinked and blinked and in the final grip of life, blinked one last time, and then went still, never to blink again. The small bulb of its belly slowly dimmed across all six letters of a word, exactly the length of its body, which I believe it chose for that careful passing. One word, maybe a little too eerie to share.

But when you and I have our first daughter, I already know her name. We will call her Wonder. She will have wings of her own. And when we throw back the shutters, she will light up the night.

Francis Looks Down at Bob Temple.

"You're looking pretty ugly there, Bob."

"Just let me be."

Temple lies in the shade of a willow tree, one of many in a small cluster about an hour's ride north of Modesto. The gang camped here for the night. Pursuers never arrived or showed any sign of pursuing. And Temple shows no sign of rising anytime soon, though the sun is directly overhead. His face is swollen beyond recognition. He is pale and sweaty. He rolls about on his bedding, clutching senselessly at the air like an inebriated starfish.

"What do you think we should do?" asks Samuel.

Francis turns in place, looking about. The surrounding fields lie brown and fallow and rutted like a mile of corduroy in every direction. He doubts anyone can see them in the shade of this copse. He hears the mournful whistle of a train, somewhere east, and then he sees it chugging into view like a great grey snake spouting smoke over its shoulder. It whistles again.

"You think we could catch it?" says Francis.

"That train? You mean right now, without Bob?"

"I think we can catch it. We can head it off."

Samuel deliberates barely a moment before nodding. "Okay. Sure. We can do this."

"Yes we can."

"I'm actually excited."

"As you should be. We're about to rob a train."

Samuel is energized in a way Francis hasn't seen since they were kids. Samuel jogs off to locate a wandering Ned, and then turns in place.

"Hey, brother," yells Samuel.

"Yeah."

"I got a feeling about this."

"Me too."

"It's going to be good."

"It is going to be good," says Francis. "It's going to be real good. And make sure Ned brings along the rest of that dyno."

❖

They saddle their horses, saddlebags and all, hastily preparing for their adventures while the rhythmic grunting of the locomotive grows louder. They hear the whistle again.

"You ready?" says Samuel, jumping saddle.

"Ready," says Ned.

Hidden this side of the horse, Francis glances once more at the clay lamp in his hands. No one sees the lamp, or what Francis does before he slips it back into the sock and wraps it once and tucks it into the bottom of his saddlebag. He jumps saddle himself and adjusts his hat.

"All right," he says. "Bang bang shoot."

Spirit of Misadventure

The brakeman is standing on the ledge out front of the engine, just beside the grill, hauling back on the giant brake lever as the locomotive shrieks to a laboriously vivid halt in the middle of a potato field twenty miles northeast of Modesto.

The train sighs in a great wash of smoke and settles down on the tracks like a nest hen. The brakeman inspects the twisted wreckage of the tracks before him. Only dynamite could have done this kind of damage. The iron rails reach and twine like the tentacles of a kraken or some other antique leviathan emerging from the earth. He regards the three boys sitting their horses beside the tracks.

"Howdy," says the brakeman.

"Howdy," says Francis Blackstone, touching his hat.

The brakeman assesses their horses—perhaps the three most beautiful animals he has ever laid eyes upon—and then the condition of the tracks again, and finally the sky above as though the weather on this day were of equal importance.

"Is this a holdup, or are you boys here to repair the tracks?"

"Little of both," says Francis.

"How does that work?"

"I figured we'd come aboard. Do our thing. And afterward, if you got the tools and supplies, we'll pitch in and help you on your way."

"You boys armed?"

"Yeah."

"Let's see what you got."

Francis points his Cooper at the sky. Noting this, Samuel and Ned quickly follow suit.

The brakeman peers at them from his roost beside the grill, shading his eyes with one hand. "I can see yours is real. And yours is real. I'm not too sure about yours."

Ned turns the pistol sideways, displaying it with both hands.

The brakeman squints. "All right. You're good."

❉

Once aboard the engine, the brakeman introduces the gang to the conductor. The conductor is a smallish, bright-eyed, congenial man in his elder years and not particularly concerned with the details of their plan, only when the gang might be departing and how soon they can help with repair of the tracks. He is a conductor after all and his god is a clock. "Just let me know if there's anything I can do to speed this along," he says.

"You got any lawmen aboard this train?" asks Francis.

"None famous enough I was made aware."

"So you got passengers?"

"Oh, plenty."

"All right," says Francis. "Could you direct us to the money, or anything else you got of value?"

"May I make a suggestion?" says the conductor, who appears to know his way around a holdup.

"Please do."

"This is your first attempt on a train, is it not?"

"It is," says Francis. "How would you say we're doing so far?"

"Fine. Just fine. But I was going to say, start with a schematic. The actual schematic. Get a visual for the thing, if you know what I'm saying. Then you can figure out your priorities. In this case I'd say go straight for the express car. Seventh car back. Then you can think about the passenger car, the mail car, and so on, working your way down the list. But you got to prioritize. You can't go at it all haphazard. That'll save us both some time and keep things moving."

"So where's this schematic?"

"Right here. I was about to grab it."

"This will do fine," says Francis, studying the card in his hand. "Why don't you get some spare rails together, maybe a few more hands, and we'll meet you back here shortly."

❖

The gang climbs to the roof and walks down the line, counting cars as they jump. Five. Six. Seven. They descend the ladder to the door of the express car and Francis knocks and puts his ear to the door.

"Are you able to open this thing up?"

"No sir, I can't do that," says a voice on the other side.

"What if I told you this was a holdup?"

"Wouldn't change a thing."

"All right."

Francis and Samuel and Ned briefly discuss their options. Francis knocks again. "You still in there?"

"That's my job."

"We're going to plant some charges on this door."

"Oh dear."

"You got some place you can hole up in there?"

"Give me a moment."

"All right. Let me know when you're set. We're going to get started on this side."

"Since when did you become the gentleman?" says Ned.

"No point in being rude."

They work together with the paraffin and place their charges on both hinges of the express car's iron door. They lay a length of detonation cord that reaches to the roof of the next car forward.

Francis knocks on the door. "You all set in there?"

"One moment! Almost ready!"

"What's that?" calls Francis.

"Okay, I'm good!"

"Okay, here she goes!"

❁

Pow.

Ned Gets Tough

Through the smoking ruins of the doorway, then, and into the express car. The expressman emerges like a balding mole from his protective mound of passenger baggage.

"You okay?" says Samuel, steadying the man in his rumpled suit.

"Quite. Quite."

Francis glances about. "Where's the strongbox?"

"There is no strongbox. Look around you."

"I don't believe him," says Ned. "I think he's lying."

"You got me," says the expressman. "The strongbox is over here."

The express car is essentially a boxcar with an open layout, locked from within, where passengers store high-value baggage. But there is a strongbox, which the expressman has cleverly barricaded behind crates. They dig it out. They look at it.

It's a sturdy specimen of squat dimensions, fully iron. It has a solitary combination dial and a steel crank like a mariner's wheel.

"Are you able to open it?" says Ned.

"Yes and no."

"You understand we're outlaws, right? We're the bad guys. Breaking every law in the book is our middle name."

"Somehow I don't believe that."

"Oh yeah? Then feast your eyes on this. You know what this is?" says Ned.

"It's a gun."

"That's right. Now what do you think?"

"But you just put it back in your holster."

"Oh, it can come out again. Don't think it won't."

❀

It turns out dynamite, like honesty, budgeting, and practical knowledge of the wheel, can solve more problems than you'd expect. Once again, pow, and the contents of the safe are revealed.

Inside they find a stack of ten-dollar bills amounting to twelve hundred dollars. There is also a small canvas of a landscape signed by someone named pcézanne, a leather dossier of notarized land deeds, and a harmonica-case housing a fine meerschaum pipe.

They take the cash, shut the safe, and pat the expressman on the back for his troubles.

Next stop, the passenger car.

So It Begins

They enter through the back door and find the passenger car is loud and buoyant like a dinner party with everyone engaged in some form of exchange while a waiter in a tuxedo pushes a drink cart down the aisle, taking orders and pouring elaborate colourful concoctions into long-stemmed crystal. No one appears to notice the gang.

Francis steps forward. He asks aloud for everyone's attention but his voice, unfortunately, fails to crest the din of merriment in the car, and he may as well be reciting Shakespeare to a tree full of toucans for all the good it does. Francis raises his Cooper above his head and fires a single round through the roof of the car. All conversation ceases. This is an important moment.

I'm now fully born, he thinks. I am ready.

"My name is Francis Blackstone, and we are three-quarters of the Blackstone Temple Gang. I'll kindly ask you to put your hands in the air, for this is a San Joaquin County train robbery."

New Development

Samuel walks down the aisle with his upturned hat before him, working the passengers to the right. Ned walks directly behind, working those opposite. Francis continues his announcements from back of the car.

"If you're a workingman with calloused hands you have nothing to worry about. You can keep your effects. Women: wedding bands, heart-shaped jewels, any items from your sweetheart are yours to keep. All else goes in the hat. Thank you, folks, thank you. Just place them in here. Thank you."

An old woman touches Francis' wrist as he goes by.

"I just want to say it's so wonderful, how you're going about this."

"Well thank you, ma'am. We do our best."

"Not like this other riffraff calling themselves outlaws. No manners whatsoever. It's young men like you who give us hope."

Francis pats her hand.

"And you have such a fine smile," she says.

"You are too kind, ma'am. You truly are. Now if you could just empty your other pocket there. Perfect, I thank you."

Ned reaches behind a child's ear and a silver brooch materializes in his hand. There follows a smattering of applause.

"Now the rest of you," Francis calls out, "there's a list going round. Put your name and address down, and we'll pay you back when we can. If you're not sure how to write, see my brother Samuel and he'll get you settled. Put your hand up, Samuel. That's him there."

A portly, red-faced man with heavy jowls and a cheap suit raises a hand as Francis comes even with his seat.

"Gus Simons, *Daily Journal*," says the man.

"Yeah."

"Would you mind," says the man, removing a notepad and pencil from his breast pocket, "if I ask you a question or two?"

"How we doing on time?" says Francis to Samuel.

"I think we're doing all right," says Samuel.

"All right," says Francis. "Shoot."

"Just a few more moments," says Gus Simons, standing behind the tripod with his head buried beneath the camera's cloth hood.

"This pose is getting heavy," says Francis. "It looks like nothing, but you hold a pistol out long enough and it's like a bucket of bricks."

"I hear you," says Gus. "I hear you. These tintypes are slow as molasses. But we're almost there."

Francis turns his head, addressing the car in general. "Sorry folks, I didn't realize this was going to take so long."

"No bother at all," say the passengers.

One of them, a finely dressed gentleman with pomaded hair that's parted down the middle, a smudge of a mustache and little brass-rimmed glasses, has volunteered to stand opposite Francis' Cooper with his hands in the air, though the man's face is turned to the camera.

"And...we got it," says Gus Simons, emerging from the hood. "Now let's get another with the three of you together.

Right over here, by the window. And let's see, let's try some-one new. Who'd like to join us for this one?"

Gus taps at his chin. How to choose?

Row upon row, a sea of hands waving like posies in the breeze.

Let It Be Shown

After the holdup, the gang rejoins the conductor outside
and begins repair of the tracks. Gus Simons follows close
behind, tripod on his shoulder, huffing about and trying
to play it smooth. The truth is he can't believe his luck. It's
finally here. The big one. The scoop every reporter lives for.

By ones and twos, the passengers disembark, out of
interest, out of boredom, and before long most have begun
pitching in with the tracks. It's a work party. Earnest,
broad-shouldered men throw back their suspenders, grab
shovels and sledgehammers and crates of iron ties. Women
cluster beneath parasols and wave half-moon fans while the
waiter in his tuxedo — a suit of fantastic origin, impervious
to wrinkles, odours, insects, spills — goes about in his
solemn prance delivering trays of cold pork sandwiches and
lemonade.

Gus Simons is in a state. He is everywhere at once, taking photos, scribbling, sweating. Whenever he stops long
enough to consider the image plates within his satchel his
heart pounds so hard he can barely breathe.

Forget the *Journal*, thinks Simons. He's going straight
to *Nat Post* with this one. They'll reprint in Washington,
Philadelphia, Boston, Chicago...

It doesn't hurt that the kid is a natural-born celebrity.
Francis Blackstone is polite, loves the camera, and photographs like Adonis. He has the longest lashes, woman or
man, Simons has ever seen. You don't generally think of
outlaws as having pretty eyes, but there you have it. In fact

the whole package is a damn glittering casino. By some luck of the draw, Gus Simons has been granted first interviews, first portraits, first exposure and reportage, and all of this on the gang's *very first job*.

Simons glances about for another shot, something he may have missed, but feels confident he's covered everyone at this point; passengers, train-staff, the gang. He has group shots of every possible combination too. Posed and freestyle, silly faces, human pyramids, everyone jumping at once.

He's got a great shot of Samuel, towering above the others and smirking like a schoolboy with a hundred pounds of steel rails balanced across his shoulder.

He even has a chummy one between the conductor, a petite, adorable, white-bearded old man in a black felt bowler, and the soon to be irrevocably famous Ned Runkle. The conductor is sunny and cheerful, with an arm around Ned's waist. Ned points a pistol at his own head while making rabbit ears behind the conductor and grinning like a whiskeyed buffoon.

The only one Simons can't seem to capture is the old Indian on the train. The man sits straight-backed and stoic and entirely alone in the passenger car, staring rigidly at the seat before him. The man wears his hair in an unusual bundled fashion, like a topknot. Every time Simons attempts to photograph him, the shutter jams, or the tripod tilts, or a bevy of women jump out front and mug for the camera.

He returns his attention to the standout, young Francis Blackstone. If he plays this right, hitches himself to the right star, Gus Simons will never have to introduce himself again.

"Let's get one last photograph of you, Francis, alone with your Cooper," says Simons, dipping his head beneath the hood. "Just aim it at the sky. Perfect. Hold that."

An idea strikes him. It's accompanied by something like a sizzling blue current. Also a general intimation of success. Otherwise Gus Simons has no way of knowing he is about to take the single most recognizable photograph of his century.

"On second thought," says Simons. "Let's have you point that thing at the camera."

Ned Makes a Mistake

Triumphant, giddy, and loaded with loot, the gang rides back to the willow copse to find Bob Temple still asleep in the shade.

"Should we even tell him?" says Samuel, climbing down from his horse.

"Let him sleep," says Francis. "We'll give him his share when he wakes."

Temple is in no condition to outrun any lawmen that might be on their scent. The gang therefore decides to stay hidden in the shade of the willow copse for a few days, despite being two miles from the tracks, gambling on their pursuers roaming far and wide in search of a gang on the run.

They gather remainders from a potato field, eating them unwashed and raw. The horses find plenty of shade grass and at night they ride out to the irrigation pond for water. By the third day Temple is much recovered. He is bruised and raw but otherwise moving about, gazing squint-eyed into the villainy of daylight. The sun has just crested a boundary line of sycamores in the east and it's already hot, waves of light wobbling the fields. Ned leans against a willow tree, writing on a piece of paper with the nub of a pencil.

"What are you working on?" asks Francis, rolling his blankets into a bundle.

"My autobiography."

"Your what?"

Samuel grins. "It's the book he's writing about himself."

"Let's take a look," says Temple, holding out his hand.

"Busy," says Ned.

Temple snatches the paper from Ned's grip and reads quietly to himself, his lips moving as he scans the page.

"Nope," says Temple, setting the paper down. "Nuh uh. You can't do this to people. It's not right."

"You ever heard of a first draft?"

Temple just scowls at the paper. "Look here. You even misspelled *boy*. How in God's name do you misspell *boy*?"

"Let him be," says Francis. "He's not hurting anyone."

Temple ignores this, turning the page over. The other side is a handwritten reward notice for a missing dog. It turns out Ned pulled it from the community board out front of the hardware store back in Modesto for the paper it was made of.

"You took this?" says Temple with obvious disgust.

The notice reads:

REWARD! IF YOU HAVE MY DOG PLEASE RETURN HIM! I WILL NOT ASK QUESTIONS, I WILL MEET YOU ANYWHERE. PLEASE TAKE CARE OF HIM! ALL I CARE IS GETTING MY DOG BACK. HE IS MY BEST AND ONLY FRIEND.

Ned looks suddenly pale and wretched. He turns to Francis. "Is it that bad?"

"It's pretty bad," says Francis.

"You didn't even think about it," says Ned. "You just said 'pretty bad,' but is it really that bad? Now that you think about it?"

"What do you want me say, Ned?"

"Well what about him?" says Ned, pointing at Temple. "At least I never shot anybody."

"I don't know," says Francis. "This is different. This is a different kind of bad."

"Jesus, this is bad," says Ned. "This is really bad. What should we do?"

"We?"

"We're a gang, aren't we?" says Ned.

Bob Temple doesn't say anything. He just mounts his horse.

On the Road Back to Modesto

"You know we could get caught because of you," says Samuel. "This is the last place we should be going right now."

"In and out," says Temple. "We repost the notice and we're gone. Before anyone sees us."

They tip their hats low over their eyes as they ride into town. No one appears to pay them any mind. Out front of the hardware store, Ned dismounts and hurriedly tacks up the notice. Then he stops, staring at a discarded newspaper on the bench.

"What are you doing?" says Samuel, still sitting his horse in the road.

Ned just stares.

"Take the paper and let's go. Come on!"

"It's the *National Post*," says Ned, blinking dumbly at it.

Samuel dismounts, hissing with frustration. He marches over to Ned, fully prepared to pick him up and return him bodily to his horse, when he too stops, staring at the front cover of this morning's edition.

Mr. Cassidy, We Need to
Borrow This a Moment

They ride all four, side by side, passing the newspaper back and forth as they head vaguely north in the direction of Sacramento but with no fixed destination as of yet. They come to an olive grove. Olives, as if they now wander through Galilee — the trees' squat, contorted limbs gesturing like minstrels.

"Can we eat these?" says Ned, yanking a handful of pods as they pass beneath.

"I don't think so," says Temple. "Something needs to happen to them first. Boiling or something."

Ned chucks the handful away. "Well I'll say it then," he says. "Since no one else cares to."

"So say it," says Samuel.

"All right. I have little love for this article. There it is."

Francis says nothing. He's said nothing at all, in fact, since the article came to light.

"And do you know why, Francis?"

Francis says nothing.

"Because it is entirely about you," says Ned. "Barely a mention at all about me and Samuel. As though we weren't even there. And none at all about Bob."

Ned lifts the paper and reads aloud. "'The young desperado with a gentleman's charm, bewitching blue eyes, and a matching Cooper.' And after all those photographs they only used the one."

"I can't help any of that," says Francis. "I'd change it if I could. But there it is."

"And what's all this about 'Anything for love'?" says Ned, scanning the paper again. "Did you tell him we're robbing trains for love?"

"I did."

"When did we agree on that?"

Francis shrugs. "I was speaking for myself. He didn't ask my opinion on your motives, Ned."

Ned passes the paper to Temple. "I just don't see why I'm the only one's got a problem with this."

"You're not alone," says Temple. "Just the loudest. Me and Samuel here, we've been biding our time, knowing if we waited long enough you'd speak it for us."

"I want you all to listen for a minute," says Francis.

"All right," says Ned.

"If you could just get past the photograph on the cover," says Francis, "you'd know two county marshals are already on task, hoping to catch us further down the line."

"All right," says Temple.

"So we are not further down the line. We are here. They weren't expecting us to stick around, posting notices on billboards in Modesto."

Temple scratches his neck. "What are you suggesting? We hold off on the bank, hit another train?"

"Not another train," says Francis. "The same train. It has to come back some time."

No one says anything for a while, just thinking on the matter. Then Temple says, "All right. Where would we hit it?"

"Where?" says Francis. "Well, the last spot worked just fine."

Sometimes, in summer, two storms collide. The heavens amass in a roving grey sea, supernatural with light. The distant downpours are like a thumb-smudge.

Bob Temple and Francis Blackstone ride up front. Ned and Samuel are just behind on the trail. They are all four quiet until Ned says aloud, to any and all, "All right. Tell me this. If you had a time machine would you go into the past or the future?"

"Future," says Samuel.

"Past," says Temple.

"Neither," says Francis. "Because neither would work."

Ned stops his horse. "It's a game, Francis."

"That's fine. Still won't work."

"It is *my* time machine, Francis. I made it in my head. And if I say it goes back in time, then that's what it will do."

"Well it won't," says Francis.

"Well tell me why not!" says Ned.

"If a man gets in a time machine and goes back in time," says Francis, "then it's not the past anymore. It's the present. If you can't see that, I don't know how you find your legs in the morning."

No one says anything for a while. Just riding, the light going gold.

Francis leans forward, resting his chin on the horse's withers. "Hey, Bob."

"Yeah."

"What would you have done if we'd found our fortune already?"

"You mean back at the mine?"

"Sure."

After a long, thoughtful pause, Bob Temple says, "You wouldn't believe me if I told you."

"Now you have to tell me."

Temple says, "I was going to give it to someone."

Francis is shocked. "You're kidding. Who?"

"Doesn't matter. We didn't find it."

But Francis isn't letting up. "There's another fortune waiting for us in Chesterville. What then, Bob Temple?"

"Then I guess I'll return to my original plan, Francis. And that's all you need to know."

"All right," says Francis. "Then tell me this. You ever wonder what you'd be doing if you weren't an outlaw?"

Temple is quiet for a long time. In fact Francis figures the question was ignored and they are now riding in a sort of companionable silence, when Temple finally says, "We call men outlaws because they have grown free in their displeasure with the world and are therefore hardened to it. Or else they simply cannot abide within the laws of a given land. For any number of reasons. Could be on principle. Could be convenience — or sloth. Dereliction of heart. Some men just don't like to be bossed around. Whatever the reason, whatever the crime, there's really just the two kind of outlaws. The angry ones and the broken ones."

"Which one are you?"

Temple peers up at the sky, at the clouds smirching the barrens. He says, "You got the devil's own luck, Francis."

When Francis glances at Temple there is something beaten in his eyes. Something woeful and beyond repair.

Temple says, "Don't know where it comes from. Wish to God I did."

Francis wonders what has to happen in a person's life. What has to go wrong. Certainly a soul doesn't go bankrupt all at once. And then with a sort of clairvoyance he does not understand, he understands Temple all at once. "You're both of them," he says. "You're both kinds of outlaws. And it's tearing you up."

Temple is still looking at the clouds. He doesn't respond.

Francis thinks: Here's another way of living I must not make mine.

Round Two

Steam chugs from the stacks as the engine creeps to a halt. The whistle blows. The train settles and sighs and the conductor comes out on the grill. "I was wondering if we'd see you again."

"This here's Bob Temple," says Francis from his horse. The gang sits mounted beside the tracks, much as they had when they encountered the same train four days prior. "Bob Temple couldn't make it last time but he'll be joining us today."

The conductor removes his hat and swipes his brow. "Hot today. Was it Bob Temple, did you say?"

Bob Temple leans forward slowly. He spits. "I did not say."

Temple is apparently unfamiliar with the friendly persona the gang has worked to create, and Samuel frowns at the comment. To the conductor he says, "You must forgive our friend here. His mother was abused by coyotes, and he got the misfortune of his father's manners."

The conductor ignores this, or doesn't hear it, immersed as he is in the condition of the tracks. "You boys really tangled the lines this time."

"Our apologies for that," says Francis. "Ned was in charge of dynamite."

"Just tore it to hell, didn't you."

"Yeah. I'm not sure what to say," says Francis. "We'll do better next time."

The conductor just exhales. "All right. Well let's get things moving." He calls out for the brakeman to begin gathering material for repairs.

"Oh yeah, before I forget," says the conductor, turning back around. "You'll want to check in with the mail car this time."

"We tamper with US mail and this thing goes federal. Brings in a whole other kind of marshal," says Francis. "We're doing just fine with state charges, thank you."

"No, no. They have something for you," says the conductor. "This one's actually yours."

❧

The express car blows like a dream. In and out, cash in hand, and off to the mail car. After a brief repartee with the postman, the contents of this car too are made welcome to them.

"Let's see here," says the postman, sorting through enormous canvas sacks stencilled with destinations. The sacks cover the entirety of the floor, arranged three-high in places.

"Modesto. Modesto. Here we are," says the postman. "And what did you say your name was?"

"We're the Blackstone Temple Gang," says Ned. "Heard of us?"

But the postman is already about his job, untying the drawstring and rifling through the sack. "Blackstone. Blackstone. Aha. This must be it. All sent poste restante."

He withdraws a sheaf of envelopes wrapped in twine. "I'll need you to sign for it."

Samuel extends his hand. The postman regards him briefly and then passes the sheaf over.

"What are they?" says Ned.

Samuel thumbs through the first five or six letters, flips to the middle, then to the last letter. He slowly reties the twine.

"It's fan mail," he says with no discernible emotion.

"Let me see," says Ned, shouldering in.

"I don't think you'll care to," says Samuel, extending the sheaf past Ned and on to Francis without looking.

Francis accepts the sheaf wordlessly. He studies the packet in his hands. He feels within himself the correctness of willpower needed to quell his curiosity and then he doesn't, and he is passing the sheaf back and forth before his nose.

"They're perfumed," he says. His wonder is entire.

❧

"Could I have your attention please," says Francis and every passenger in the car turns around in their seat to find the gang standing back of the car with pistols raised.

"My name is Francis Blackstone and we are the Blackstone Temple Gang. This here is a San Joaquin County—"

"Hey now," calls a man from midway down the aisle. "Hey, are you the one they're calling the Dynamite Kid?"

"I don't think so. That's someone else, I think."

"No, look here," says the man, overcome with excitement. He raises a newspaper for all to see and points to the photograph. "It's him right here. It's the Dynamite Kid! See for yourself!"

The man hands the newspaper to the passenger in the seat behind him, and so on, until the paper makes its way back of the car.

Ned takes the paper. "I'll be damned," he says, turning the page with his pistol.

"Which paper is it?" asks Samuel.

"It's the *Washington Post*. And look, Samuel! They got a picture of us!"

An old fellow turns to Bob Temple. "Which one are you? I don't believe I saw you pictured."

Temple looks hard at Francis. "Can we move this along?"

"Right, well you know the deal," announces Francis. "Stick 'em up if you can. If you're too old to do so, just enjoy the show, this one's on us."

Women remove mirrors from their purses and powder their faces. Men begin unhooking their watches. The gang strolls down the aisle with upturned hats in their hands.

"Thank you, ma'am."

"Thank you."

"Oh, and that's a pretty one."

"Just drop it in. I thank you."

No one sees where it comes from — somewhere front of the car perhaps? — but it's while they're robbing the Modesto line of the Central Pacific railway that the first pair of lady's underpants hits the floor at Francis' feet.

So begins a new tradition.

CHAPTER SEVEN

Then Throw Back the Shutters

"I'll kindly ask you to put your hands in the air, for this is a Solano County train robbery..."

"A Yolo County train robbery..."

"A Placer County train robbery..."

"My name is Francis Blackstone, and this is a—the hell are we?"

"Plumas County, son. We're just outside Quincy, about thirty mile. Nice to meet you, by the way."

"Right," says Francis. "Well, you've all read the papers. You know the routine. Samuel's got the list for recompense. Bob Temple will look after special requests. Rest of you, hands in the air with sleeves rolled back. And today we're in a bit of hurry, as we got the marshal on our tail, so we'll be saving all photographs till the end."

The northern chapter of the Dynamite Kid Fan Club is advertised in the back of the *Baltimore Citizen*. Another chapter quickly follows in Umbrage, Illinois. Before long it's a craze.

Mail depots across the west are inundated with bags of fan letters from as far away as London, Tokyo, Moscow,

Tangiers, each sack filled with requests from young ladies wanting Francis' nose in their ear but unsure where he'll turn up next.

It seems the world has been waiting for a champion, someone to personify their restless, reckless, innermost desire for love that knows no bounds.

"I don't get it," says Francis.

"Which part?" says Samuel.

"Any of it. None of it."

"Well, you're a goddamn sensation, Francis. I suggest you run with it while you can."

In the fall of that year, the first dime novel goes into print. It's titled *A Thousand and One Adventures of the Dynamite Kid*. Francis reads it. The book is terrible.

"You ever feel like…like maybe we've sidetracked?" says Francis.

"Sidetracked?" says Samuel.

"I don't know," says Francis. "Just a feeling I get. Like maybe we lost something. Or something."

He's looking at himself in the grandly framed oval mirror of the Lilac Lounge in Macondo, California. He checks his teeth. He adjusts his hat. Samuel leans in, and together they gaze at the trim figures staring back.

"Anyhow," says Francis, tugging the lapels of his coat. "We're looking pretty slick in these new duds."

What Happens Next Is

Two drinks appear on the walnut wood bar before Francis and Samuel. The brothers share a look and turn over their shoulders to find a thickset, roguish-looking fellow in a dusty flatcap seated at a table behind them. The man beams splendidly in their direction. He hefts a beer and crosses the lounge to join the brothers at the counter. He clinks their glasses.

"Francis Blackstone?" queries the man, smiling brightly.

Francis nods toward Samuel. "And my brother Samuel here."

Samuel warily places both hands upon his hips, the action pulling back his coat and revealing the pistol there.

If anything the man smiles wider. The teeth in his head are spaced like tombstones. He wears a corncob pipe on a string about his neck and the knees of his trousers are shiny as glass but he has clear, cool eyes, and no fear in them, which will form the primacy of any first impression.

"So these are the Blackstone brothers," he declares. "Alive and in person." He sips his beer. His swivels his gaze between them, his agenda unknown.

"You know, I have a brother," he continues, innocent enough. He lifts his glass and then lowers it before drinking. "Tom is his name. Four years my elder. He was thrown from a wagon just outside Virginia City. Knocked his head on a root and didn't wake for a year."

Francis remains still, waiting to see what comes next.

"The following winter," continues the man, "Tom wakes in bed, refreshed, cheerful as a goat. He greets everyone around like he's just woken from the most glorious nap. But now he's got this accent nobody can place. Some European accent." He gestures obliquely with his mug. "Turns out to be Lithuanian."

"Go figure," says Francis.

"Go figure," the man repeats, leaning back against the bar. He examines Francis. "You don't know who I am, do you."

Francis simply gazes back.

The man laughs abruptly. He clutches Francis by the shoulders and gives him an affable shake. To those at nearby tables, he exclaims, "He doesn't know who I am! Not a clue!"

Then into Francis' ear he whispers, "Or do you…?"

The man gives Francis a meaningful wink. He slugs back the rest of his beer, wipes his mouth, and sets the empty on the counter. He offers a casual salute and heads out the door.

"Who the hell was that?" says Samuel, watching the man depart.

"It's what I'm talking about. Things are sliding out of hand."

"But who was that?"

"I have no idea," says Francis.

"You really don't know?"

"Nope."

And here's the thing:

He never will.

Unknown Lands

Francis Blackstone is ten years old. He enters the den to find his father seated at the desk with oil lamp gleaming. What does his father look like?

Out on the street, among the people on the street, picture a man in a black derby with a sourdough baguette under his arm. In the comfort of his home, behind the desk of his study, picture the opposite.

His father is peering at a map stretched full-length on the desk and weighted at the edges with both volumes of Sir Richard Francis Burton's translations.

Or rather, he's peering at a map of a map. It's a two-dimensional representation of the Lenox Globe, the oldest known globe on earth, created in 1510, none of which concerns Francis. It's paper, a paper world, and at first glance he understands none of the appeal. He's more attuned to the command, both palpable and peculiar, it appears to have over his father's attention.

Has his father, Francis wonders, ever gazed upon him with such interest?

From the threshold Francis says, "What are you looking at?"

"Come closer. See for yourself."

His father moves the oil lamp to make way for Francis. The two lean together over the map.

"It's not finished," says Francis, referring to the white spaces dominating the image.

His father says nothing at first. And then very carefully, very distinctly, as though tasting each syllable: "Terra incognita."

Francis asks what his father just said.

"Means unknown lands."

"Why are you looking at it?"

His father considers the question. "I suppose," says his father, "I like to think of terra incognita like a..."

He massages his cheek, his chin, looking for the words. "It houses everything we can't see but is real nonetheless. Everything that's waiting to be known."

Which happens to be exactly how Francis feels when in his father's company. Waiting to be seen. Waiting to be known. And today for some reason — or a whole assortment of reasons he's simply too young to parse out — this waiting cuts deeper than ever.

"Maybe one day," begins Francis, pondering the white spaces on the map. "Maybe one day they'll see it all — and then they'll be happy with what they have. And there'll be nothing left to look for."

"Oh, it could happen," says his father. "It's a big world but it could happen. It's bound to happen. But not in my time, I think."

They look at the map together, each to a side. It's one of those instances where two people are looking at the same thing, and seem to be saying the same thing, when really nothing could be further from the truth.

Dearest girl,

I want to apologize. I did not expect this fortune
business to take so long. It turns out gathering one's
future into a saddlebag full of cash is no simple
thing, but many things — and none of them simple.
I'm nevertheless confident the money we need to
begin our life together is near at hand, and I expect
to see you soon.

I am also aware you have probably seen my name
in the papers. There are many stories about. I want
you to know some of them are true, and some are
not. It may be hard to understand but everything
I do, everywhere I go, brings me closer to you.

My brother Samuel keeps asking me, why this
girl? Why her, and not some other? I cannot make
him understand. I did not choose you. A person does
not choose their own body. Their own arms and legs.
Do you agree?

But I am no good with words. It is so hard to
explain.

When I was young my mother spent each
morning in the garden. She wore wide-brimmed hats
and flower dresses. She wore leather gloves too, like
a man. She was very beautiful. Her eyes were like
glittering crescents. One morning in spring, I helped
her with the planting, and she said, Francis, you are
to be happy in life. Not like me. She had about five
black freckles beneath her left eye and nowhere else.
She said, Francis, do you love your mother?

I said I did. I loved her more than myself.

My mother turned aside then. She placed another seedling in the ground and the way sunlight flashed across her shoulders I knew I'd said the wrong thing. She said, Two people can only be the same distance apart. One cannot stand further than the other.

No matter where you are, I said?

I'm going to show you, she said. Watch closely. She entered the space between us and drew a circle all around. Now look up at the sky, she said. Who stands underneath?

For the longest time I thought she meant me — because it was me looking up. But of course we were standing together, she and I. And looking up as I was, I could not see either of us. As though we were one body. One set of eyes drinking in a milk-white sky.

I apologize for not sending any of the letters I have written. I do not think I will send this one either.

Yours faithfully,
Francis

Pure Gone

They are an hour's ride outside Burl. The gang should arrive early enough for a drink in the saloon, maybe a nap in the hotel, and still have plenty of time to ride a few miles down the tracks to hit the 4:21 train to Arcata Bay.

The desert here is unremarkable, uncreative. Very possibly bored with itself. Francis reins up, middle of the road, gazing at the dust of the road.

"What's going on?" says Samuel, turning his own horse about.

"We're going the wrong way."

"There's only one road to Burl, and we are upon it."

Francis shakes his head. "It's all wrong. We've gone sideways with this whole train business. It's been almost ten months now, and who knows how many scores. I know the trains were my idea, but it's time we get to Chesterville. I feel it in my bones."

"Oh, come on," says Ned. "We got a rhythm going."

Ned floats the dreamy conviction that they are safe from all, and cannot be caught, and will moreover find the Arcata train fully packed with bigwigs coming up from San Francisco tonight.

Samuel pulls alongside his brother, their horses now juxtaposed.

"I think I'm with Ned on this one," says Samuel. "To tell the truth, I never did understand Chesterville. These trains are jackpots. A couple more and we could be set for life."

Francis sighs, gazing out at the sagebrush and chaparral in all its uncontested whateverness. There are no trees till your eyes reach the hills, ten miles distant or more. "You know, I have close to eighteen thousand dollars cash money in my saddlebag right now. If that doesn't appease Governor Whitmore I don't know what will. I'm only saying Chesterville because that's where it ends. And my heart says we're done."

"One more," says Samuel. "Give us one more and then we decide."

"Aren't you ever the late-blooming rebel."

Samuel shrugs. "I found my calling."

Francis shakes his head in thought. "What do you say, Bob Temple? It's your fortune in Chesterville too."

Temple sucks his teeth. He is thinking. He nods to himself amid this thinking. "Last train," he says. "Last train tonight. And then, by God, we head straight for Chesterville or—"

Temple stops midsentence, twisting abruptly in his saddle as though in response to some sound in the sky. He blinks vaguely at it, a parade of inscrutable emotions working the features of his face, one after another.

"Or what?" says Francis, watching with fascination.

But Temple is pure gone, irretrievable in his examinations.

And that, thinks Francis, is why we finish this now. He says aloud, "There is no way in hell I'm becoming like you, Bob."

Temple just nods, his gaze fixed on the clouds. The subtle radiations issuing from them like coded instruction.

Back in the Den

His father appears to have forgotten him, having returned his attention to the Lenox map while Francis remains standing beside the desk. But Francis has one more question. There's an illustration of a dragon on the map. It's depicted near the eastern coast of India. Beside the dragon, the words HC SVNT DRACONES.

Francis points. "What's that mean?"

His father starts, as though surprised to find Francis still present. He peers at the Latin beneath Francis' finger.

"Means don't believe everything you read."

He scoots the oil lamp between Francis and the map.

HC SVNT DRACONES

Bursula Carter fans out her cards. She arranges the suits red to black and collapses the hand and lays it face down on the table. She pushes a stack of dimes forward on the table and glances into the eyes of the dealer and then the four rubes sitting either side of her around the table. They're in the backroom of the Haymaker Drinkhouse in Burl, California. The room's furnishings, odour, lighting, and decor are precisely as you are picturing them in your head.

Bursula turns sharply as the door crashes open. Jack Bilworth is standing there, breathing hard, having come at a run.

"What is it?" she says. "I'm working."

Bilworth is grinning. He has a newspaper in his hand. The little animal in his pocket turned out to be a mink. It looks like a kitten with a silky brown pelt and beady black eyes peeking out from his breast pocket. Bilworth instinctively cradles the pet with his right hand, slapping the newspaper onto the table beside her cards.

Bursula is annoyed. "Not them again," she says.

"Go on," says Bilworth, scrubbing the creature's tiny forehead. "Read it."

Bursula's annoyance is worsened by lack of sleep. Also, her body's thermostat is out of whack. For mysterious reasons it's come under the recent command of a zinc-plated box with a long wooden lever. The lever has two positions, really hot and really cold. The whole thing is affixed to the floor of a steel cage filled with screeching monkeys, and Bursula can only watch helplessly from the outside, yanking at her hair, while monkeys throw the switch back and forth without mercy.

"Fine, pass it here," she says, mopping the cold sweat from her brow and then snatching up the newspaper. Her lip curls on the instant. It's an op-ed piece, written by the Blackstone Temple Gang themselves and published today in the *Santa Rita Gazette* as an open letter.

Dear Bursula Carter,

We are writing to inform you there is no further need to slink about in our footsteps, attempting to catch us at some inopportune moment. Please understand your husband's death was not an act of aggression, but self-defence. Given the misinformation at your disposal, we sympathize with your desire for revenge but henceforth ask you to set aside your wrath and find some new form of diversion, of which life provides many, you degenerate, butt-faced mandrill. Furthermore we can recommend a fine saddler out of Yuma who specializes in high-quality leatherwork, similar to that presently in your possession, should you be in need of repair to your saddles and so forth. We have left a credit of $300 at his establishment made out in your name.

Sincerely,
The Blackstone Templars

Bursula stares at the paper. She glances up at Jack Bilworth, her face scrunched with bewilderment, and then scans the paper once more before setting it down and staring at the opposite wall for some time.

"What the fuck!" she yells at no one in particular.

While many questions remain, what she gathers foremost is that Yuma is in fact the diversion, and therefore the last place she will go. Where then could the Templars be headed?

"There's more," says Bilworth, tentatively stepping forward to turn the page. Bursula reads on.

It seems the letter is followed by a full-page editorial commenting on the rivalry between their two gangs, as well as an interview with the Blackstone Templars regarding their meteoric rise to stardom. It follows:

Q.— Francis, one of the most frequently discussed aspects of your work is the inclusion of live music. It certainly distinguishes the Blackstone Templars from other cooperatives pulling similar jobs right now. Can you discuss how this decision came about?

F.B.— It just sort of happened really. I don't recall any discussion around it. There was this one passenger on the San Benito line — he just climbed up onto his seat and started playing real loud, making up lyrics as he went.

Q.— And the passengers responded?

F.B.— Instantly. They just loved it. Tied the whole thing together really, is what everyone was saying.

Q.— Did things evolve quickly from there?

F.B.— I think it was our next run ... Yeah, it was the next run, we started putting out a call for musicians. Dollar a gig. It just became a thing ever since.

Q.— But an artistic collaboration of any kind would affect your initial concept, yes? What can you tell us about your process?

F.B.— In the beginning, it was first passenger to raise a banjo got the job. They'd follow us around, going car to car, serenading as they went. But like everything else, it quickly got out of hand.

Q.— How do you mean?

F.B.— Well, we never expected the bands, for one.

Q.— You're referring to the string quartets?

F.B.— I don't know what they're called. But yeah, they started showing up around June, I guess. Now I'm told every train west of Winnemucca has their own load of musicians—just riding about, waiting to get robbed so they can strut their stuff.

Q.— In his most recent book, *Pioneers of the Dead Horizon*, author Koshiro Nakamura puts forward the notion that the Blackstone Templars are not *thieves* in the purest sense, but rather "concept thieves." An idea he likens to "concept art" in that both occupy "that rarified junction of popular culture and its transmission through sociology and mysticism." Would you agree with this description?

F.B.— Ned, you want to take this one?

N.R.— That's definitely us. That's us to a T.

Q.— Which brings me to my final question on the topic. According to Roland Green, music editor and columnist at the *Denver Cauldron*, these self-styled train heist ballads have inspired an entirely new genre of music. They're calling it "Gasoline Banjo" for its raw, explosive, improvisational sound and the way it's strafing the nation like wildfire. Any thoughts on where it could go next?

F.B.— Not even one.

Q.— Thank you, Francis. Next question is for you, Ned. Can you confirm the story that you once swallowed six bullets and a cigarette at the suggestion of a gypsy healer from...

And so it continues, eventually moving on to the gang's thoughts on politics and whether they've chosen a front-runner for this year's election. The interview concludes with a rather detailed discussion of the Templars' plans for the future.

Q.— One last question for you all. I know you have many fans out there still hoping to catch a live showing... Any hint as to where you will be heading next?

It's here Bursula Carter tosses the newspaper aside, staring into space.

"The Arcata?" she says. "The Arcata Bay train out of Dunhaven?"

"Told you," says Bilworth.

"Why on earth would they announce it?"

"I can think of two reasons," says Bilworth. "First because they're the nation's darlings right now. Beyond reproach or so they believe. Never harmed a soul on the job. Handing out candy to children. Even the railroads are saying we need more men like them. Look there, bottom of the page. They're saying Francis Blackstone 'embodies the spirit of America.'"

Bursula just stares at the words, uncomprehending in her fury. How is it that her husband's murderers are now lauded as heroes?

"The spirit of America?" she hisses.

It seems absurd at a glance. But if Bursula were to unroll these statements beneath the cold light of history she'd know the papers are correct in their estimation of young Francis. The foundations of America were penned by a small band of dynamic men just like him: gutsy, spirited, driven, individualistic, steadfast in their defiance of imperialism and its laws. Men who by modern standards would be branded as "terrorists" but who nevertheless incanted an ideology of such mythological proportions that the world has yet to contain its progress.

Bursula Carter, confined to the knowledge in her brainstem, is unaware of this link, comprehending only that a moment of dire reckoning is at hand.

She spits on the floor. "And second?"

"Second is they don't plan to hit the Arcata Bay train out of Dunhaven," says Bilworth.

"No?"

"They plan to hit it out of Burl." Bilworth slips the folded train map from his pocket and spreads it in the air before her. "If they featured in today's *Gazette* from Santa Rita they would have interviewed there yesterday at the latest. Which puts them nowhere near Dunhaven. See this? The closest rendezvous with the Arcata Bay line is right here. In Burl."

"Son of a bitch," she whispers.

"Guess you can't believe everything you read, huh?"

After a moment's consideration, Bursula nods, and then reaches across the table with a decisive movement and sweeps all bets into her lap.

Cries of outrage, then, from her opponents at the table.

"Now, now," she says, forestalling further protest with her palm. "I was going to win anyhow. And had I lost, you would have lost more." She stands and adjusts the gun belt on her mighty hips.

"Round up the gang," she says to Bilworth. "We're headed down the tracks."

"Finally going to kill those upstart bastards?"

"Yes we are," says Bursula. "But first we're going to kill their name."

"Their name?"

"Their reputation. I will see it licked by the dogs. There is no way in hell my Stanley's assassins will go down as heroes."

The Evolution of Evolution

Francis sits his horse, middle of the tracks, watching the train approach. Little puffs of smoke wash forward about the grill as the train commences its halt.

"You almost done?" he says to Ned. "You're going to get hit."

Ned finishes laying the charge. "Ready."

Ned lights the charge and hops his horse and the gang gallops a short distance away. The tracks blow, and the train redoubles its screeching.

When the engine completes its halt Francis just sits his horse, looking at the train. He counts four passenger cars. One of them has a handpainted banner strung between the first and third windows. It reads: Anything for love!

The silhouettes of faces appear at the windows, wholly obscured by sunflare. A solitary pane slides down in its track and a feminine hand dangles vigorously a small cloth something—Francis can't say what, though he can guess—and tosses that something onto the tracks. The hand waves at Francis and slides the window home with an audible click.

"I don't know," says Francis. "I got a not-good feeling about this one."

It will be another ninety years before someone can look up from this very spot, the spot Francis presently sits his horse, and see the image of a skyscraper warped and abstracted in the windowed face of another just like it. That someone will shout words Francis has never heard, their meaning contingent upon invention. They will express gladness at alien concepts and neon signage.

For now, Francis must accept the humiliation of linear time and the crushing inevitability of consequence and fact and all the physics of causality that confine a person to one coordinate in space whether they choose to agree with the arithmetic or not.

It all just happens. With or without us.

"Look lively," says Samuel, riding close enough to slap Francis' thigh, and then he too joins Ned and Temple, who are already hooting and firing pistols in the air as Temple kicks at the door to the passenger car.

❦

The moment the door crashes open, the whole car erupts with chatter. A few cheers go up. A solitary hat loops through in the air. The Blackstone Templars enter the car one at time, saluting like celebrities, theatrically pointing pistols at this person and that, bowing to applause. But before they can even make their customary announcements, the passengers are squawking at Francis like magpies.

"Fire one off, Francis!"

"Yeah, let's hear one from the old Cooper!"

Francis brushes them aside. "Not today. Next time maybe. I promise."

"Oh, come on!"

"Just one, Francis!"

Samuel nudges him with an elbow. Somewhat shyly, Francis blasts a hole in the ceiling, waving down further requests with his free hand. But the reverberations of his gunfire knock something loose, some flange or sprocket in the complex mechanism of female logic, and send two young ladies sprinting down the aisle, squealing his name.

Samuel intercepts their affections with an outstretched arm.

"Let's just address this up front," he announces to all. "My brother Francis here, so you know it, he's dedicated his heart to another. He appreciates your many generous offers of courtship but he refuses to budge on this one. What's that? Nope we don't know her name, but you can be assured we are working on that. Over here, the fellow in shirtsleeves—little louder please—yes he'll still be doing autographs."

A Premonition

Gus Simons pries the back door open, stuffing himself through before it slams shut again. He had to race through all three passenger cars to get here in time, and by the sound of it, he's already missed the inaugural pistol fire.

Simons climbs atop a seat, waving both hands frantically to gain Francis Blackstone's attention. "Hey! It's me, Gus Simons! I got an assignment!"

"Hey, I know you," says Francis.

"The *New York Times*!"

"That right?"

"I've been riding this train two days straight!"

Francis winks, raising a fist in solidarity, and Simons nearly drops his pencil in excitement. He swipes the sweat from his gleaming brow and presses a tiny notepad to his thigh, scribbling impressions in a frenetic scrawl:

door breached approx 4:32pm
general mood of levity in car
  young woman beside me sobbing: happy? sad?
  F.B. winks   *S.B. puts out a call for banjos,*
tosses player a coin
  N.R. hair parted on opposite side
  repeatedly checks reflection in window

Simons has been issued an unheard-of advance of two hundred dollars from the *New York Times* for fifteen thousand words on the Blackstone Temple Gang. It's practically a novella. The paper aims to position Simons as the foremost

Blackstone biographer, ensuring future publications acknowledge the *Times* with first credits. It's bold, visionary, and requires Simons submit to yet another robbery, for which he is all too glad. The *Times* has even provided four Swiss pocketwatches to this end, hoping to secure private interviews for Simons with each of the gang's members.

"Oh yeah and before I forget," says Samuel Blackstone, who appears to be leading this particular show. "The Dynamite Kid is a little downcast of spirit today, so let's go easy on him. Give him some space."

It seems a reasonable request, and the passengers nod and mutter in good-natured consent.

Samuel moves down the aisle, liberating passengers of their valuables. Behind him is Ned, the happy dunce, his fulsome grin and pillowcase outstretched. The banjo player follows, adopting his role with aplomb — and then Francis, his mood as described.

But Simons' eye is drawn foremost to the fourth member of the gang. It's the first he's seen of the infamous gunslinger and somehow the actuality of Bob Temple does not square with the legend. His presence is both diminished and erratic. He waves his pistol about, independent of provocation, some spark in his complexion, his eyes, in the volatility of his mien, at once indecipherable and wholly understood. For the first time since signing the contract, Simons is afraid. His chest goes hollow, and he commits his attention to the notepad as a means of distraction.

Simons jolts in surprise as a hand clutches his shoulder. He's relieved to find Francis Blackstone at his side, casually working Simons' watch from his wrist. "Do me a favour," says Francis, his gaze roving about the car.

"Sure, Francis. You name it."

"Skip this one."

"This one what?"

"This article," says Francis. "Don't write it."

"But...I got a contract...fifteen thousand words! We need to get an interview and—"

Francis shakes his head. "Skip this one," he says. "Trust me." He pats Simons on the back. "Something real bad is about to happen."

But for the Vivacity of His Doubts
He Would Certainly Be Certain

Gus Simons' head is awash. He sits on the train's benchseat, staring at the notepad with pencil in hand. What to do?

Despite Francis' warning, and the unnerving inclusion of Bob Temple, the event went off without a hitch. The gang finished their business with the passengers and now the car is in bloom with a pleasant chatter. Beyond the smudged windows, Simons can hear the dull ring of hammers on steel as the final repairs are made to the track. The train should be on its way any moment.

Shortly thereafter the car engages with a metallic clank and the train jolts forward a few inches. A whistle blows. The locomotive swells with steam and they're off and chugging, on their way to Arcata Bay once again.

So what could Francis Blackstone have been referring to?

Simons glances about the car and sees folks signalling their contentment, regaling each other with the private thoughts and excitements that accompanied their adventures of a few moments past. No one appears injured, physically or otherwise. Simons resolves to write the article. He sees no reason not to.

On the instant his mood brightens. He is visited by happy images in his head. It becomes certain that Francis' foreboding won't hinder the story but rather bolster it with a hint of mystique the editors will no doubt — *big money red carpet genius all mine* — appreciate, and if Simons can follow up with another article of similar calibre his career will almost certainly flourish.

Gus Simons crosses his legs, forcibly smiling as he glances out the window.

And he earned this, for godsake. He earned this.

Simons' hand goes involuntarily to the press card affixed to his hatband, touching it, his eyes roaming the scenery beyond the window. A few oak trees roll past. The silver thread of a river. A rickety water silo grows larger in the distance as they approach a ranch.

"But then again," Gus murmurs aloud, "even I hate my own writing."

His fist slams abruptly against the wall, surprising even himself. Several passengers turn in their seats. Simons smiles apologetically.

"I am a writer," he explains, the noble fragmentation of his soul implicit.

His gaze returns to the window, his cheek pushed against it. The stencilling on the silo becomes huge and legible, great white dispatches roaring toward him like the slogans of Zeus. They shoot past the window and are gone.

The truth is, Simons is trying desperately to sustain his convictions. But the only thing more secret and haunted than a writer's certainty he is good is the nagging sense he is wrong. What Simons needs most is a sign. Something to distinguish himself from all the rumpled, erudite bozos of the world, tottering about like a plague of penguins.

Gus feels a tap on the shoulder. He turns to face the woman in the seat beside him. She is offering him a baby.

"Oh," he says.

"Can you take him a moment?"

"Certainly. It's just that—"

She passes him a swaddled lump. Gus Simons holds it like a cake. The woman drags her valise into the aisle and wrestles it open, digging about. She piles items onto the seat, one after another, until she retrieves a baby-sized blue blanket.

Gus looks down at the infant in his outstretched hands. It can't be older than a week. Its little face is pinched and mottled. More than anything it resembles a fist. A squeaking, snuffling fist. Or a gourd.

Yes that's it. A winter gourd.

"Precious, isn't he?" says the woman, retrieving the baby and wrapping it with the blanket.

Gus Simons smiles awkwardly. He nods.

And then he wonders to himself: perhaps we call a newborn precious because *precious* draws no attention at all to the odious shape of its head. Its ill-formed limbs. Its odour.

"Precious," he agrees, logging the word away. He again feels certain that one day soon he'll be kissing ugly babies left and right. Such a hazy endearment will come in handy.

The train jerks violently to a halt. Simons is thrown forward in his seat. Around him passengers are similarly discomfited. Simons climbs back onto the padded bench, adjusting his coat, catching his breath. He assists the woman and her infant as they resettle on the bench. She appears shaken but otherwise uninjured. From up front, somewhere several cars forward, a pistol shot.

The shot is followed by a brief pause, and then two more just like it.

Gus Simons holds very still. Tentatively his pencil goes to the pad. Without understanding the how of it, he knows the conductor of the Arcata line is now shot and killed. He writes those very words and then stares at them.

Blackguarded

Two days later the gang reaches Sacramento. It's a hard ride over barren country but now they are here in the state capital with its doublewide avenues and effusive streetlamps and all the clean, convincing shapes and sounds that accompany such places.

They split into two groups to disperse attention. Ned and Temple purchase feed for the horses. They look into a known buyer of jewelry, pocketwatches, and other illicit oddments—their primary incentive for visiting Sacramento. This goes well and without disturbance from the law. They come out many dollars ahead.

The Blackstone brothers go for general supplies. This includes more dynamite and det cord, hair tonic, balloons, apples, and beans. After finishing their purchases, Samuel picks up a paper from the rack. His face sours on the instant.

Francis doesn't even ask. He says, "I knew this was coming."

"No you didn't," says Samuel, still reading.

"I knew something was coming."

Samuel shakes his head. "Not this you didn't."

He hands Francis the paper.

Francis is made to understand he is now wanted for murder. The paper is filled with scurrilous accusations, including the coldblooded shooting of a train conductor on the Arcata line.

Samuel takes the paper back, pointing to the corpse photographed on the front page. "This wasn't us, Francis. We've been blackguarded."

"We most certainly have."

"You know who did this, right?"

"I do."

"They won't let up. They aren't going to stop."

"I know it."

"I always knew we could beat a robbery rap, Francis. With your luck, and your…whatever. But this is different. This is big different."

"I agree."

"What do you plan to do about it?"

"Not a lot."

Francis is less concerned with the legal ramifications than the impression it may make upon his beloved. When it comes down to it he doesn't know the first thing about her, which extends to her commitment to Francis should he prove a felonious ogre.

"I guess we're just outlaws, through and through," says Samuel. "All there is to it."

"No," says Francis. "That's just an idea. A something in your head."

"Sometimes I don't get you."

"That's fine."

They don't say anything for a while. Just looking out at the cobbled pavement from the shaded porch of the general store. "Is it Chesterville or Chesterfield?"

"To be honest," says Francis, "I don't recall. They both sound right when you say it."

"You don't know?"

"It's one or the other."

"How we going to find it?"

"I got a map."

They load their purchases onto the horses and Francis digs out the map from his saddlebags. "There it is," he says. "Chesterville."

Samuel studies the map, his finger drawing out routes. "Looks like maybe another couple days' ride. Three at most. I still don't get it. You got plenty money now, Francis. What is it about this fortune?"

If only Francis could explain. He thinks about his fortune from the moment he wakes and in a dozen ways he doesn't think about it at all.

"It all ties together. With my girl," he says.

"How so?"

"I have no idea. Just have to go and see."

"You have no idea."

"Not really."

"Just some witches told you."

"That's about it."

Samuel shakes his head. "Meanwhile we leave a goddamn fortune in a cave — that whole Carter Gang stash. You know what I think?"

"I know you'll tell me."

"But do you want to know?"

"I don't even care all that much what *I* think, Samuel."

"I think you're as confused as the rest of us. About this whole girl thing."

"You're probably right," says Francis.

"Not probably."

"All right. I'm confused. But not in my heart."

Samuel scoffs, shaking his head.

"I mean it," says Francis.

"Oh, I know you do."

"Look around you, Samuel. All anyone really wants in this world is to live for something worth dying for. I think I've found that. If that makes me confused, or if that upsets you somehow, well."

Samuel doesn't say anything for a while, just watching his brother. Then: "You ever think about that treasure? Back in the cave?"

"Yeah. I think about it a lot actually."

"What are your thoughts on it?" asks Samuel

"I think so long as the Carter Gang's out there, no one's going to get away with it. There's too many of them."

"Yeah," says Samuel. "And I doubt we could ever find it again."

"Yeah," says Francis, pointing to a small, handwritten *C* on the map. "That's why I marked it here."

That Night, Francis Blackstone
Dreams He Is You

And you are alone.

You stand before the pearly gates of a carnival. Beyond the gates, rising high into the sky are fantastic creations; mechanical wonders that spin and spin. They make no sound.

You approach the ticket booth at the gate. The man in the ticket booth is asleep. He lies face down on the counter in a puddle of his own drool, ticket stubs clutched in one fist. You select the ticket printed with your name and wander in.

The carnival is enormous. But mainly there is a pavilion beside the path. Also a midway filled with rides, the same rides you observed from afar. You turn about. It is so quiet. So pleasantly, peacefully quiet.

On the lawns, throughout the galleries, draped like ragdolls over ponies, everywhere you look: The sleeping. The profound hush of the sleeping.

You meander past gentlemen in their fine hats and powdered women with fat babies — even the clowns, their stupefied grins — everyone slumped and beautiful and dreaming one dream. The very dream Francis is having now.

Within the pavilion, where spotlights of red and blue sweep randomly about the tent, you look up. The acrobats in their sequins are asleep on the wires. They swing limply from the trapeze. They are blasted out of cannons, snoring spread-eagle through the air. It is magnificent.

And then you are outside again, wandering beneath the laudanum of sun, everything asleep, the roustabouts asleep, the taffy vendors, the prized pigs in their corrals. The ringmaster sits flopped against the fence rails like a decommissioned robot.

You turn in place to witness the passage of a Ferris wheel. It has broken loose and rolls slowly, freely, proudly in the sun, past the carousel, the funhouse, past the Dunk-O-Matic, its anodized steel flashing like starbursts as it goes round. And then it is gone from view. It is forgotten.

You continue on.

And then a terrific splashing as the contraption tumbles into the sea, some unseen sea, the Ferris wheel forcing itself upon your awareness once again, the tremendous splash of it, and then it is truly gone this time. As though it never was. In fact it never was. You realize you did not see this thing. It was actually the sound of music you were seeing all along.

From where does this music come?

You stroll through the midway, following the haunting trail of this melody. You are certain it's an accordion. No, an organ. The sound of an organ. The carousel goes around, endlessly around, while sticky-faced children, as though drugged, nuzzle the withers of carved stallions.

You halt abruptly, making space for the roving oddity of a stilt-walker. The man mumbles in his slumber, chin slack against his chest as he scissors by on long, pointed legs. When the stilt-walker has passed, there he is.

The Organ Grinder himself.

The Organ Grinder is a fat man with a walrus mustache and a derby, a bullet-shaped cigar clenched between his teeth. He is not asleep. His eyes twirl like parasols. He stands alone in the dust, surrounded by fabulous rides. The box-organ hangs from a strap about his neck, balanced upon the girth of his round belly.

And hopping atop the organ is a little monkey in an impresario's vest and matching red fez. The monkey screeches at you and shakes a tin cup. You hear the rattle of coins inside the cup. Pennies perhaps?

Somehow you understand they are pennies.

Something Before You

They ride from Sacramento to Lodi, where the air is perfumed with fertilizer. Lodi to Vallejo, and then across the
Carquinez Strait by ferry, eventually stopping for the evening in Walnut Creek, a magical grassland of no walnuts and
long, muscular hills and valley oaks with great hoary limbs
that dip into the earth and rise again elsewhere like another
tree entire. All this in view of Mount Diablo.

"You think they're still following?" says Ned, stirring the
coals of their fire. They're camped along the creek that runs
through these hills. All along the banks, bay trees and their
heady smell of camphor.

"You mean the marshals or the Carter Gang?" says Francis.

"Either. Both."

"Both," says Samuel. "They're both coming."

Ned tosses his stick into the fire. "How are we going to
set this straight? We didn't kill any conductor."

"Put your heart at ease," says Temple. "This is the path
you've chosen. Just walk it."

"Just walk it."

"That's what I'm saying. Just walk it."

"Maybe I'm not cut out to be a bad guy," says Ned.
"Maybe I'm something else."

Temple clicks his tongue. He is thinking again. He's
thinking that he too is something else. We are each of us
something else. But what? This is the issue. And then the
bells commence ringing and Temple stands of a sudden, gazing off into the woods where the shadows coalesce.

"What is it, Bob?"

He shakes his head. He wants to describe it. To try and describe it but—

And there it is again.

"Bob, what did you hear?"

Like a tolling in his heart.

"Bob?"

Like something far, far away is approaching.

Three-Dollar Boat

Late that night, while the gang lies curled in their bedding about the sputtering fire, a traveller wanders into their camp, having traced out their chimney of sparks from the road.

"Mind if I join you? Cold tonight."

"Help yourself," says Francis, lifting his head from his blankets and then resting it again.

The traveller squats and rubs his hands beside the fire and glances about at the gang.

"Where you all headed?"

"Chesterville," says Ned without opening his eyes.

"Chesterville! Well you're close. You'll be there before tomorrow noon."

The newcomer doesn't seem to appreciate they are sleeping and not the least bit interested in conversation. Francis turns away, rolling deeper into his blankets, when the sky brightens in a spasm of light. A moment later, thunder, as though the moon has collided. Francis sits up, taking stock of their camp, its readiness for rain, finally taking in the newcomer as well. This is what Francis sees:

An older gentleman in a grey duster, handlebar mustache, bright blue eyes and wavy brown hair that hints at having once been red. He wears matching pistols at his hip and the star of a marshal on his lapel. He smiles at Francis, setting a blackened kettle among the coals. "Hope you don't mind if I make some coffee."

"Help yourself," says Francis, glancing at Temple who is now sitting as well, taking in the situation.

Temple says, "Ned, Samuel, wake up. We got a visitor."

The marshal introduces himself as a Mr. Maximilian McMillian. He goes about his business with the kettle, making small talk all the while.

"You fellows sure know how to pick a camp. I'll have to remember this one. Lovely view of the creek. Plenty of firewood lying about." The marshal tips a handful of coffee grounds into the kettle and brushes his hands together with a scuffing sound. "Good cover from the road too."

Temple meets the marshal's eye but says nothing.

"Now you remind me," chuckles the marshal, wagging a finger at Bob Temple. "Now you remind me of a man I once knew. That look you just gave me. It was just like him, I swear to God."

Temple sucks his teeth. Without turning away he spits into the fire.

The marshal studies him in turn.

"No. No I believe you are the handsomer fellow. This was years ago, and I must now apologize for the comparison. But anyhow, this man, I'll always remember him because he bought a three-dollar boat. I kid you not. Thought it was the greatest bargain ever, poor fellow. It was like, it was like he was so smitten by the promise of an opportunity, by the notion of it, he just completely failed to understand the consequences. Now can you imagine? I mean, can you imagine a man whose, whose faculty of foresight has so completely abandoned him that he does not comprehend he is doomed? That he has doomed himself, in fact?"

The marshal looks at each of them in turn.

"Well of course you can't. To men like ourselves, men of reason, such lapses in judgment are appalling. We are as mystified," proclaims the marshal, spreading an arm in demonstration, "as by the parting of the Red Sea. But I assure you. There are others out there who look upon the outcome of their choices with all the clairvoyance of a flowerpot. Or a clump of wet wool. I am serious. Three-dollar boats going down left and right. Even as we speak."

The marshal pries open the kettle's lid with a twig and peers within. "So anyhow how you all liking California?"

No one answers at first, and then Temple says with a distinct edge, "How you know we aren't from here?"

"Just a guess," says the marshal. "And your ponies aren't branded. We brand just about everything around here. Even our criminals. And look at that! Coffee's boiling!"

He wraps the kettle's handle with a rag and raises the kettle from the fire. "Anyone? No one?" With his free hand, the marshal waves at the night butterflies that throw themselves, one after another, into the hissing, popping flames.

"Lucky me, I guess."

Courage Has No Memory

When asked about his gumption, his general can-do attitude, Bob Temple likes to credit his father, who sent him out to milk a bear when he was six years old. This actually happened.

In the telling, Temple helps his audience to assume he succeeded in this task. He did not—though the entirety of the affair would arguably exist as a standout event in the formative years of any child.

The truth is Temple hasn't a got a clue how courage works or where it comes from. Or more importantly, where it skips off to when you need it most.

He presently lies quaking in his blankets, palms between his knees, hypnotized by cowardice while the marshal sits beside the fire, drinking cup after cup of black coffee. Temple knows he must act now. He must get up from this bedroll and do what he does. The marshal only came here to confirm his suspicions, which he's done, and he's clearly alone or others would have joined by now.

The problem:

The canny old bugger has the drop on anyone who dares go for their pistols. So he'll just sit there beside the fire, watching each of them in their bedrolls, and come sunrise he'll gallop straight away to gather a posse.

Get up, Temple whispers to himself. Get up now, you old toad.

He glances at his pistol belt, coiled an arm's length away. Slowly, carefully, Temple twists around to check on the marshal and the man is staring right back, grinning.

Temple twists away, cursing in his blankets.

He's considering his options when he notices Francis similarly awake and curled in his bedding. Concealed from the marshal, Francis has some item in his hands. Temple can't tell what it is. He squints, looking closer. A clay item. A lamp? Temple is still trying to understand what he's seeing when Francis does something—Temple can't say what, for the moment Francis does it, Temple goes out like a light.

※

Temple wakes just after dawn. He's surprised to discover he slept at all. The fire is already banked with kindling and Francis is rolling his blankets.

"Where's the marshal?" says Temple, sitting up straight.

"Lit out," says Francis. "Just before dawn."

"What marshal?" says Ned, rubbing his face and peering about with the scrunched look of confusion. Apparently neither he nor Samuel paired the newcomer with the trouble he was and returned to sleep shortly after his arrival.

"Shit," says Temple. He glances around, rubbing his jaw. "We got to pack up."

He launches into a flurry of activity, loading his kit double time. "There's a posse out there or I'm a fool. We've got to move. How long ago did he leave?"

"Not long," says Francis.

"Are we talking hours? Minutes? What time is it? And you're drinking coffee! What is with you?"

"We're all right," says Francis. "Take it easy. He left a whole pot."

"We have to run!"

"We got plenty of time. Chesterville isn't going anywhere."

"I don't get you," says Temple. "Do you understand the situation?"

"I understand it just fine," says Francis. "I understand Chesterville is a half-day's ride. That's where my fortune lies, and that's where I'm going."

"That man last night," says Temple, "that was Maximilian McMillian, United States Marshal."

"You know him?"

"Yes I know him. And he knows me, and once he gathers his folk he'll be headed straight to Chesterville. He'll noose us in a heartbeat."

"Not if we get there first."

"Well you certainly aren't firsting about here, drinking your coffee. I'm telling you, he's here to noose us."

"Then I guess he'll noose us, Bob. What that marshal does, or does not do, is none of my business. I have to do what I know to do. I'm sure he'll do the same."

"I don't get you. Not one bit."

"That's fine," says Francis. "I've never even asked you to."

✥

They start the horses slow, warming them up with a trot. By the time the sun peaks over the hills of Walnut Creek they're at a full gallop, racing down the road to Chesterville. The oak trees, individually, stand revealed in morning light. The grass either side of the road is tall and green and pearled with dew. They startle a whitetail. It's a mature doe. She has a look of expectation, like she's been standing there with chin cocked in the air, waiting to see what order of creature turned up and attached itself to the scent. She crashes into the underbrush and disappears.

Within the hour they reach a shallow creek running crosswise over the road. They slow the horses for a drink. The horses stand steaming in the water when Francis hears the jingle of horse tack and around the wooded bend come two men on chestnut mares pulling a wagon straight toward them. The men are dusty and grizzled, their eyes shaded by hat-rims. Adventurers of some sort. They don't appear alarmed to find the Blackstone Templars on the path before them.

They're hauling a large iron cage back of the wagon. Francis spies clumps of hay spilling through the bars but can't tell what's housed within. As the wagon draws near, Francis tugs his horse aside. The man nearest Francis tips his hat. Francis does the same. The wagon rolls past and Francis peeks through the bars of the cage. He sees a jaguar in there. It's lying on its side, its yellow eyes peering luminously about. And then the wagon is splashing through the creek and up the next hill and it's gone.

The Blackstone Templars resume their journey, again starting their horses at a trot.

"Did you all see what's in that cage?" says Ned.

"That was a big cat," says Samuel. "I've never seen one that close."

"I have," says Francis, quietly recalling the encounter. Recalling, too, the old Indian's suggestion that such a creature might, at some later point, figure into their collective path.

Samuel is surprised to have not heard about Francis' sighting. He's about to inquire further when Temple says, "Remember that old dynamiter I told you about? Hun Chow? He saw one once, a jaguar. He tracked it even."

"Did he get it?"

"Nah," says Temple. "What happened was, the way he tells it, one time all his charges froze up. All his dynamite. It'll freeze before water does, so it's not uncommon in winter. So his whole box of dynamite freezes up and he sets it near the fire to thaw and next thing you know he gets blown out of his clothing. Literally. He was thirty yards away and it blew his trousers clean off. Boots. Socks. Trousers."

"What's that got to do with jaguars?" says Ned.

"He was tracking a jaguar when it happened. Said it was bad luck. He was all about luck. Lucky this, unlucky that. He'd never seen a jaguar before and then he saw it and then this happened. So he turned around and left the animal alone. Said the pelt could have bought him a whole string of fresh horses."

Bob Temple Has a Secret

Once again just speaking Chow's name brings back a whole flood of memories, wild recollections from that time in his life. He and Chow shared quite a few. There was a period, some years ago, when Temple even considered him a friend.

But then there was that business with the map.

For the record, Temple never felt good about stealing it. It was just that the map was already rotting to pieces, as Francis pointed out. If the map wasn't used soon it wouldn't be used at all.

The trouble started back in San Francisco. About this same time last year. Temple had been staying in the Chinese quarter, just a few blocks off the piers. He'd managed to earn a little money on the boats. Mostly loading and unloading cargo. But Temple was a sucker for the exotic underbelly of that city: the gambling houses, the women. He spent most of his pay before it even came in.

Against all advice, he fell into particular favour with those miserable, deviant little dens that crowded like blackened teeth about Portsmouth Plaza. Temple enjoyed their sultry, sleepy atmosphere, their silken canopies, brocaded pillows. He enjoyed a certain unguarded avarice in every person he met, and most of all the anonymity. No one knew who he was—reclining peaceably across a daybed, smoking pipe after pipe.

Temple was mostly unaccustomed to the world of oriental leisure. And this world, newly articulated to him through narcotics, was perhaps a damn fine spot to stay a while. He discovered that after an hour on the pipe he could pass one hand through the other. After a day of it he reincarnated.

It didn't take long before Temple had a pretty problem on his hands. The problem grew, so to speak, and surprised all when it had nothing to do with his habit, and everything to do with the slender black-haired girl who packed his pipes.

The girl had this way with her hands. It was how she rolled the soft black putty between her fingers. How she held the burning straw tip to the bowl. Everything she touched had this magical charge, so precise, so delicate, it almost hurt to watch.

Needless to say the bigger the problem grew the harder it was to conceal, until the girl finally gave up the charade and waddled about the hazy den with her great round belly, cigarette dangling from her lips like a sailor. The family got involved. Temple offered a little money. It wasn't nearly enough, so the uncle was brought in — Hun Chow, whom Temple had known many years. Negotiations recommenced and promptly fell apart. Things got confused, then excited, and then downright ugly. Hun Chow vowed to carve Temple's liver from his body and feed it to the dogs. Such honesty! And the man half his size, like a stump of gnarled wood. How could Temple not respect such a vicious little gnome?

In the end Temple skulked out of town with a stolen horse, a satchel full of Chinese beef and noodles and the legendary map of Hun Chow in his saddlebag.

Presently Temple glances over at Francis, who sits quietly in the saddle, his eyes fixed on the road before him.

Temple adjusts his hat. "You once asked me what I'd do with the money. Any money we got from the coalmine."

"I did," says Francis. "You said you'd give it to someone. You ready to say who?"

Bob Temple considers how strange it is that he, of all people, is now a father. Why should he be ashamed? There is no disgrace in paternity, in taking responsibility for the girl and the child that is now his. He was already considering some kind of change before all this came along.

"No," says Temple, slowly shaking his head. "No I am not. Just wondering if you remember."

The gang soon enters a gorgeous tableland of purple wildflowers and swooping, chirping swallows. Insects buzz with seasonal madness. The road meanders through the meadow, flowing random as a watercourse, which maybe it once was. Hardwoods flash and glimmer in the salmon-hued rimlight. They crowd in from either side, slowly pinching off the meadow until all the pretty flowers are swaying at their backs and the sky goes dark and the gang is riding through the dense understorey of an ancient oak grove. The ground is bare, as though swept clean of all life, with only crackling brown leaves and golden acorns and puzzling grey orbs called oak gall which are in actuality made of tree fat and house the larvae of clever bugs.

Francis hasn't said hardly anything since they crossed the creek some miles back, and now he stops in the road. He sits quietly in the saddle, as though parsing some thought. He nudges the horse around and heads back the way they came.

"Where you going?" says Temple.

"I'll be just a moment."

"This isn't an outing," says Temple. "There's no time to fool about."

"I understand," Francis calls over his shoulder.

"We're not waiting for you!" Temple yells back at him. "There's not a moment to lose! Do you hear me! We're not waiting!"

Francis mutters something in response. Temple sneers. "What did he say?"

Samuel scratches behind his ear, looking a little put out himself. "He says that's fine."

Francis and the Jaguar

Most people don't know it, but the American southwest has always harboured small populations of jaguar. It would remain legal to hunt them until 1969, and to this day rogue cats wander the Santa Rita and Peloncillo Mountains in Arizona. Maybe elsewhere too.

Francis Blackstone has never found it easy to discuss his own place in the world or his aimless wanderings or, most of all, the decisions he makes. Mainly because he doesn't understand them himself. In his estimation, the comprehension of a thing is vastly overrated. Far better is to *know* it, as one might the heart of a close friend, and thereby move forward in this subtler orientation while the chips are falling everywhere at once.

Francis catches first sight of the adventurers a half mile beyond the creek. He observes a wisp of smoke rising from a cluster of oak trees at the edge of a meadow, just off the road. Francis walks his horse directly into their camp, where the two men sit around a fire, a pot of eggs boiling on a tripod. The first man stands.

"Morning," he says.

Francis touches his hat. He glances at the wagon parked in the shade of the oaks. Nothing of the beast can be seen in this light save the twin eyes glowing like moons.

"That's a pretty cat," says Francis.

The second man stands now. He sniffs elaborately and spits into the fire.

"Yes it is," he says. "May I ask what you're about?"

"Just came to see about the cat."

"What about it?"

"Is it for sale?"

The man scans the grass around his feet and then stoops and when he comes back up he's holding an oak limb, about the size of a club. He snaps off little irregularities, his gaze entirely on the limb, all the while speaking to Francis.

"Heard of P.T. Barnum?"

"Sure."

"Well, this cat is his. Or will be soon enough. He pays quite handsomely on his commissions and somehow I doubt you're in a position to outbid him."

"How can we know unless you give me a number?"

"There is no number."

The man is now standing before the cage. He thrusts the limb through the bars and jabs the cat's belly. The cat rears and hisses, baring its teeth.

The man smiles at this. Something cruel and primal stokes the light in his eyes — some cold spark that is older than man and yet finds completion of itself within him.

He jabs the cat again, harder, and this time it roars.

"Whoee! Hear that? Cougar don't do that. Never hear that from a cougar."

The other man has by now peeled an egg and stuffed its entirety into his mouth. While chewing, he shouts around the doughy mass that the other should do it again.

The first fellow sticks the cat a third time, and now the men laugh idiotically while the jaguar thunders and dances and swats at the bars.

"Well, it's a pretty cat anyhow," says Francis. He touches his hat again and walks his horse out of camp without either man acknowledging his departure.

It is perhaps five minutes later—for that is all it takes for the sincerely wicked to forget their offences—that Francis gallops directly through their camp at full speed, depositing a half-stick of dynamite into the fire.

The earth blooms in a fantastic black halo. The explosion rattles the oaks and showers the grass with green leaves. The cat's tormentors scatter in fright, sprinting into the meadow beyond. They halt midway across it, turning at a distance perfectly measured by cowardice to yell obscenities at Francis without reprisal. He walks his horse to the cage, parking before it. The jaguar bares its fangs. It hisses.

"You sure are pretty," says Francis.

He angles himself in parallel to the door and removes the Cooper from its holster. He takes aim at the iron lock and fires a single round into it. The lock deconstructs with only an iron U hanging upside in the ring and Francis pulls it from the ring and tosses the fragment into the grass.

He grips the bars on the door, looking one last time at the cat. Muted shouts reach him from the meadow.

"Pretty as all hell."

He yanks the door open and kicks his horse into a standing gallop as he races to catch up with his brother.

Bottom of the World

There is something, says the old Indian, I need you to understand.

He beckons with his hand. It takes a moment but you realize he's addressing you. He opens the very book you hold now.

Look, he says, pointing to these words. There is something precious at the rim of silence, where you stare at ink prints and see only me.

So look.

What do you see? Do my many veins wrap you in clover?

As a young man I burned like many things, a dreamer. Each burning a story: to walk and burn, to speak as though burning, to sing.

Now as an old man I find the blood is too loud. My hopes evolve backward, toward meaning. From the Nations in Oklahoma to my people in the west, nothing remains.

Just perfectly good furniture, splintered with an axe.

So who am I? When I am last of my kind? I will tell you.

I am the Old One. I am the Genie. You may call me Scheherazade. It does not matter. Go deep enough—to the very bottom of the world—and you will know the place all names become one.

You are made of rest.

It is your floor and your dreaming.

Man with a Tomahawk

Francis rides hard. His horse is slick with sweat in the noon-tide heat when he reaches the gang. They've pulled back to a trot again, the horses running hot and ready for shade. Francis draws alongside his brother. Samuel glances at him.

"I'm all set," says Francis, eyes forward.

Samuel nods.

"Told you we weren't waiting," says Temple.

After a few moments, rocking side to side in his saddle, Samuel whispers from the corner of his mouth, "We waited."

Francis grins. He then notices Ned is oddly withdrawn and somber.

"Anybody seen Ned around?" says Francis, coming alongside him.

"Just thinking is all. About life," says Ned.

"It does not become you, this thinking. Return to your tactless ways."

Ned just stares ahead.

"Ned Runkle is going to rob a bank," says Francis.

A slow smirk crawls across Ned's face. "Going to rob a bank," he repeats.

"There you go. We're all accounted for."

The hills are round as shoulders and covered in lush grass with a solitary oak tree like a majestic sentinel crowning here and there and also clustering in the clefts of valleys where little streams tinkle unseen through a riven green.

They come upon the foundation stones of a bygone structure, overgrown with weeds and moss, half a chimney tumbling to the earth, and then the first habitation enters into view. A few more homes crop up alongside the road and then a series of orchards, mostly nut trees and grape, and within the minute they're trotting their horses into Chesterville proper.

They really have no idea what they're walking into, whether the marshal arrived first and so forth. At a glance it's a nondescript town. There are many streets, uniform in their variety. There's a clocktower in the square and a steeple, and rising broadly to the south, always in view, the marvellous brown fin of Mount Diablo.

Of note are the many people about, on the streets and boardwalks lining the storefronts and also riding horses and buggies, and they are all moving like a current in the same direction. The gang trots unnoticed into the general tide, moving with it, much aware of its mystery.

Francis leans over and asks a woman in a chinstrap bonnet what the fuss is about.

"There's a bank robbery," she says. "Happening right now."

"Go figure," says Francis, glancing at his brother.

"They're catching him now. Man with a tomahawk."

"Which bank did you say?"

"Piscataqua Exchange. End of this road. It is a crazy world, I'm telling you."

"Yes, ma'am. You got that right."

"I mean if it's not one thing it's another."

"That seems the way of it."

"Plus last week my kitchen caught fire. They said it was a oil fire, which is the worst kind of fire, but I was just baking geese and next thing you—"

"Could you direct us to the Manhattan Company Bank?"

"Coming up on it now," she says, pointing to the facade on the right.

Sure enough, Francis recognizes the logo painted in white on the windowfront, and the letters *M* and *C* printed in two-foot font.

Francis parks his horse before the single-storey building, looking at it. The others stop beside him.

"Any idea what's going on?" says Samuel.

Francis shakes his head.

A commotion erupts behind them. The crowds veer either side of the road as four horsemen gallop heedlessly, rifles in hand, straight for them. The metallic star of a sheriff glitters on the coat of the foremost rider.

"Here we go," says Temple, hand hovering at his hip.

The horsemen gallop past in a cloud of choking dust. They continue to the end of the road and dismount and rally with other men just like them, milling in what appears to be a confusion of lawful intent just outside the Piscataqua.

Temple turns to the gang, sitting unmolested upon their horses out front of the Manhattan Company Bank with nothing at all to prevent their progress. Temple looks pointedly at Francis, and then they all do.

Francis lifts his hat and scratches his head and returns the hat to his head. "No clue," he mutters.

He dismounts. The others do likewise.

The bell on the door jingles as they stroll into the bank.

The Stonewaller

"Hello, gentlemen."

The teller raises a hand in greeting. He sits behind the counter as though awaiting their arrival. He is entirely alone. The bank is empty.

"Hi there," says Francis, glancing about. There are several stalls for tellers but only the one is occupied. The benches along the back and sidewalls sit vacant.

"You open?" says Francis.

"Certainly."

Francis looks about for some hint to anything at all. Failing that, his gaze returns to the cheerful man behind the counter. "For business, I mean. You're open for business."

"Yes, sir. Right and ready!"

The teller appears eager to help in every capacity. He crosses his hands and smiles at each of them in turn. "Welcome to the Manhattan Company Bank," he says, pushing his glasses higher on his nose. "You're the Dynamite Kid. I recognize you from the papers."

Francis says, "I have the feeling you're not surprised to see us."

"Of course not. We've been waiting for you."

"We?"

The gang spins in place, each doubly on guard.

"Oh don't worry. Your timing is fine. Just fine. In fact, if you'd come a moment sooner, it'd be a whole different story. The marshals had this place staked out, saying you'd be here on the instant, and then some fellow marches into the Piscataqua with a tomahawk! Go figure! This place cleared out fast, let me tell you."

Francis walks to the window. He pulls back the curtain and peers down the street. "Just down there, huh?"

"I saw the man myself," says the teller. "Walked right past that window and I didn't think a thing of it. Old Indian fellow. With his hair all bundled up like so. And now they can't find him! Like he just disappeared!"

Ned is peeking over the countertop, glancing into each of the tellers' stalls. He calls out, "Empty! Everyone's gone!"

Temple stands by the door with pistol drawn, intermittently peering through the door glass into the street beyond, and then scanning the interior of the bank. Outside, inside. Outside, inside. It's like some metaphysical exercise. Outside, inside. He's struck by the simultaneity of both worlds, and also their dissonance, and it seems for a moment he can bridge this gap and tie it all together, everything, his life, inside and out, the haunting emptiness of his future, the bells, the tedium of decline and the nagging sense of displacement and irrelevance and doom as though he had, by accident, a mere slip of the hand, disembowelled a rainbow and must now watch its colours writhing in the dirt, gasping, convulsing in hideous —

"Hey! They got slot machines!" calls Ned.

Sure enough, there are three plum-pot slot machines against the adjacent wall.

"Part of a marketing campaign," says the teller. "About federal banking versus private. Pretty effective actually."

"Do they work?" asks Ned.

Samuel looks at him. "We're holding up a goddamn bank, Ned. You want to play penny slots?"

"I've never actually seen one."

Samuel shakes his head and spits on the floor. "Enough of this." He takes two steps toward the teller and pulls his pistol. "You seem a happy fellow. Let's see if we can keep it that way. Just put your hands in the air where we can see them. We are the Blackstone—"

The man grimaces and waves the pistol away as if such gestures are unnecessary between friends. "I know who you are, sir," says the teller. "And let me just say, you're all right with me. I'm staring at a pistol bigger than yours, right here on the counter. But will I pick it up? Of course not! I'm here to fill this seat only!"

Samuel lowers his pistol. "I confess your intentions elude me."

"Think of me as your personal stonewaller."

"My what?"

"I'm your stonewaller. It's what I do."

"That's a job?"

"It is indeed. My job is to filibuster. To perplex or otherwise distract and oppose through congenial repartee."

"I think it's time you brought out the manager."

"He would tell you the same thing."

"Then the person supervising the manager. Can we talk to them?"

"Yes, but again. That person would abide by similar job descriptors."

"Look, we need to speak with someone who has the authority to think for himself."

"Oh my. You'll have to go pretty high up for that."

"On second thought, you'll do just fine." Samuel levels the pistol at the teller's forehead. He cocks it this time. "Take us to the strongbox."

Heart of Creation

The back room is wallpapered in arabesque designs right down to the wainscotting. There's a small desk with a lantern and paperwork, and a number of filing cabinets marked A to Z. The strongbox is a tremendous iron rectangle squatting in bullish contempt against the far wall. It's so large it has dual locking mechanisms with twin handles and the smug, wilful air of a streetboxer, tattooed arms crossed, toothpick dangling.

"That's a big safe," says Ned, partly in excitement, partly with the realization that the dynamite needed to open it will likely disassemble the building.

He removes four sticks from his satchel. "How you want to do this? All four edges of the door?"

"Oh, no need for that," says the teller with Samuel's pistol at his back. "I'll just open it for you."

"I thought your job was to not open it."

"My job is to engage you until the proper authorities return. But whether I open it or not it's all the same. You'll understand in a moment."

The teller crouches to work the combination on the lower lock, humming tunelessly as he rises to work the one above it. There's a distinct click within. A nervous giggle escapes Ned, who stares intently at the door. The teller grabs hold of the first wheel and instructs Ned to spin the second in unison.

They struggle on the first rotation and then it goes easy, and then the wheels knock simultaneously to signal the retraction of the inner bolts. The teller hauls on the handle, leaning back with the full force of his weight, and the door swings wide.

The strongbox's interior is large enough to stand within. There are little pegs in the sidewalls to convey eleven trays from top to bottom. Every one of those trays is gone. Missing. The vault is empty.

In response to the gang's look of shock and disbelief, the teller offers this: "We all knew you were coming."

"How so?" says Samuel.

"Well it's been in the papers for months. You sort of announced it."

"We did do that," says Francis, appearing more amused by the moment. "Ned, I believe it was you who told Gus Simons."

"It was just a matter of when," says the teller. "Just the when of it. So when the marshal arrived this morning with his posse, we cleared the vault. It's protocol."

Temple just stares into the strongbox. He doesn't appear to have heard anything the teller said.

"There's nothing in there," says Temple.

"Yes well it's empty," says the teller, scratching the back of his head. "As I was saying —"

"But it's completely empty," repeats Temple, refusing to understand. He rounds upon Francis. "Why are you smiling?"

"It's nothing," says Francis, his mirth undisguised.

"Damn right it's nothing. There's nothing at all. Where's the fortune, Francis? Where's the goddamn fortune?"

Francis is awash with a tinkling joy.

"It's perfect," he says.

Temple doesn't agree, and slams his fist through the wainscotting in demonstration of this.

Francis doesn't even look at him. He's still gazing into the emptiness of the vault. Though he would never describe it this way, it's the moment his biographers would in later years say young Francis Blackstone was touched by God.

"Nothing!" hollers Temple, placing his other fist in the wall. "Nothing!"

"Yup."

"Not one goddamn thing!"

Francis nods slowly to himself.

It's while gazing into that esoterically charged vacancy that Francis realizes: he is *knowing* nothing. Actually knowing it. Touching it. Breathing it in—like some living substance without beginning or end.

Amid his absorption, there arises in Francis a sort of collision of impossibilities. And from this collision, a spark. Like a fleeting perfection.

And within this perfection—in its code, you could say— Francis peers into the featureless heart of creation.

And he is thinking:

Broken Bell

The Blackstone Templars exit Chesterville beneath a mass of looming brown clouds. The sun, like a petrified toad, sits dull and bloated on the distant, rounded hills. They take the road east, following the creek.

For Francis' part, he's headed directly to Nowhere to find the Whitmore girl. He got what he came for, and there isn't anything in this world to hold him back. In his saddlebag is the money he requires to win the governor's favour, and in his heart is something else. Something new. A thing that has no name because it looks like nothing at all — but he knows it. And it's even bigger than love.

Francis can't speak for the others or where they're headed, though for the moment their four paths are in union. Thunder rolls in from the east. The first pellet bounces off Francis' shoulder. Another thumps his hat and then hail is clicking all around. The grass shushes and fries with jumping white tablets. The trees roar as their leaves are ripped asunder. And then the hail turns to rain, and it plunges in solid sheets. The gang is drenched on the instant. The road turns to stew.

Bob Temple rides out front, impervious to all weather. He's said nothing since departing the bank. His general person is crackling with menace and no one has yet dared approach it.

They pass a derelict mission of white adobe, glowering heroically atop a hill; a reminder this coastland was not even part of America when Bob Temple was born. The mission's bronze bell totters perilously in its cove, its axle fractured and jutting. Bob Temple was once told the bells of San Juan Capistrano rang themselves in times of tragedy. He doesn't know what it means to see a broken bell, right now, with his heart governed by animus, but he believes some significance lies harboured therein.

The deluge slackens, and now the trees drip in a steady cacophony. The road is carved with countless little rivulets. Mud flecks the horses' legs and stripes the backs of their riders.

Bob Temple falls back to ride beside Francis. He doesn't look at him or speak at all. Francis senses a new phase in Temple's mania. A cool lucidity, which is more threatening than any violent sulk.

At last Temple speaks. He says, "I want to know why."

Francis doesn't answer at first. He understands he is at a crossroads here. He's not clear on what kind, only that the words he chooses now will affect the path ahead.

"Just because we don't know the reason doesn't mean there isn't one," says Francis. "Who knows how these things work. We may never know the answer."

Temple remains silent, staring forward, the reins in one hand.

"All I know," says Francis, "is you don't go connecting dots, pulling shapes out of nothing, just because the mystery scares you. Let the stars be stars without them needing to be constellations. You know what I'm saying?"

Temple appears to think on this. Francis believes he's reached him. But then Temple says, "I know it was you."

"What was me?"

"You are the witch. Not them. You did this."

"I don't even know how to speak to that, Bob."

"Nothing to say. Because I know."

"What do you know, Bob?"

"I saw you," he says. "With that lamp in your hands. I didn't know what I was seeing, but now I do. And I warned you. Back at the mines, I warned you. You remember what I said?"

Francis remains silent.

"I told you then," says Temple, "if I find out you're swindling me, you will not like it one bit. And now here we are."

Temple removes his hat with tempestuous calm and swipes the puddles from the rim. He returns the hat to his head and glances at a break in the clouds.

"Oh, la-di-dah," says Bob. "The songs we sing."

Hope Is the Gambler's Tyrant

That night, around the campfire, Ned announces he is done. He has no complaints but he is done. Finished. Anyhow they can't do this forever, banging through life like drunken Minotaurs. Burning bridges. Heckling fate. With the money he's saved Ned will go back to Nowhere and open a saddler's shop. Or a confectionary. Yes, a confectionary, and he'll sell every kind of sweet thing. And dynamite. Because why not. And he might embark on the odd adventure or two but he's feeling unexpectedly satisfied and quite ready to hang up the spurs.

"Samuel has already agreed to be my partner in business," Ned continues, though no such arrangement is in place. "There's going to be a sign out front. A big one, with bright blue letters. Runkle & Blackstone. Purveyors of Fine Confections. We'll be known throughout the world. We'll travel to Paris for conferences. Eat chocolates and pastries, and then retire somewhere with about a million dollars in our pockets, and write a great big book called *Crazy Shit We Did with Money*."

Samuel grins good-naturedly. But the truth is, he feels as lost and disconsolate as when they first set out. There was something he'd hoped to find out here, some part of himself—call it certainty, call it purpose—and though he's glimpsed it at times, almost reached out and touched it, he has never once grasped it with both hands. When he thinks of home there is only an immense white page with no writing at all. He can't see himself there. He can't see himself anywhere.

✻

Bob Temple sits around the fire, staring into it. He speaks not a word.

A Much-Anticipated Fiasco

When Francis wakes next morning Bob Temple is gone. The fire is out, the ashes soaked and sunken and grey. Ned is some distance away, urinating among the trees, and Samuel is lying on his back with one foot in the air, pulling on a boot.

Francis stands there in his long underwear, staring pensively at the ground. "I don't like this."

"Let him be," says Samuel, yanking at the boot's collar. "Bob's done here. He's on to something else."

Francis shakes his head. "I don't think so."

"What are you worried about? He's gone."

Francis pulls on his own boots and mounts his horse directly. "I'll see if I can find him."

"At least let's pack up first. I'll join you. You're not even dressed."

"I won't be long."

The sun lurks behind gunsmoke clouds, its motive uncertain. The earth is wet and soft and there's a dead light on the trees, their brown leaves rustling in an icy breeze.

Francis leads his horse the short distance to the road. He has no difficulty finding Temple's tracks, him being the first rider upon the road since rain. Francis pauses to inspect the depressions in the mud. Even as Francis looks, the prints are infilling with water. A series of hoof-sized puddles leads up the road.

Francis stands there, thinking about that. He begins to shiver and crosses his arms against the chill. The ragged petals of his breath hang in ravelled suspension.

Then the reflection of a crow in flight skips across the puddles in the road. He's never seen that before, and it gives him pause. After some moments, he urges his horse in the same direction.

The puddles stretch the length of a mile up the road and then veer off into a copse of madrone wood. The grass is sodden and lies flat to the ground where Temple's horse trod by.

It's only after Temple's trail cuts again that Francis has the first suspicion of trouble.

"He's looping around," Francis mutters. "He's going back to camp."

It dawns upon Francis like a peal of thunder. He was meant to follow. Temple was leading him all along.

Francis kicks his horse into a gallop, and then slows abruptly as Temple's trail weaves through the understorey of oaks, their discarded limbs littering the ground and impeding Francis' progress. Cursing, Francis jerks on the reins, crashing directly into the brush until he reaches the road. He rides hard, his flight unhindered. He's approaching the last bend when he hears the flat pop of a pistol. He listens for return fire but hears nothing more.

Francis yanks off his hat and swats his horse's flank. The horse grunts softly, rhythmically, its legs pounding like pistons.

❖

Francis flies into camp, leaping off his horse and running to Ned who lies back against a log, clutching his left leg. He rocks side to side, moaning piteously and without shame.

"That son of a bitch!" cries Ned. "He shot me in the knee! Just outright shot me!"

Samuel is crouched over Ned, trying his best to calm him. But the truth is, nothing short of oblivion can staunch Ned's exclamations. This is his moment, his spectacle, the one he's been waiting for, and no one's going to take it away.

Samuel rises as Francis approaches. "You weren't kidding," says Samuel. "That crazy bastard came back all right. He was muttering about how you swindled him and started rifling through your bags. He got your money, Francis. He took all your money. I tried to stop him and then Ned jumped in and that's when—"

Francis stomps over to his saddlebags. His possessions are spread in a haphazard circle about the bags as though exploded there. He scans the grass and stoops to pick up a solitary sock.

Samuel says, "We'll split my share. The money's yours, Francis."

"Keep it," says Francis, staring down at the sock in his fist. The sock is empty—the lamp is gone. In its place is a brief note, written in an unexpectedly meticulous hand:

Ha!

-B.T.

Francis stares at the note. Meanwhile Ned's moaning has grown louder, particularly now that their attention has strayed.

Francis wads the note into a ball and tosses it aside. "What's done is done. Let's get Ned taken care of."

Francis pulls on his pants, then his shirt. As he's setting his hat, Samuel steps into his path. "I'll take care of Ned. He'll be fine. Trust me."

"I do trust you. And I'll help you too. Ned isn't going to make this easy on either of us."

"Listen to me, Francis."

"I am listening. You're just not saying much."

"Bob Temple isn't through with you."

"That's fine. I'm not through with him either."

"No, Francis. He lit out. Said he's going back to Arizona."

"Arizona? What could he possibly —"

"He's going after your girl. He's headed there now."

From There, Who Knows,
Maybe Wings Begin

Francis stands rigid. His brother's words hit like a brick. He has barely a moment to register when the first bullet sings past his ear. Francis instinctively ducks and then dives behind the log, lying shoulder to shoulder with Ned. Samuel throws himself down beside them, squeezing in close.

"That was no pistol shot," says Samuel. "Someone's got a rifle out there. Anyone see where it came from?"

"Top of the hill—back there," says Ned. He piles a handful of bullets on the grass beside his injured leg. He digs out his pistol and begins chambering the empty chambers. "Probably the marshal, and whoever else he's brought. I saw about six of them up there. Maybe more."

Samuel tries to peek over the log and jerks back down as several more bullets thud into the wood, sending fragments over them all. "That's not the marshal."

"Who is it then?" asks Francis.

"Who do you think?" says Samuel.

Ned curses and sighs.

"They're all spread out on the hilltop. Bursula's got the rifle. Maybe others too," says Samuel. "Temple's pistol shot must have drawn them in."

Ned glances about their camp. "They got us penned like geese."

Francis too scans about, looking for an escape. His horse stands at the edge of the wood, restlessly huddled with the others. All three horses are probably twenty yards away over open ground. Francis wonders if they can make it. He glances down at Ned's leg and his stomach drops. Ned's trousers have a small triangular tear at the knee, and he can see a little purple hole going straight into Ned's knee. Almost no blood. It's a weird thing to see.

Voices rise on the hill. Lots of them. They're coordinating up there, calling out to each other.

Francis says, "We'll have to make a break for the road. And just hope they don't have that covered too."

Ned finishes loading his pistol. "Oh hell, Francis, you know me and Samuel can't work a candy shop." He snaps the chamber shut. He reaches over his head and fires three shots, blindly, at the hill behind them — pop, pop, pop. He rests back against the log. He appears oddly resigned. "You're going to have to let us be the handsome heroes for once."

Francis just looks at him. "What are you talking about?"

"I'm talking about —" Ned shakes his head as he reloads. "Listen, Francis, don't make us spell it out. Me and Samuel already talked about this. If it ever came to this."

"Ned, shut your goddamn mouth," says Francis. "I'm not leaving you two."

At that moment the voice of Jack Bilworth calls down from the hill.

"Hello boys! Quite a spot you're in! But I think we can work something out!"

"It's not so bad!" Ned yells back at the hill, and then he grins at Francis. He actually grins.

Bilworth continues. "I think you should know we got several men swinging around both sides of your camp! You'll be surrounded in a moment. Any chance you want to throw down your arms?"

Samuel responds by resting his pistol across his chest. He cocks it. Without looking at Francis, he says, "Here's how this will go, little brother." He takes a long breath. "In about five seconds, me and Ned will start shooting like mad. You're going to run for the horses. Grab whichever one's nearest. Ride like hell."

"Samuel, I'm not—"

"This one's not up to you, Francis. It's me and Ned making the call."

Bilworth yells down at them. "You got barely a minute to decide, and then this gets real ugly! How you want to do this?"

"Just give us a second you son of a bitch!" yells Samuel. He turns back to Francis. "We're going to hold them off. And you're going to run."

The log jitters and jolts, and wood chips fly as a several more bullets bite into it. When the barrage lets up Ned hisses loudly. "Francis, goddammit." He fires two more rounds over the log. "Me and Samuel need something for the poets to write about. Not just Francis this, and Francis that. You selfish bastard. If you're still here when this starts I'll shoot you myself."

Ned pumps fresh bullets into his pistol.

"It doesn't have to go like this," argues Francis. "We can carry Ned. Or even...I don't know, give ourselves up, or—"

"I *want* to do this," says Samuel, his voice faintly hoarse.

Francis will later recall how his brother appears to phosphoresce in this moment. As though Samuel has genuinely, with all his heart, chosen the path before him, abruptly altering what he is, and whatever he was before. It's like seeing Samuel for the first time.

Samuel takes another long breath. "Ready Ned?"

"Goddamn, yeah. You know I am ready." Ned barks a sharp laugh, and then stifles a sob. He positions his pistol on the log. He sights the barrel with one eye, and then wipes that eye and sights the barrel again. "Going down in a blaze of glory," he whispers through a trembling grin.

Samuel's chest is heaving. "Anything for love, right?"

Francis nods.

Samuel grips the pistol in both hands and stands with an adrenalized yell. He fires several rounds, one after another. Ned roars unintelligibly from behind the log, his pistol bucking and thundering. The rifles on the hill go silent. Francis breaks for the horses.

He jumps his black mare and slaps the white stars on its haunch. The horse rears and bolts, Francis holding on for dear life. They pound through the woods, kicking up turf. The racket of gunfire is a storm at his back. Francis doesn't look back.

CHAPTER EIGHT

With Wings Like These

For the first hour Francis rides so hard he thinks he might kill his horse. The foam from her mouth flies across his trousers, soaking them black. But she is indomitable and recovers her breath before Francis does when he finally veers from the road. They take cover behind a ruined millhouse on the banks of a creek. The horse drinks greedily.

Francis remains saddled, scanning the surrounding hills. They are long and sinuous and curved as hips, while the dales are sharply furrowed and wreathed with oak. If Francis crosses the creek here he could quickly disappear among them, but he is of two minds. He can't shake the Carter Gang if he keeps to the road. But nor can he catch up to Bob Temple if he leaves it.

Francis tugs lightly on the reins. "That's enough," he chides, pulling her back from the water. "We're not done yet." He decides to risk the road. They set out at a good clip.

Headed east on a lane with barbed-wire hedging its sides, Francis passes a rough-hewn signpost for Martinez. He doesn't know if that's a town or a person. A few miles further he passes a sign for Pleasant Hill, and then it's on to

Walnut Creek again, and the country goes wild with oak. Trees crowd the road and darken it.

And it's only now, in the relative calm of the forest, amid the rhythmic clomping of hooves, that the stark hard reality of what just transpired catches up to Francis. It bores into his thoughts. Francis doesn't try to stop it. He wouldn't know how. The felt image of Samuel as he was at their last parting sizzles into his heart like a firebrand.

Six Miles Up the Road,

on a tremendous oak limb overhanging the road, an owl sits placidly watching Francis ride just beneath. When Francis turns over this shoulder he sees the owl has done the same.

A little further on he comes upon a coyote. The animal is lanky and lean with a cloud of flies about the muzzle. It stands upon the grey stems of its shadow, middle of the road. The coyote holds its ground until the horse forces it aside, and even then it is reluctant, moving only just enough for Francis to tread by.

The path climbs a hill, offering views of many more — they rumple the distance like soft waves on a blanket. A sharp descent follows, and then a hairpin turn, and now Francis startles a peccary. The beast screeches and snorts, crashing through the underbrush with a terrified ruckus.

Francis sits his horse for a solid minute on the road, his heart pounding in his chest. It's a goddamn menagerie, he thinks, starting his horse again, only to complete the turn in the road and find a lone piglet, abandoned by the peccary in her haste, and this time Francis has his wits about him.

Francis washes the kill out at the next creek crossing. The creek is loud and cold and he checks his shoulder repeatedly, wary of the road behind him. He checks the sky.

He notices the buzzards first, circling high in the sky.

A Curious Encounter

At first Francis thinks the buzzards have caught wind of his supper. But that doesn't make sense—the piglet is too fresh. The buzzards continue their approach, however, appearing to follow the exact course of the road behind him. This is curious.

Francis watches the road until a man appears. The man is single-handedly hauling a two-wheeled oxcart. The buzzards keep pace above him like gloomy black kites.

As the man draws near, Francis notes a tall, skinny, dejected looking fellow with a ragged Stetson and threadbare trousers. The man's cheeks are hollow and his skin is rough. His eyes sit too far back in his head.

Walking alongside the man is a girl-child with wild staring eyes and tangled blonde hair. She's as lovely a child as one could ever encounter but in her dingy grey dress and no shoes to speak of she and the fellow look like refugees from some biblical blight. In the cart behind them is a rectangular box.

Francis sits his horse, middle of the road.

The man halts his cart some yards away. He sets the cart stems on the ground. He leans back, stretching his back. Whatever the man is hauling, Francis can smell it from here.

The man introduces himself as H.R. Mulligan, headed east with no want of trouble. He inquires politely of Francis' intentions.

Francis puts the man at ease, asking this Mulligan if he might have met other riders on the road. Thirty-eight of them, to be exact.

"Haven't seen them," says the man.

Francis nods. "And when did you set out?"

The man removes his hat and swipes his brow. "I am forty-one years old."

Francis thinks that might be the most miserable answer he's ever heard of. He again studies the cart. He studies the buzzards overhead. He tries to contain his curiosity but simply can't.

"So what's in the cart?"

"That would be the missus," says the man, turning over his shoulder as though to double-check this assertion. "Made me promise not to bury her west of the Missouri."

"The Missouri River? How long will that take?"

"Oh a month perhaps."

Francis rubs his lips. "That sounds like a long road," he says.

He reassesses the man, this time with a thought for his soundness, and then he looks at the child. There is a haunted, hungry look about her, so lost in this world she can't even begin to know it.

Francis sighs inwardly, knowing he will regret this. "Are you all hungry? Because I got a little pig. All ready to cook."

Your Worst Ever Idea

Francis and the Mulligans move off the road, taking cover in a stand of eucalyptus. Francis is reluctant to halt so early in the afternoon but the little pig must be cooked, and daylight is best or the flames will beacon in the dark.

In a small clearing within earshot of a rushing stream, and therefore covered by its song, Francis gathers a bit of kindling. The oily, aromatic wood catches fire with a single match, and the whole pile goes up in an impressive whoosh. The child climbs into the cart and sits quietly atop the coffin, looking about with those owl-like eyes.

H.R. Mulligan is content to luxuriate on a log, observing Francis at his preparations. Whatever politeness or congeniality he displayed on the road is now all but gone, a nice piece of theatre. The man says without preamble he dreams every night, and always has. But ever since the missus died his dreams are boring as hell. He just walks around, doing nothing. All night long, just walking about, so help me God. Mulligan says the best part about boring dreams is he is living his dreams, and how many out there can say the same?

"Well that's something at least," says Francis, and H.R. Mulligan agrees that it is.

But the thing about this man: the more he speaks, the more you want him to stop. He fared so much better as a nameless traveller on the road. If he could just somehow return to that bland, unspecified state, and thereby withhold all evidence of his personality, he might inspire another's sympathy to good effect. Anyhow he is eager to share his story and Francis is now resigned to the man's company.

"Started out with two oxen and a wife," says Mulligan, his knees spraddled wide, leaning forward upon them. "I was a prospector."

Francis erects a simple wooden spit with a pair of forked branches. He sets the piglet to roast. "What were you after? Gold? Silver?"

"Makes no difference. I'm out." Mulligan ferrets a smoking pipe from the deepest recesses of his coat. He does this like a man settling in to oblige a receptive audience, but there is no such audience. His fingernails are black and the pipe too is black with a corresponding grime, altogether suggesting a certain loyalty to neglect.

Mulligan packs the pipe with a generous load and drives it down with a tar-brown thumb. "A prospector! So help me God. Nothing on earth could kill a man's prospects faster." He leans forward to remove a fire-tipped twig from the fire. "But really it's inspiration that's the killer. Like a disease," he continues. "It's like a poison. It will drag your ass out to the middle of nowhere. Tell you to dig a hole." He sets the twig to the pipe and puffs it alive. He exhales out the corner of his mouth. "Two years later you realize you're indentured to a whim, and there is no hole on earth that goes deep enough — that can reach the place you're really trying to get."

"Well you gave it a try," offers Francis. "That's better than most."

"And it all comes down to the smallest thing," continues Mulligan. "The smallest goddamn thing. Just take Adam and Eve — you ever think about that? If they never even met? No? Eve stays home to wash her hair. Adam goes out with the boys. Their paths never cross, two ships in the night. Where would we be then?" he asks. "Everything hangs upon the smallest choice. The unconsidered choice."

Francis says, "It sounds like you've had a particularly —"

"Take me for example, I'm fucking smart," says Mulligan, spitting into the fire. "You wouldn't think it to see me but there it is," he says. "So I'm smart — *twice as smart* as any of these other, these, pear-shaped articulate apes. These so-called *prospectors*. Dragging their hairy knuckles over the earth. And the gold just jumping into their sluiceboxes, just jumping up from the ground. So I'm smart, hell — but do I excel at even one skill that would make a life easier?" He snorts and shakes his head. "Now that's a story for you," he says, jabbing a finger in Francis' direction. "That's the story behind the answer to the question you've been wanting to ask."

"Well I wish I could offer you —"

"And those dirty preachers!" he croaks, waving a filthy hand before him. "They'll tell you how it is. Oh, they'll tell you. But until you've witnessed your worst ever idea come rippling to life in gigantic fucking form you just cannot possibly appreciate. So take my advice," he says. "Inspiration comes knocking at your door. You empty your shotgun into her. No hello, no goodbye. Let her speak one word and you're done for. You'll aim that barrel at her heart-shaped mouth, and you say—"

At this, Mulligan mimics the shouldering of a shotgun, sighting down its invisible length with one eye.

"You'll say, 'Get back, you shining, fraudulent, honey-tongued leech of a whore.' And then you slap that trigger like your life depends upon it, because it does."

At the end of this little speech he laughs loudly and coughs wretchedly and knocks out the ashen contents of his pipe against the side of the log.

Francis feels no sense of delicacy at present. He cocks his thumb back at the child who sits motionless upon the coffin. "Is she yours?"

"Hell," says Mulligan, his gaze now fixed upon Francis' horse, possibly admiring it. "She doesn't speak a word. Just sits there by her mama. Head full of fireflies. You don't believe me, watch this. Hey. Hey."

The child sits motionless, saying nothing. It's clear she's avoiding Mulligan's glance. Mulligan picks up a twig from the ground. He tosses it into the child's lap. "Hey. Eat that stick."

The child does not eat the stick. She simply sets the stick aside without comment, directing her attention elsewhere.

Mulligan shakes his head. "See what I mean?"

Francis sees, all right. He sees all too well, but he opts to keep his mouth shut, stirring the coals with a stick.

"Now her mother, God rest her soul, was the best human being I ever met in my life. Hands down."

Mulligan insists his deceased wife never once uttered an unkind word, refusing all opportunities for rudeness and disdain. "She's the one who set me straight. Got me off drink. My wild ways. Now that she's gone, frankly speaking, I'm just not sure what the future holds."

"If you don't mind my asking," says Francis. "What happened to her?"

"Shot herself," answers Mulligan. "Twice."

Francis winces. He shakes his head at the fire.

"Didn't even know she had the damn thing."

It's here H.R. Mulligan reaches into a second pocket of his coat and this time removes an unmarked bottle. The bottle is dark and ominous. He uncorks it with care, as though its contents are precious, or volatile, or both. He doesn't drink right away but rather considers the moment and what he's about to do. Then he takes a long swig. He makes an awful grimace as the stuff grips his shoulders, his eyes pinched tight, his spine twisting slowly until it appears it might snap, and then a beautiful shiver runs through him. A light shines from his head.

"Holy god-awful demon mother of hell," he gasps, face down in the crook of his arm. He extends the bottle blindly in Francis' direction.

"I'll pass," says Francis.

"Go on now. Don't be like that." H.R. Mulligan taps the bottle against Francis' knee until Francis accepts.

Francis raises the bottle reluctantly and tips it back. His throat ignites on the instant—it's even worse than he feared. He can taste it in his eyes. In his elbows. In his socks.

Mulligan grabs the bottle away and takes another long pull. He goes through the same motions. It's like watching someone get possessed by the Holy Ghost. He corks the bottle, his movements less steady this time, and slips it back into his pocket.

"Little rough," he admits, "but better than nothing."

There are all kinds of nothing Francis would rather have. He returns his attention to the pork. When it's well turned, its skin crispy and black, he slides it from the stick and rips it into thirds. They eat quietly around the fire, each to their own thoughts.

Francis doesn't say so but whenever he eats pork he can't help but picture the animal itself snuffling about in its own muck. The image sits firm in his mind, sometimes producing phantom flavours that may, or may not, be true to the source. As a child he once climbed the fence rails of a sty and asked his father beside him why any creature on earth would so greedily devour its own dung. His father replied that they're called pigs for a reason.

Presently H.R. Mulligan turns his head and spits a wad of gristle. In the midst of said turning, the sight of Francis' horse again catches his eye. He examines it for some time while chewing. "But look at the white markings on that haunch," he comments. "They look just like little stars, don't they? I'll tell you what. That is one stunning mare."

"Yes she is," says Francis. "And I believe she's calling to me." He is eager to get back on the road. He stands and wipes his hands on his trousers. He realizes he is unsteady, just from that one swig. The child remains seated, watching him. "If you want the rest of that piglet," begins Francis, turning about, but the man is nowhere to be seen. Francis turns about again, and then he feels a clunk on the head.

A Foretelling

Francis Blackstone is eleven years old.

It's late at night. He is lying in bed, watching the moon through the window, when he hears the floorboards creak at the threshold. By the sound of them, the particular rasp and groan, he knows it's his mother standing in the doorway. But she doesn't enter. She remains there so long he eventually dozes off. Francis wakes some time later to find her silhouette crouched over his sleeping brother, whispering into Samuel's ear.

Francis can't hear the words, only the click and murmur of her voice as she presses some mysterious dispatch into his brother's dreams. This goes on for a time, longer than Francis would expect, and all the while Samuel snores softly.

When his mother finally rises from this task Francis shuts his eyes and feigns sleep. He maintains this illusion as she sits upon his own bed, the mattress giving faintly with a squeak.

She bends close to his ear, and he feels the heat of her breath.

"Francis," she whispers, "whatever bees in their frenzy cannot live without, you will have always and in plenty."

Francis remains perfectly still, his eyes pinched shut.

"Francis," she whispers, "you will marry in a rose arbour. You will bounce daughters across your knee. Their eyes will gleam out from a garland of curls, the same ice-blue as your own."

His mother gently combs fingers through his hair.

"Francis," she whispers. "I've waited till now. Till you were ready. Now you are strong and have no more need of me. I will miss you, Francis. I will always miss you. Only some things cannot be helped." A teardrop, hot, taps the side of his cheek.

"I hope you never understand."

She rises from his bed and glides to the door.

Francis lies curled in his blankets, refusing to watch her go. He will not call out. He will not open his eyes. For all he knows this is a nightly visitation, something his mother does and has always done, baring her heart in the dark and thus shaping him, hauling up from his slumber the wet ingots of what's to come.

But she isn't done. For presently she is beside him again, having returned on silent feet, bending close to speak in his ear once more.

"Francis," she whispers, "you will ride horses always, and fear no man."

And then she is gone. Not just gone from his room. Not gone from his thoughts.

Gone.

Francis and the Tessellated Heart

When Francis comes to, his horse is gone. His Cooper is gone. The map to the Carter cave, the oxcart, Mulligan — everything, gone.

His head is ringing like a bell. He sits in the dirt, gathering his senses. He glances groggily about. The sun is still in the sky, though now in its westerly quadrant. Evening is in the air. He touches the lump at the back of his head, exploring the wound. It feels like a knee.

Francis only ever had one picture of his mother. He kept it in his saddlebag throughout the journey. It was taken by a tintype photographer, long ago — back before there was anyone to grow up without her. Now that picture is gone too. He quite literally has nothing left. Not even the matches for a fire.

Dry leaves crunch at his back and Francis glances over his shoulder. The girl-child stands there among the trees, forlorn and abandoned, a small leather valise in hand. The valise is scuffed and mottled and possibly rotten. Twine holds it all together like a scrapbook. The child watches him. Francis turns back around, ignoring her.

For the next several minutes Francis says nothing, his face in his hands. Thoughts of his brother come crashing in. Then his mother again. Then the Whitmore girl, who feels so far away. All of it swirling about in a storm of futility. Everything has gone wrong. The distance to his home is like a living thing.

The child remains silent at his back, presumably watching.

Eventually Francis sniffs and stands. He doesn't even bother to wipe the tears. He approaches the child and crouches before her. He looks at her a moment. Her eyes are wild and blue. He's keenly aware that she's standing in the place his life used to be — the whole thing blown apart and brought back together in the apparition of a miserable child.

He says, "I guess you are with me now."

After a moment, the child nods.

"I got a long way to go. And I have to move fast. You'll have to keep up."

She nods again.

Francis eyes her valise. "And we have no horse. So we can only carry what we need."

A look of alarm crosses her face and Francis softens. "All right. Let's see what you have in there."

Reluctantly the child passes him the valise. Francis lays it flat on the ground and unties the twine. He opens it up. He stares within, rubbing his jaw. He is not sure what to make of it.

There's no clothing inside. No blankets or dolls. The only thing in there is a little broken guitar, just big enough for a child.

Which everyone knows is about the saddest thing on earth.

Back on the road, Francis sets out at a solid pace, the child's valise in hand. It bumps against his leg with each step. The child walks just behind.

The sun is going down, burnishing the trees in flashed hackles of light. The sky gleams red. "Pretty, isn't it?" says Francis, expecting no answer from the child. But she comes alongside him. She tries to match his steps, and then the shadow of his steps, and there is just the tiniest, faraway hint of amusement in her stride.

A mile further down the road, Francis hears a horse approaching. He pauses a moment and looks down at the child. Without a word between them they step clear of the road. They wait. When his Appaloosa mare, riderless, comes trotting into view Francis steps out again and greets the horse, halting her with a hand. He coos to her. He pets her broad neck. A man's hobnail boot is still lodged in the stirrup and Francis removes the boot, turning it over in his hand.

"Recognize this?" he asks the child.

She nods.

Francis tosses the boot aside and lifts the child into the saddle. He finds the remnants of a second harness hanging loose from the mare's belly — likely the evidence of some attempt to tether horse and oxcart. Francis unbuckles this and cuts a set of straps and secures the child's valise to the saddlebags. He opens the saddlebags and smiles to himself as he peers within. Here, the photo. There, the map. He removes the Cooper and cracks the chamber and checks it and snaps it shut, slipping the pistol back into its holster.

"I guess we're all set."

He climbs into the saddle with the child behind him and urges the horse into a canter. He hopes to make up for lost time.

❧

Francis rides through the night. The hills feel endless, as there is no horizon in the dark. Nor is there any way to gauge the distance travelled. By next morning he's exhausted, though still unwilling to halt. His sense of haste is unusual in that, like said distance in the dark, it has no measure. Bob Temple could be close, or around the next bend even. He could also be on a different road altogether.

Francis' plan is to intercept Bob Temple if possible. Failing that, he will beat Bob home and spirit the Whitmore girl to safety. Both plans require speed and nerve, and he has the horse for it. He has the will. What he does not have is the ability to forgo sleep entirely without losing his head.

"Can you steer a horse?" he asks the child.

They trade places on the saddle. He passes her the reins and shows her how to hold them. "Just follow the road, and wake me if you see anyone. Anyone at all."

Francis closes his eyes. He sees vivid images of Samuel and Ned, both as they were when he left them in the clearing. He can hear the clacking of their pistols. He can hear them shouting. Telling Francis to run, run.

Francis jolts awake in the saddle. The child holds the reins exactly as she was told. But she is approaching what is obviously a discarded oxcart in the road—and she's still looking askance, as though she has not noticed.

"Whoa," says Francis, halting the horse. He climbs down from the saddle. He draws his Cooper. He glances about for any sign of others. The oxcart appears unattended.

He looks up at the child. "You didn't see that cart?"

Francis studies the child for some reaction. She in turn squints over his shoulder, and then gasps aloud in recognition. He realizes she is half-blind.

"Wait here," he says.

Wary of an ambush, Francis levels his pistol as he approaches the cart. Rounding the cart, he stops short and crouches. The body of a man lies twisted up among the leaves. Francis glances over his shoulder to see if the child is watching. "Stay where you are," he calls to her. He slowly approaches the body.

A miracle of white butterflies has gathered there. They cluster upon the ground, and on the body as well, fanning the air with soft, powdered wings — open and closed, slowly open and closed — their long probing snouts feasting on blood-salt.

Francis flips the body over and the butterflies rise about him. He steps back and looks at the body. He can see two bullets to the chest. A third in the face. Just the one boot, toes aimed at the sun. Francis goes next to the oxcart. The coffin is overturned and the shattered lid sits some feet away. The stench is god-awful. If there were any other possessions in the cart they are now gone.

Francis' first thought is that Bob Temple must have done this. But then Francis notices fresh horseprints in the dust, many of them. It would appear the Carter Gang is no longer behind him but ahead, laying waste to all they find. Could it be possible they are in pursuit of Bob Temple, just like himself? With Francis just behind? What a mess.

Francis climbs back into the saddle, taking the reins this time.

"It was nothing," he says over his shoulder. "Someone's cart must have broke down."

He urges the horse into a canter. He can feel the child trembling at his back.

Whatever Francis offers, the child accepts. Food, water, blankets. She has no agenda of her own and so poses no burden. She is literally along for the ride. The child sits quietly behind Francis when he guides the horse, and sits in front of him when he sleeps.

"Can you write?" Francis asks her one morning, just after dawn. They are in the saddle, rocking to and fro. The foothills of California fall away in layers, their distance marked by brightening shades of silhouette.

The child shakes her head. Francis was hoping she could write her name at least. He's already got a fiancée and a horse without proper designations. This whole business of no names is getting tedious.

"I'm going to call you Lily."

The child says nothing of course. But a moment later he feels a pair of small, timorous hands reach around from behind and clutch his waist. He smiles to himself. For all he knows, he guessed her name exact.

Francis hasn't really spent much time with children. He's happy to discover he enjoys Lily's presence. It comforts him. Not even a week ago, he would have dreaded the encumbrance. Now it feels normal. As though she slipped in next to his heart before he even thought to prevent it. How strange life can be.

"Listen, Lily, I'm going to tell you something. I'm going to teach you to write. How does that sound?"

She nods.

"That way you can keep your tongue and still get your point across."

She nods.

"We can start right now. Why don't you dig out that old ledger from my saddlebag."

Francis finds something confiding in her silence. Rather than push him away, it offers a kind of inclusion, the way a small room brings even strangers together.

"Now see if you can find a pencil in there. You'll have to sharpen it. Here's my knife."

So long as they can keep the mare moving, and it doesn't distract Francis from his course, he has no objection to teaching Lily from the saddle. They set about learning the alphabet. Lowercase first, capitals to come later. She dutifully accepts his instruction. Francis finds this remarkable. He's reminded of a time when he was very young, probably no more than four or five. Samuel invited him to visit the candylady.

The Candylady

lived alone in a small cabin about a mile outside town. How Samuel first learned of her, Francis has no idea. He was too young then to even wonder, having the impression she was known to all. A natural phenomenon, like the Grand Canyon.

Arriving on her rickety porch, Samuel and Francis knocked at her door and were greeted by an energetic, endearing old spinster in several layers of garment and a tartan shawl. She never asked their names. She never asked what brought them out to her cabin. Instead she accepted their visit as though arranged by invitation and immediately showed them about the kitchen where she kept a collection of kitchen witches. The little witches were made of bundled straw and dressed in a variety of seasonal outfits. They hung on hooks on the wall around the cookstove. The woman spoke in kooky voices as she introduced each one, and Francis was delighted. He'd never met an adult who seemed so much like a child.

After the tour the old woman led them back to a lone table in the middle of the cabin. On the table was a jar of peppermints and Francis and Samuel were invited to help themselves to a few. The candies were so old they'd fused to their wrappers. What's more, Francis never even cared for peppermint. But the whole experience was so interesting and pleasant that he returned several times on his own. He even brought along some neighbour children on a few occasions. Each visit was the same. The candylady greeted him like a dear old friend, showed him about the kitchen, offered him a sweet, and waved farewell when he left.

People are always saying how curious children are. How they ask so many questions—too many questions. But what strikes Francis most about childhood is all the questions we never even thought to ask. All the magical little moments we just accepted as so.

Just West of the Colorado River,

Francis and Lily come to the foot of a remarkable hill. It's like the carcass of a colossal humped beast curled up beneath a blanket of grass, a few knobby trees on the spine. The road flows about its base, winding crazily around boulders and mounds of green moss. It eventually crosses a trestle bridge over a boisterous creek and enters a copse of manzanita—this last presenting a new oddity for Francis, as the strange shrub appears less plant than animal, its smooth red limbs like the wrists of skinned deer.

Francis and Lily ride warily through this wooded grove, Francis at the reins, when they come upon another wreck in the road; the second such wagon in a week of travel.

This one lies on its side, middle of the road. Most of the panelling is splintered and the horses are gone. Clothing is scattered everywhere, as are the contents of several large steamer trunks and even furniture: a wooden bedstead, a pair of endtables, the smashed hull of a desk. Francis halts the horse in the road, observing from afar. It is very quiet. No one is about.

"Should we have a look?"

A rogue gust of wind combs through the leaves in the trees. It sends a single wheel, suspended upon an upturned axle, spinning freely in a cadence of squeaks. It's as though they've stumbled upon the set piece for some elaborate last act, and all the performers have vanished.

The child shakes her head, clutching Francis' shirt.

"Come on," he says. "We'll be quick."

Francis dismounts. He lifts Lily from the saddle and sets her upon the ground. They begin picking through the litter but Lily stays close, refusing to leave Francis' side. He searches the desk. He finds all the drawers have been yanked out and emptied in the road. A skirt of tattered documents surrounds the desk, fluttering in the breeze. He kicks through the pile and turns up nothing of interest. And then:

A miniature bronze telescope, green with patina.

Francis plucks it from the wreckage. He slides it open, all three sections, gives it a peek, and his vision inflates with the detail of faraway trees.

Lily tugs at his shirt and he turns about. "What'd you find?"

In Lily's hand is a small leather sack. She passes it excitedly to Francis. He unties the drawstrings. He lifts the sack to his nose and then glances at Lily, bobbing his eyebrows with theatrical flair, and then smells the contents. He pretends to sneeze.

"Pepper! You trickster!"

The child laughs loudly, almost uproariously. It's as delightful a sound as Francis has ever heard.

"Good find, Lily. Pepper is good." Francis pats her shoulder and stuffs the sack into his pocket.

Francis likes the idea of pepper. Pepper means you no longer have to accept the world as it is. You can alter it. You can dress it up. Also, only adults use pepper—and though Francis hasn't given it much thought, he supposes he is now an adult. He has charge of his own life. He has a child in his care. Yes, pepper is the thing.

"Whoa, look what you almost stepped on."

Francis stoops to retrieve something in the road. It's a pair of spectacles, miraculously unscathed. He huffs across the lenses and wipes them on his shirt.

"You could use a set of these. Let's see how they fit." Francis crouches down, facing the child. He slips the spectacles over her eyes and her eyes go huge.

A tiny gasp escapes her. She goes very still.

"Do they work?" asks Francis.

She appears to be in shock. She just gazes about at the trees and the trees. She takes hold of Francis' hand. A tear rolls down her cheek.

Not Keen on Strangers

Three or four miles further down the road, the manzanita grove far behind, Lily signals for a halt. These little stops come frequently. It doesn't seem to matter how much water she drinks. But this time, rather than dismount and quietly disappear into the woods, she points at the road ahead.

Francis is surprised to discover there is a man up there. He's seated in a ditch. There is nothing else around, no crossroads, no ranch, not even the ruins of old fences. Strangest of all is the man himself, for he doesn't appear to be the sort one finds in a ditch.

The fellow wears a pair of fine woollen trousers and a pecan-coloured vest. His bowtie hangs loose in a celebratory fashion. But there's a rivulet of blood coursing down his forehead. The man's suit coat is spread out like a picnic blanket in the dirt and he sits upon the coat, hugging his knees, looking like:

a) a man who's lost his way home after one hell of a
   wedding
b) a shipwrecked survivor on a desert isle.

Both scenarios are intriguing enough for Francis and Lily to draw the horse up before him.

"Could I bother the two of you for a bit of water?" asks the man from his seat.

Francis considers the man a moment, observing him for signs of falsehood or malice. Wordlessly Francis unhooks his canteen. He holds it out to the fellow, who in turn pushes himself laboriously to his feet, brushes off his rear, and makes his way to the horse.

Francis makes a second observation. This man is one of those men who, while sitting, appears intelligent enough, happy to converse on any number of subjects. But walking reveals a distinct shuffle to his gait, and his arms refuse to swing, so that his intelligence appears halved upon rising from the ground.

The man accepts the water and drinks deep, and drinks deep again before wiping his mouth and returning the canteen. He nods at the child. "I see you found my spectacles."

"Those are yours?"

"No matter. She can keep them." He taps at a second pair, identical, resting low upon his nose. "My thanks for the water."

Francis inquires into the event that left this man stranded. It turns out he is a doctor by the name of Paul Laslyn-Smith, en route to his new place of employment in the town of Redville, California — which he estimates to be a few miles further up the road.

Francis inquires of Bob Temple, and Laslyn-Smith immediately recognizes the description, saying Temple passed him on the road just yesterday. However it was not Temple who stole his horses and wrecked his wagon but a large and rowdy clan of horsemen, led by a three-hundred-pound Gila monster named Carter. Bursula Carter.

"She's the one who cracked my skull," declares Laslyn-Smith. "Left me cold in the dust. She had a few questions for me as well. About that same man you asked about. And possibly about a boy like yourself, if I have my memory straight."

Francis considers the man, this doctor, and where things might go from here. Bob Temple once told Francis that when gambling, begin by asking yourself what you're willing to lose. Don't put up more than that. Which is good advice, except that Francis is always prepared to lose it all. It's his nature, his predilection. Some part of him understands that in the final tally there is really nothing to lose — so why not risk it all?

"Listen," says Francis. "We're not keen on strangers. But you're a doctor. We got a horse. I'm going to suggest an exchange of services."

"I'm not really in a position to bargain," says Laslyn-Smith. "If you can get me into Redville I'll do what I can for you."

"That's fine. Then what do you know about belly aches?"

"Well I've seen just about everything in my time. I've been practising medicine close to fifteen years now."

Francis looks skeptical. "That's a long time to practise at something."

"No, I'm —" The doctor waves a hand dismissively. "What's ailing you? Just tell me what the problem is."

"It's not me," says Francis. "It's the little one here."

Francis dismounts and helps Lily down. The doctor clears his throat, acquiring an erudite squint as he lowers himself to the child's height and looks her over. Any air of wisdom or authority he might convey is unfortunately cheapened by the dangling bowtie. The bloodied left ear. The child looks up at him with those enormous blue eyes, all the bigger with her new spectacles on.

"She looks healthy enough," observes the doctor. "Could use a wash. What's the issue?"

"All I know is her belly is all bloated," says Francis. "And she gets real sick each morning."

The doctor looks at him. Then down at the child's belly as if noticing it for the first time — her condition so obvious now, it can only be that his eyes had refused to accept it.

"She's mostly fine by afternoon but mornings are real rough on her. Can't keep anything down."

The doctor sniffs and straightens. He looks off down the road, shaking his head. He appears to be in pain of some sort.

"Jesus," he mutters. He glances down at the child. "She's how old?"

"I don't know. Young."

"Jesus."

The doctor stares at her belly, anguished and bewildered. He crouches down for a better look. He seems to be speaking to himself when he says, "Never in my life did I think to see this. Not with my own eyes, and certainly not here." He stands again and removes his glasses and wipes his eyes and puts the glasses back on and returns his gaze to the child, blinking at her. "I mean there's the literature, sure — girls young as this. Maybe even younger. But that's Africa, for godsake. The Orient. Not right here in ... And you have no idea how far along she is?"

"How far along what?" asks Francis.

The doctor looks at Francis for some time. He appears to be deliberating the foundations of despair, its buried purpose and origin, at last giving way to the thing itself.

"It will pass," he says with finality.

"That's it?" says Francis. "You don't need to . . . I don't know, check her belly? I mean look at it. It's big as a melon."

"It will run its course. There's nothing to be done now."

Francis exhales in relief. He pats the child's shoulder. "You see? Told you it would be fine."

But the doctor appears more disgusted than ever. He falls into a grim reverie, shoving his hands into his pockets, staring off at the trees. He can be heard whispering, muttering aloud to some invisible other—something about the state of the world, the loss of decency and so forth. Something about what in God's name is even he doing out here. Wandering about in this miserable desert. When Laslyn-Smith turns back around, the once placid features of his face are now the picture of forbearance.

"There is one thing I can do."

He asks for a piece of paper. Francis digs out the ledger from his saddlebag and tears off a sheet. The doctor writes something down, folds it in half, and hands it back to Francis without looking at him. "Take this to the apothecary in Redville. I've signed my name to it. They'll give you what you need."

"I thank you," says Francis, lifting the prescription in gratitude. He tucks it away. It's uncomfortable but they all three manage to find space on the one horse. They set out for Redville without a word between them.

❧

The town of Redville is small and unremarkable, set back against the foothills of the Mojave's easternmost frontier. It presents as six straight blocks of horse manure, austere storefronts, and small, cheerless houses like so many crates laid in a row. A few have glass windows. The whole town, every building, is painted red. That's because our galaxy is dying.

Once extinguished of life, each star within it slowly converts into iron — making iron the most common element in our universe, as well as the stuff that makes paint red, and therefore the most economical colour to cover a large unfashionable structure, like a barn. Or a town.

And so Redville. Because our universe is doomed.

"You can let me off here. I'll find my way."

Doctor Paul Laslyn-Smith climbs down from the mare. An awkward moment follows wherein he looks up at Francis and Lily, still seated in the saddle. He appears to be torn between expressing his thanks and some prior disposition.

"Well. I believe I'll go begin a new life."

"Best of luck to you," offers Francis.

Doctor Paul Laslyn-Smith walks down the street, looking about at the newness of his surroundings, the place he will now call home, and Francis thinks, I will never see that man again.

Powders & Elixirs!
Tinctures & Tonics!

The signboard out front of the apothecary hangs cockeyed from a rusty chain. It bears the engraved image of a mortar and pestle. There's another, smaller sign, hanging from the first, announcing: THE CHEMIST IS IN!

But Lily won't go inside — not without her valise. She gestures repeatedly at the saddlebags where the little suitcase hangs.

"Your guitar will be fine," Francis assures her. "Just leave it with the horse."

Lily glares at him, eyes smouldering like a matador's.

"Look, I know it's hard to believe. But there's not a soul on earth who wants to steal that thing. You'll have to trust me on this."

Lily huffs indignantly. She performs exactly two jumping jacks in the road and squares both fists upon her hips.

Francis is of course powerless against this show of obstinacy. He submits, untying the battered valise from the horse. He carries it in one hand, leading Lily with the other.

A string of bells jingle as they enter the apothecary. Francis and Lily stand there a moment, their eyes adjusting to the gloom. The cluttered space is without windows and the atmosphere sits close. The odour is downright over-powering — a heavy mélange of exotic roots and spices. As if a hermit's dreams have caught fire. A hermit's dreams of the moon.

Behind the glass counter is an entire wall of dark hardwood drawers. Each drawer displays some devilishly decorative title like *Panax quinquefolius* or *Salix alba* or *Coccoloba uvifera,* all inscribed in cursive script across rectangular bronze tags. The adjoining walls are stacked with shelves, and every shelf is crowded with glass jars and pots of various sizes, each containing powders, tablets, mysterious twigs and berries, even leeches.

On a stool behind the counter sits an elderly gentleman in a leather visor. He wears twinned garters on his sleeves and a monocle in one eye. He's reading an impressively large manual of some sort. It makes a satisfying thunk as he drops it on the counter—this manual still open to the middle— and removes his monocle and drops that too onto the open book to mark the place of interruption. He steps down from the stool, which makes him taller, and places both hands upon the counter and leans forward against them.

"Good afternoon to you, sir, madam."

He introduces himself as Mr. Jay Duncan Spencer, second-generation chemist and full owner of this establishment, as well as the real estate office next door, and how might he be of service?

Francis slips the prescription from his pocket. He unfolds the paper and spreads it flat on the counter before him.

Jay Duncan Spencer retrieves the monocle from its place and, with just a touch of ceremony, fits it to his eye and reaches for the prescription, bringing it closer, and then further away, making the face of one who finds annoyance in small lettering.

More abruptly, he sets the prescription back down and removes his monocle. "Who might this be for?"

Francis looks down at Lily. She stands beside him, as open and true to the world as a tiny bird. He makes a decision in that moment.

"It's for my daughter," says Francis, and it's done.

Lily smiles up at him and Francis can't help but smile back.

But when Francis returns his gaze to the chemist, the man's face has gone sour. Baleful, even. He sniffs loudly, glaring back at Francis. "Young sir. You may leave the premises."

"Your pardon?" says Francis.

"I said you may leave. Now. Or I will call the sheriff."

Francis reaches for the script but the man snatches it away. He holds it high in the air, his hand quaking with emotion. "There is no future," he declares, "in which I allow this prescription to be filled! Whoever wrote it should be jailed alongside you!" He then proceeds to shred the script into tiny bits, all the while staring Francis in the eye. He points to the door.

Reluctantly, Francis leads Lily out to the street.

"And pray!" the man calls after him. "For in the Lord there is forgiveness!"

Francis and Lily stand there in the road, the sun beating down. Neither knows what to do next. They feel like the only two people on earth. As lost and bewildered as the day they were born.

❧

Despite their confusion, and the urge to flee town, Francis knows the road ahead will be stark and hard. Before departing Redville he waters the horse at a public trough outside the general store. Lily sits quietly on the bench out front. She's picking at a scab on her elbow, the valise at her side. It's generally hard to tell about her, but she appears mostly content.

"Looks like they got it all," observes Francis, taking in the vast array of storefront signage. The clapboard wall behind her is literally covered in placards, posters, handbills, banners — they're like wallpaper.

One reads: Ladies' clothing. Men's sizes.

Another: Baths! Fifty cents for fresh water. Half price for used.

Another: NOTICE! The Carrying of FIREARMS upon the Streets is PROHIBITED except by duly Authorized Representatives of THE LAW.

Francis says, "Anything you been pining for? This may be our last outpost for a while."

When Lily shakes her head Francis glances back at the apothecary across the road, and then at the storefront again. Certain facts, realities, have begun to dawn upon him. "Maybe I'll try this one alone," he says. "You're good here?"

Lily nods.

"All right. I'll just be — what are you eating?"

Lily stops chewing. She opens her mouth and points within. A mysterious grey mash sits lumped in there.

Francis looks at her. He nods. "Got it," he says. "Back in a minute."

Lily remains on the bench, chewing whatever she's chewing. With the valise at her side she looks like someone waiting for a train — her whole life stretched out before her, bare feet swinging beneath.

❧

"And there you go. Ten pounds of horse feed," says the proprietor, setting a small gunnysack among the pile of purchases upon the counter. "Will there be anything else?"

"There will," says Francis. "I'd like to see a selection of dresses."

"Dresses. Excellent. Are we looking for a particular style? Pattern? Fabric?"

"For a child," explains Francis. "Or…an expectant mother."

The proprietor gives him a sideways glance.

"Actually boots is what I'm after. Is what I meant to say."

"Naturally."

"For a person smaller than myself."

"But of course."

When the proprietor turns about to fetch a pair from the storeroom Francis pushes the horse feed aside and lays his pistol conspicuously upon the counter.

"And I hate to do this — but how would you feel about setting up some sort of payment plan?"

❧

Late that night, in the lee of a gully ten miles east of town, Joshua trees all around, Francis spreads his poncho before the fire. He stretches out and Lily curls up beside him. Francis has been thinking the day through and he believes he's put it all together. It is an ugly story but the doctor was right. There's nothing to be done now.

Francis wonders if the Whitmore girl will feel the same. Then he almost laughs aloud. Won't that just bowl her over, he thinks, when he explains they are now the parents of this child, soon to be grandparents too, and how about that?

Francis closes his eyes. Instantly, in the darkness that follows, a rocking sensation, as though he's still in the saddle. Some echo of the day's motion released all through his body. He turns on his side and the feeling quickly subsides.

He hears a whisper in his ear. It's so soft — the sound of her breath almost louder than the words themselves.

She says, "I'm all done being quiet now."

"Okay," says Francis, and the child puts her arm around him. They fall asleep like that. It is the most beautiful sleep one can imagine.

The Fabulous Travels of Francis and Lily

For the next two weeks, Francis and Lily rise before dawn each morning and ride deep into the night. They hunt food along the way. Small game mostly, quail and hare. On one occasion, a little speckled sidewinder that drops from his boot. Lily helps with what she can, which amounts to little. Francis is just happy to have her along. Really he can't imagine it any other away. Who knew it could be so heartening to look after a child? To fall under the spell of her innocence? And become a guardian of the same?

"I think she's tired today," says Lily, glancing at the horse. They're walking the mare, each to a side. A dark awning of clouds moves in from the south where the road branches off to Mexico.

"She might be tired," says Francis. "Though she did have a good rest last night."

"I think she's tired. And she's thinking about her home."

Lily is often reading the horse's thoughts and feelings. Francis enjoys this. He encourages it. Since finding her voice, Lily has shared all kinds of interesting ideas.

Lily says, "See how she keeps lifting her chin? And turning it sideways?"

Francis adopts a studious look. He cradles his jaw, examining the horse from different angles. "You know, Lily, I think you're right. Does that mean something?"

Lily nods. "It means she's longing for the stars again."

"Longing for the stars. I didn't know that about horses."

"She does though. She misses them."

"Okay then."

"That's why she has that patch of stars on her rump. So she can always find her way back."

The other thing about Lily is she keeps feeding the horse stuff — like stuff horses shouldn't eat. Pine needles. Eggshells. Bits of stew. Dry leaves.

"Lay off those acorns, Lily. They're not good for horses."

"Oh, but she likes them!"

"They'll give her gas. See how much you like that."

"Just a few more? Please?"

Despite fair skies and a shady path through mesquite, the remainder of their morning is characterized by horse farts — so densely sour it burns the eyes.

"What did I tell you," says Francis.

"I don't mind," says Lily.

❧

Sometime in the afternoon they dismantle a barbed-wire fence and cross into Arizona. Francis predicts they'll ride through an assortment of lands with very few settlements. Some stretches will be downright forbidding. It's nonetheless a gorgeous country of yawning gullies and velvet dunes. Lily keeps asking to stop or slow down at least but Francis feels the need for haste, knowing all the while Bob Temple could be just ahead.

Lily rides up front on the saddle, leading the horse. Francis guides her hands from behind. Her belly is getting big. She keeps thumping it with her finger. *Thunk*. Francis watches her do this. *Thunk*.

"I don't think you're supposed to do that."

"Why not?" *Thunk*. "I like the sound it makes."

Francis says his brother Samuel used to do that with melons. Samuel could tell you if they were ripe. He even won a contest once, and was offered twenty dollars to tell the crowd how he does it — because believe it or not, a true and honest-to-God melon thumper is rare as rubies.

"Did your brother tell?" asks Lily.

"He didn't."

She turns to Francis with a look of genuine confusion. "Then what's the point in telling me all about it?"

"Well," says Francis, "I guess the moral of the story is you are not a melon."

"I already *know* that," says Lily. "I've known that since I was a baby."

"Just making sure. I hear it's a common mistake."

Francis falls quiet and they ride for a bit. Then he says, "You would have liked my brother."

"Was he like you?"

Francis considers the question. "In some ways. But mostly he was better than me. And he was really smart."

"You're smart too," says Lily.

"You just think that because you're a kid. But I'm more like average."

Lily twists in the saddle and peers back at him, a dubious look on her face.

"Turn back around, you little monkey. You have to look where you're going or you might fall into a canyon."

Lily's face lights up. "I love monkeys!"

"You do not."

"I do! They're like little gross people."

"When have you ever seen a monkey?"

"On a poster. For the circus."

Francis thinks about that. "Maybe one day I'll take you to the circus."

Lily looks at him as though Francis is the circus. Right now. It's a look of such adoration and awe it literally puts a lump in his throat. Francis urges the horse into a canter.

Lightning flashes to the south, where the undersides of clouds hang dark and mute. The air turns cool. After a while Francis clears his throat. "You know I have to ask," he says. "What's your real name, anyhow?"

"Mary."

Francis halts the horse. He sits there, unmoving in the saddle. He peers down at her belly, her left hand upon it — the airy enigma of her conception like a winter haze.

"What's wrong?" she asks.

"Let's just say I'm used to Lily," he says, starting the horse again. "We'll stick to Lily."

"Okay."

Ring Finger

On the last day of April, with the evening air burning pink and twilight's wedge on the horizon, Francis and Lily direct the horse up a scrubby ridge somewhere north of the Buckskin Mountains. The sun descends behind them, casting the long shadow of their movement against the reaches of the slope. Topping the rise they hit a headwind damp with distant weather. The horse puffs and snorts.

Francis halts abruptly, looking about. He dismounts. "Stay up there a moment," he says to Lily.

With reins in hand, he walks the horse to a sandstone outcrop and scouts the far side. He sees a narrow band of cottonwoods running the base of the ridge. He hears a creek but can't see it. He can see the campfire though, or the reddish glow of it upon the surrounding canopy. He watches for a while and the firelight grows brighter as the sun dips the horizon.

"That's him," he whispers.

"The man you're after?"

Francis nods. "I'm going down there. I can finish this now."

Francis and Lily left the main road some days ago, opting for this shortcut. Francis knew there was a good chance of this encounter. Now that it's here he feels somewhat unprepared in himself. He continues to study the fire below. He can make out the vague movements of Bob Temple roving about the small camp. In the back of his mind Francis is also wondering about the Carter Gang, and whether they made the shortcut as well. He supposes there's nothing he can do about that right now.

"All right," he says, handing Lily the reins. "Here goes. I'll be back in a moment."

"No."

"Lily, this is what we're here for. Why we rode all this way."

"No," she repeats. "What if you don't come back?"

Francis sighs. He wants to argue but something tells him she has a point. Perhaps it's because females, no matter their age, tend to always have points.

"What else can I do?" he asks her.

Lily tells him to forget Bob Temple.

"I can't do that. It's not an option."

Lily says it is too an option. Because really it's the Whitmore girl he needs to get to, and get to first, and to this Francis has no good argument because of course she's correct. He considers it a moment. He supposes aloud they could, in theory, probably stay ahead of Bob Temple at this point. "Four or five more days and we could be home."

Lily looks relieved. And Francis is perhaps a little relieved too. But he also knows he can't just leave Bob Temple in peace down there. Not without a little mischief.

"What are you doing?" asks Lily as Francis digs through the saddlebags.

"Just saying hello. Bob Temple will understand."

Francis roots out two sticks of dynamite and a small spool of det cord. He tucks both sticks beneath the sandstone outcrop and lays the cord, stepping backward as it unspools.

"Walk the horse this way," he says. "Park it behind those boulders over there." Francis likewise takes cover, and Lily soon joins him. Then he blows the whole thing.

The ensuing rockslide is small and unlikely to have caused harm. It's more of a calling card.

Francis squats in the dark with Lily at his side, listening to the changes in the creek. It's gone quieter, almost silent. Presumably the slide has dammed its flow and redirected it into the trees.

Francis can picture Temple cursing in the darkness of an extinguished fire, racing about to preserve his camp as the creek washes in. Just to make sure Temple understands the situation Francis draws his Cooper and fires once in the air.

Satisfied, Francis pats his horse and tightens the saddle. "I think we're all set," he says. He lifts Lily back into the saddle. He figures they'll maintain their advantage if they walk all night and begin riding at first light.

Francis glances down into the trees once more and sees the fire has indeed gone out. He removes his hat and slaps it against his leg to clear the dust and at that moment hears a distant report from the trees and feels his hand jerk back. The hat drops involuntarily to the ground.

Francis bends to retrieve the hat and notes with cold wonder the complete absence of his ring finger, knocked clean from his hand like it never was.

Francis and Lily Travel On

Their horse, uncomplaining, bears them over varied country, all of it rugged. They encounter hard blue skies and improbable mesas. They cross a broad white saltflat where the glare off the crust is so bright it burns. Francis and Lily shut their eyes and ride blind for an hour.

When Francis opens his eyes they are still out on the salt, but they're now passing a boulder — big as a house. The boulder is black quartz. It burns darkly in the sun. While all around, as far as the eye can see, a land as flat and bright and white as snowpack.

They travel on.

The nub of Francis' finger bleeds down his leg and across the horse and dries in hard dark clumps on the horse's pelt. Each time Francis glimpses the nub his mind lurches in confusion. Then comprehension seeps in and the surreal absence is resolved.

"Does it hurt?" asks Lily. She can't seem to take her eyes off the wound, at once horrified and riveted.

Francis shakes his head. "Not like you'd think."

He tries not to attach any significance to the loss of that particular finger. His ring finger. Still, he can't help but wonder where his wedding band will go. Certainly it's just a coincidence.

"Do you think she'll love me?" asks Lily.

"Who? My fiancée?"

Lily nods.

"Of course she'll love you. She's going to be your mama."

"But what if she doesn't?"

"Then I'll set her straight," says Francis. "I'll say, 'Look here. Young Lily has been sent to us from the angels above. And if you don't love her proper, they'll throw sand in your eye. And call you mean names. And switch out all the forks and the spoons till you think you've gone batty.'"

Lily smiles and Francis says, "Don't worry about it. You're with me."

He glances down at the finger again. He suspects the injury needs attention. The surrounding desert, however, seems to have its own narrative — its own hardscrabble concerns. None of which include helping Francis find a physician.

Late in the afternoon on the second day following his injury, Francis halts the horse atop a rocky arroyo and marvels at the broadening horizon. It oscillates in the heat and the distance has gone liquid. Every living thing in this desert lies hidden from the sun in some cool shelter. While far to the east, where the foothills shimmer and quake, Francis notes an unnatural flare against the greenery. It's hard to tell but he thinks it's windowglass.

Night falls before they reach the cabin. Francis sets their course through the dark by the solitary lantern emanating from the window. As they draw near, but are yet quite far away, the front door opens momentarily and a figure appears within, framed by interior light. Then the door shuts and the figure is no more.

The horse freezes at this occurrence and Francis and Lily are pitched forward. After a moment, Francis urges the horse on.

From the yard out front where Francis and Lily sit their horse, they can see the cabin in full. It's a one-room construction, surrounded by square plots of potato, all laid and marked in orderly rows. There is a wagon beside the cabin and a paddock with two horses. Juniper trees connect the property to the hills.

"I want you to wait here," says Francis.

"But I want to come with you."

Francis shakes his head. "It may not be safe." He glances about the yard. "Listen, I want you to hide over there. Just behind that paddock. If anything happens you take the horse and —"

"Anything like what?"

"Like if I die or something."

"Okay."

"But don't worry."

"Okay."

"So listen, I want you to find a spot behind that paddock. I just need to get some fresh bandages and I'll be right back. Okay?"

"Okay."

Francis dismounts and starts across the yard and halts abruptly, turning about. "Lily, what are you doing?"

"I don't want to be alone."

✻

Francis and Lily climb the steps of the porch. They stand there a moment while Francis examines her appearance, determines it's hopeless, and knocks on the door.

No one answers at first. Francis puts his ear to the door and hears movement within. Voices too. Francis knocks a second time.

Now a reticent, ornately bearded man opens the door partway. This action reveals his left eye and little more, and Francis and Lily are forced to stand there upon the door-step while Francis summarizes the purpose of their arrival, their recent misadventures with a foe, the need for medical attention if it can be provided.

The man's one eye continues to assess him. Finally the man asks to see the injury. His accent is thickly German.

Francis shows him the hand. He realizes he knows this man, or has seen him before. But where?

The man instructs Francis to lift both arms above his head and spin a slow circle on the porch.

Francis does this.

The man instructs Francis to kindly remove his pistol from its holster and toss it into the yard.

Francis does this too.

The man nods faintly, the lone eye going up and down, and pulls the door wide.

Francis steps inside, glancing about the small cabin. For one mad moment he believes his vision has gone haywire.

But no, it is only the sisters, all three in a row. They wear the same flower-print dresses as before.

The man addresses his daughters as one. "Soll ich bleiben?" *Shall I stay?*

The middle one shakes her head. "Es wäre am besten wenn du gehst." *It is best if you go.*

The man grunts softly and nods once in Francis' direction. He snaps the suspenders across his shoulders and puts on his coat, his wide-brimmed hat, and departs the cabin, closing the door behind him.

"Sit," says the middle sister, indicating a chair beside the table. There is an oil lamp on the table. On the wall above it, Francis notes the two artifacts, carefully displayed. The scythe. The bone-handled knife.

Francis sits. Lily climbs into his lap, her belly touching the table. They've brought her a mug of milk and Lily quietly sips it. The three sisters join them at the table. They watch impassively as Francis attempts to cradle the injury.

"Show us," says the one.

Francis extends the hand across the table. The middle sister takes it, turning it sideways in the light. A quiet examination soon follows wherein all three sisters work as one, silently cleaning the wound with a bowl of warm water and cotton.

Francis watches, fascinated by their movements, their uncanny coordination. Try as he might, he still can't register the slightest difference between them. He wonders if they ever have trouble. By all appearances it would seem they have mixed it up enough times that they've finally given up on being one or the other.

The middle sister holds his hand while the others scrub

at the dried blood. She says, "It seems there is somehow more of you now than when we last met."

Francis smiles to himself, watching their ministrations. "And it seems you've acquired a sense of humour."

"No. We are just reading your hand."

Francis yanks it away. "I thought that was for gypsies."

She grabs it back, forcing the hand open. "Gypsies read the palm. We read the hand. All of it. See here? See where this line comes to an abrupt halt?"

"Ow. Ouch!"

"It has been violently altered. Which means your life will be too. Very soon."

Francis feels something like a tingle. But he is not one for tingles. He says, "What do you mean altered? Are you talking about my fiancée?"

"You have expectations," she says.

"Just answer my question. Are you talking about my girl?"

"You have a picture in your mind," she says, "of the way things will go."

"So?"

"Have you asked yourself what you'll do? If things turn out different?"

Francis' heart thumps in his chest. He doesn't want to say it, but that very question has been growing in his mind.

The sisters fall quiet. They begin dressing the wound.

"I will tell you a story," says the one.

"All right," says Francis, anxiously watching the bandage go around.

"In the year 1421, the young prince of Byzantium balanced a silver spoon across the bridge of his nose. It teetered gently, nearly falling..."

One sister lifts the cotton, another cuts it. The third tucks it under and secures it with a pin.

"The prince's father, the sultan, watched from an unseen corner of the palace, when suddenly all the known world tilted to steady the boy's utensil. When the sultan spun about to square his step, the curtains were silent in the window."

Francis observes the sisters, waiting for more.

It occurs to him there is no more.

"That's it?" he says.

They nod.

"So, is that like a... like an Amish kind of story?"

They sit quietly with hands resting upon their laps, perhaps awaiting a better question.

"Well, I thank you for the dressing," he says, holding it up. "The bandage feels snug. Even the ache is gone. Didn't see that coming."

The middle sister tells Francis there is a path leading out from his mouth and into the world, and there is a little boy walking along that path.

Francis looks at her, at them.

"Now walk," says the one, pointing to the door.

"You mean right now?"

All three stare back.

Francis rises reluctantly and takes Lily by the hand. He walks to the door and opens it. He pauses, turning over his shoulder. "You know there was no fortune in Chesterville."

She replies that the story she just told him, it was about balance. About how the world will at times bring us what we need most, even when we can't see it.

"I'm just saying there was no gold in Chesterville. No money like I thought."

She tells him one event begets another, and who can say where it ends?

Francis nods in partial understanding and leads Lily out the door.

Dreamshine

Outside the cabin, Francis gathers the horse. He and Lily continue east on the road.

The moon has yet risen and the sky, like some function of his mood, is blackly churning all around.

"Does your hand feel better?" Lily asks as they ride.

Francis nods.

"Is something wrong?"

"It's nothing," he says. "Everything's fine."

"You're sure?"

Francis nods again. They ride on.

Some hours later, still no moon to speak of, they stumble upon an abandoned village of adobe. It rises up from the night, soundless and gaunt. Francis and Lily tread past the homes caked in ochre, their doorways gaping like mouths. They make no comment between them, moving mute through the village like unsolicited strangers over a charnel ground, which maybe they are.

On a low rise overlooking the village stands a Spanish mission. Much of the mud it was made from has gone away, leached out with the rains until the curtain walls have taken on a melted look. The chapel alone is in good condition, perhaps more recently restored. Francis decides they'll stay for the night. They unload all their gear just inside the double doors.

It takes some moments for their eyes to adjust to the dim. "This isn't bad, actually," says Francis, glancing about at the frescoed interior. The pews in the nave still gleam with varnish. No one has yet raided the crosses or the bibles. "What do you make of it, Lily?"

Of course Lily does not make anything of it. Her only thought is for food, anything to quiet that infernal gnawing in her gut. With predacious, prenatal industry she gets straight to it, tipping the lectern onto the floor with a grunt and a thud. There's a great shrieking ruckus as she drags the whole affair to the side of the room. She climbs nimbly atop it. She stands on her tippy toes, scavenging pigeon's eggs like a raccoon from a nest in the lowermost rafters. This is a marvellous sight with her round little belly.

"How'd you know to do that?" asks Francis and from her perch atop the lectern Lily shrugs in response, looking Francis direct in the eye as she taps an egg against her lower teeth, *crack*, and slurps back the contents.

Later still the black mare drinks holy water straight from the font and proceeds to flood the floor with her urine. Francis and Lily take to higher ground, curling up to sleep beneath the altar like two priests who've fallen down drunk in each other's arms.

Sometime in the night, Lily pokes Francis awake.

"Look," she whispers.

The once moonless, perfect dark is now disfigured by a candle flickering on the sill. Lily points to the back row of pews. A man kneels there. He wears a brown robe of the Order with his cowl pulled back. His eyes are closed and his hands are folded in prayer. He seems unperturbed by their presence, and if anything appears to be venerating them, for they are positioned directly before him upon the chancel.

Francis falls back asleep and when he wakes early the next morning, the man is gone.

"What happened to him?" asks Lily.

Francis has no idea. For all he knows, there was no such man. There was but the figment of a man shined down from her sleep. A dream-soaked mystery we call the beyond but is actually closer. Much closer.

Quietus

The night sky tilts west at the approach of dawn. Francis and Lily rise and eat what remains of their egg stash, sitting side by side in the pews. They gather their few belongings and load the mare. Lily observes that the mare with her black pelt is indistinguishable from the night, separate only in movement. As if to corroborate this, the mare goes still at that instant and appears to disappear. She swishes her tail and pops back into existence.

Just as the sun peeks out they ride past the first boundary posts for the Nelson ranch and Francis knows they're close—no more than a day's ride at most. The day heats up. Within the hour they're riding headlong into the sharp, declarative brilliance of an Arizona sun and Francis looks for water but all the washes are still dry, patiently awaiting the first rains of spring.

Around noon Francis sights a line of trees to the north. He and Lily are hot and sweaty and in need of rest. The horse too is flagging.

"I think that line of trees," he says, "marks the banks of the Little Campos. It runs all year. We can water up, have a good wash. Be all ready for tomorrow."

"You can wash," says Lily, happily enough.

"Don't you want to be all clean?"

Lily says with complete frankness that she feels just fine as she is.

"But you stink a little."

She shrugs.

Francis is a bit stumped, never having been this side of parenting, or discipline in general. "Look, this same time tomorrow you'll be meeting your new mama. I can't have you all ragged and covered in dirt. She might throw me to the wolves."

Lily eventually relents. She says she will bathe. But to Francis' ear this promise is halfhearted and he doubts the faithfulness of her resolve. He insists they seal the agreement with a handshake.

"Uh uh. Right hand," says Francis. "You always shake with the right."

"How come?" she asks. "Because of your finger?"

"Nope," he says. "It's because most folks are right-handed. When you show someone your right hand it means you're not holding a weapon. So let's see it."

She offers her right hand.

Francis makes to inspect her hand. "No guns in there? No knives?"

"I don't have those."

"No swords?"

"No."

"But what's this? Is that a noose?"

"It's a bracelet! I made it out of string."

"All right then. I guess it's a deal," he says. "A deal is no small thing. Can't go back on a deal."

"I won't."

They shake, and Francis thinks he might be getting the hang of this parenting thing.

They leave the path and head for the river. When they reach the trees Francis leashes the mare off to a limb and grabs both canteens. He ties them together with a short length of rope and loops the canteens around his shoulders like a scarf, leaving his hands free.

The banks of the river are steep and slippery and he takes Lily by the hand, leading her down. They slide as much as walk. When they reach the shoreline Francis unbuckles his holster and lays his pistol among the rocks. He peels off his shirt and pants and wades up to his hips in his underclothes and splashes about. He dunks his head. The current is strong. Lily scours the shore for smooth grey stones and tries unsuccessfully to skip them.

A few minutes later Francis sloshes back out and dries off with his shirt. He dries his hair. He puts his clothes back on. He buckles his holster. He loops the canteens around his shoulders again and then faces Lily.

She immediately gives him a look.

"A deal is a deal," he says.

"I know."

"Do you need help or can you wash on our own?"

"I can do it myself," she says. "But not here. The water is too fast."

Francis glances about. The nearest shallows are on the opposite bank, where a little pool eddies lazily among the rocks. After a moment's consideration he says, "All right, climb on."

Lily comes forward but as she does so Francis can't help but notice she's carrying a large rock.

"What's that for?"

"It's my rock."

"There's lots of them. Leave it behind."

Lily looks longingly at the rock cradled in her arms. She whispers to it, petting it with the tips of her small fingers. Francis leans in, trying to catch what she's saying. This is all he hears: "...and I will never forget you."

Lily sets the rock carefully along the bank. It vanishes into anonymity, one of a million just like it. Except there is no other just like it—adored as it is, if only for one moment in time.

"Ready?"

She nods.

Francis squats down and Lily climbs onto his back and throws her arms around his neck. She grips him like a spider as Francis wades into the river. He still carries his canteens about his neck and they float on the water's surface, rising higher and higher as he nears the middle. His pistol gets soaked but there's nothing for it. The current picks up, tugging at his balance, and for a moment Francis thinks he will fall. When they reach the far side Francis is panting and seriously questions his decision to cross.

He sits on the bank, catching his breath. "You all right?"

Lily nods serenely, poking at the shallows with a stick, apparently unaware of their brush with danger. Francis fills the canteens and takes a drink. He looks back across the river and up the bank whence they came. He can't see the horse from here, just the steep trail they slid down.

"You'll be okay here?" he asks. The little pool is protected from the current by a peninsula of boulders. A few yellow leaves turn circles in the middle.

"I'm okay here," she says.

"All right. I'll give you some privacy. Just holler if you slip or something. And don't go any deeper than right there."

"I won't," she says. "But where are you going?"

"Just up the bank here. I won't go far."

This second bank isn't nearly as treacherous as the first. It has a proper trail leading up. It appears Lily's pool is in fact a watering hole, well known by cattle. Francis climbs to the top and just sits for a while in the shade of the brush. He chews on a blade of grass. He considers for a moment the full distance he's travelled, and how close he is to home. He imagines what it will be like tomorrow when he finally sees his girl. How he will introduce Lily, and the look on their faces when they meet.

He's waiting for joy, or contentment at least, to attend these thoughts but there is only an anxious hum in his body. He can't seem to shake it.

He realizes he can't see Lily from here. He calls down to her. "You still okay down there?"

Over the rumble of the river, he hears her faint voice call back, "I'm fine!"

Francis spits out the grass blade and selects another. His mind picks up speed. He thinks about Bob Temple. In one fantasy, he is well ahead of the villain and arrives in time to rescue his girl. In the other, Temple has located some shortcut, some luck, some inexplicable wind, and all goes black from there.

Francis can't sit still. He flicks the grass blade away and rises to his feet. He turns about and scans the plain this side of the river, and immediately drops back down and presses his face to the dirt, cursing under his breath.

Not fifty yards away, in the shrill light of noon, a line of horses is approaching. At the head of the line is Bursula Carter.

Francis creeps backward through the brush, and then half-runs, half-tumbles down the bank to get Lily.

"Lily!" he hisses. "Get up!"

Lily is fully dressed, though soaking wet, sitting peacefully upon a stone.

Francis crashes to his knees before her and begins frantically unwinding the rope from the canteens. "Give me your wrists!"

She opens her mouth to speak and then shuts it. Fear ignites in her eyes, no doubt mirroring his own.

"Give me your wrists! Quickly!"

She thrusts both hands forward without a word. Francis binds them together with the rope. He slips her bound wrists over his head, pulling her up onto his back, and charges into the river. The current yanks at his knees, then his hips. When it begins tugging at the child he grabs her legs to keep her close. The river booms in his ears. He forces his way across and they emerge on the far side, huffing with exhaustion, only to hear the zang of a bullet skipping off the rocks nearby. Then voices on the far bank. People yelling. Then gunfire again. Several guns this time.

Francis bears down, grunting with the effort as he scrambles up the trail, slipping and sliding, grabbing hold of roots where he can and hauling himself up, while Lily dangles like a ragdoll from his neck. Bullets bite the earth all around.

When Francis clears the top he just throws himself down, Lily still clinging to his back. The horse stamps nervously among the trees. Francis can barely breathe. He is just trying to breathe.

"I think," he gasps, "we're good here." He takes several more breaths. "Their horses can't climb that bank."

He grips Lily's wrists and frees them from his neck. He pushes himself slowly to his feet. He offers Lily a hand, still lying there on the earth, and then Francis goes still—very still. As though the whole world has stopped, and he's just waiting for it to start.

But it doesn't start. It lies quiet as can be.

This Broken

The mare rides lightly, her muscles fluid and easy as she bears Francis east along the boundary path. Her gait is like someone's memory of a winter's tide pounding rocks. Francis can feel the gentle ministrations of her shoulders, her neck, as his own body rocks in the saddle. His mind is dead, or blank. He doesn't know which. His heart is blown ashes.

Somewhere within, he knows he can't delay. And he can never look back. There's nothing left to do but push on.

But Francis is sad to discover he's not an adult. He's just a boy after all. He never knew it was possible to feel this broken. This alone.

CHAPTER NINE
We Shall Meet It Halfway

It's hard to believe it was only six months ago Francis and the gang were riding the arid, subalpine groves of the Snake Range, high in the Nevada mountains. It was a land of scruffy grandeur, unforgiving, very hot in summer. One afternoon in particular they were traversing a ridge beneath the Bronson Gap. They halted for a rest, taking shelter from the sun beneath the stunted old pines that clung to the slopes there, each person to his own tree, drinking water, stretching out.

Francis had chosen a very unusual tree. It was so mis-shapen with age it appeared to be a singular burl, like a giant turnip, sprouting pale green needles from its foreshortened limbs. Francis sat quietly beside the tree. He placed a palm against its trunk.

This is a good tree, thought Francis. A tree to measure others.

When Francis later stood to urinate upon the tree it was an act of homage, knowing the scarcity of moisture in these parts. What Francis could not have known was that in the year 1964, roughly eighty years from that pissing, a young graduate student from the University of North Carolina would drive a coring bit into this tree's trunk, a bristlecone pine by name, in the course of research for the United States Park Service. The coring bit would get trapped in the tree before the process was complete. In an effort to free the tool, the Park Service would cut the tree in half.

It would only be later, while counting the compressed rings of the tree's cross-section that the Park, and the world at large, would come to understand they had just chopped down the world's oldest living non-clonal organism. The tree would be posthumously named Prometheus. A name originating from the word *forethought*. It would be just under five thousand years old.

Presently Francis urges his horse up the limestone ridge and spies the distant, congregated lights of Nowhere. His home. The home of his love.

It's well after midnight, almost a year to the day since he left this town. The many lantern lights form a pale halo, hovering like mist in a general vacancy of star-spangled desert.

Francis sits in the saddle, just gazing down on the plain. He holds the little guitar in his lap. He's not sure what to do with it. The neck is cracked, and half the strings are missing. Looking more closely at the neck, at the rough daubs of glue, Francis has reason to believe she tried to fix it herself.

He can't say why, but this thought stings like a wasp.

"I should have known," he whispers aloud to the night. "I should have seen what was coming." He turns the guitar in his hands, looking at it.

His brother Samuel's voice says, "There are mistakes in this world we just cannot prepare for."

Francis shakes his head, running his finger along the neck. "I could have figured it out. If I really tried. I could have taken better care of her."

"You don't know that," says Samuel.

Francis says nothing.

"Look, you're a good kid, Francis. But you don't know shit."

"I'm starting to believe that."

"And sometimes our biggest decisions, they're the ones we never knew we were making."

Francis nods. He sits quietly for a moment. "But you're still dead, right?"

"Yup," says Samuel. "Dead as a doornail."

"All right," says Francis. "And you'll look after that little girl?"

"I got her right here."

"Because she's got no one left in the world."

"She's got me now, Francis. I'm right by her side."

Francis nods. He sits alone on the ridge, looking down on the town. Just thinking about that.

And who knows? Maybe the heart is built for aching. Dying fresh each day. Each day, looking for some new bead to choke upon.

Nowhere: A Return To

There's a switchback trail that cuts down the side of the ridge. Francis dismounts and leads the mare on foot. He talks to the horse. He murmurs in a low, gentle voice, praising the animal for its skill and beauty, its many triumphs on their long journey home. When he hits the main road on the desert floor he mounts up again and starts for town.

Along the way he notices with some wonder that his melancholy has begun to lift. It's inexplicable. There's something about the nearness of home, no matter how dubious its promise, that consoles the weary heart of the traveller. Moreover, he's arrived home before Temple — or so he believes. This alone puts to rest a great worry. It's now reasonable to expect a few moments with the girl, and perhaps her father too, before announcing they must flee town on the morrow.

Francis enters Nowhere on horseback. He walks his horse through quiet streets, the rhythmic clatter of its hooves rebounding off windows, storefronts — their vigilant wood walls. He looks for changes in the town's architecture, its layout, something to mark or match all that has altered within. But he finds nothing of the sort. Everything appears exactly as he left it.

He passes Landry's, and then the post office. Both are shuttered and closed. He passes the jeweler and the Masonic lodge beside it. In time he reaches the redbrick hotel where piano music floats onto the street, and the saloon is alive with friendly disorder.

Francis halts his horse, middle of the road. He peers

up at the hotel's facade. It occurs to him that streetlamps, their mouths aflame, have a way of illuminating the dark glass of a third-floor window. He watches a moment. He listens to the piano. It all comes together in a sort of shift of atmosphere. Like the whole world in its variety — all its treasures and troubles and everything between — is passing through his heart at once. He's never felt this before. He didn't know such things happen.

For some moments he remains there in the saddle, quieted by the touch of something he doesn't understand.

When all is settled within and no one is watching, Francis tethers the horse to the hitching rail outside the saloon. He climbs his horse and stands upon its saddle and heaves himself atop the porch awning. He scales the facade to the third-floor sub-roof and goes to her window and peeks inside. Darkness, nothing but the vague and shadowy premonitions of a bureau, a bedpost, a bookcase.

Francis makes a fist.

He raps twice, lightly, against the pane.

❁

"You came back," she says, wrestling the window full open. She sweeps the hair from her sleepy eyes and stands there in her nightclothes, one hand on the sill, assessing him on the roof. She is waiting for him to speak.

But Francis cannot speak. He's struck dumb by her presence, the actuality of her. Are there even words, he wonders, to equal the enormity of right now? And she is so beautiful. So much more beautiful than he recalls.

She hugs herself. "It's cold. Aren't you cold out there?"

He just looks at her.

"Aren't you going to speak?"

"Of course I came back," he says, the words tumbling out. "Every place I ever went was to get to here. To you. To us."

There is tenderness in her eyes, and also a hurt. "You were gone a long time."

"I didn't mean for that to happen."

"I was waiting. All this time I was waiting."

"I was hoping you would."

"I thought you weren't coming."

Francis takes a deep breath. "Am I too late?"

"No," she says, shaking her head.

But then she crosses her arms.

"Look, I had some growing up to do," he says. "Far more than I realized. But that's all taken care of now, and there's not a thing in this world to keep me from being with you."

"So you got the money?"

"There is that one thing, actually. That one thing, but everything else I got covered."

She closes her eyes and turns away. "You don't understand. It will never work without the money. You don't know Father. Plus, now you're an outlaw! He'll have you arrested on the spot."

"Okay, two things then. But love is bigger than two things. Otherwise how could it ever survive marriage?"

"You don't understand."

"Look, I'm going to speak to your father. I'll explain everything."

"What will you explain? He doesn't care about your adventures."

"I'll tell him you're my girl. And that's all there is to it."

"It won't change a thing," she says, her eyes glistening. "He owns half this town. Everything. Even me. He owns me, Francis. If you can't prove to him —"

"Just come with me."

A tear courses her cheek. She is facing him. She holds very still. There is only the movement of her breathing as music drifts up from the saloon.

> *Close your eyes girl*
> *Look inside girl*
> *Let the sound take you away*

Francis offers his good hand. "Just come with me. Please"

She wipes her cheek.

She nods.

She takes his hand and climbs out the window.

❧

She sits behind him on the horse, both arms clasping his waist. They ride slowly through a starlit desert. The silhouettes of cacti strike poses in the dark. Wind whispers over sand.

They ascend the crest of a dune, walking its ridgelines. She lays her cheek against his back. Their shadows stretch long against the jeweled light on the slopes.

"I missed you," she says.

Francis feels his skin light up. His whole body is smiling.

"This sounds crazy," he says, "but I don't even know your name."

"Penny," she says, her face pressed tight.

"Penny."

"Why say it like that?"

"Just saying it aloud."

"You don't like it," she says.

"I think Penny might be the best name I ever heard of."

They ride on. The horse seems to know where to go.

Francis and Penny don't speak for a while and then she reaches forward and touches his wrist. "You haven't told me what happened to your hand."

"It's nothing," he says. "Just a finger."

"Just a finger?"

"I got more."

She slaps lightly at his shoulder. The lights of Nowhere disappear beyond the dunes.

"You're probably wondering if I read the papers," she says. "Well I did."

"You did?"

"Every day," she says. And then, as though recalling the headlines all at once, she says, "I can't believe you actually robbed trains!"

Francis shifts in the saddle. "Does that bother you?"

"No," she says. "It's just that you actually did it. I don't know anyone who would do that."

When Francis doesn't respond she says, "Are you ever scared you'll get caught?"

"No."

She lifts her head. "How can you not be scared?"

"I'm just not."

"I'd be scared. I'm scared of everything."

"No you're not."

"I am. Name something and I'll tell you it scares me."

"Puppies."

"Do a different one."

"Lightning."

"It scares me."

Francis smiles to himself. He feels the warmth of her face between his shoulders.

He says to her, "How about dying?"

"Oh, I'm scared to death of dying. Aren't you?"

"Not really."

"How is that possible?"

Francis thinks about it, perhaps for the first time. "I wouldn't say I'm fearless," he says. "It's just. There isn't anything really to fear."

"You know that?"

"I do."

"But how?" she says.

"I'm not sure," he says. "I guess it's like . . ." And then he says nothing for a while. Because it's possible to be clear about something without having the words.

He thinks about Lily. He'd like to talk about the child, and what they shared — the little shelf in his heart where she laid herself down. Because that would explain it. But he doesn't know where to begin. How to describe the way she held a cup with both hands? The quiet sway of her shoulders when she rode before him in the saddle? How her essence filled his own when she passed?

The horse descends the dune, its hooves sinking in sand. They reach the basin at the bottom and the horse halts and lowers its head and they all three remain in silence a moment with the night sky wheeling above.

"I guess it's...it's not that everything is all right," says Francis. "It's that everything is all right to love," he says. "Even the tough parts."

When she doesn't respond he adds, "That's what I learned. When I went away."

When still she doesn't respond Francis reaches into his pocket and removes a small wooden box. Inside is a comb.

He looks at it briefly and passes it to her.

The Thing about This Comb

He didn't steal it.

No, it was come upon when least expected, like so many inklings that steer the course of a life. Imagine Francis wandering the markets of Santa Fe, no purpose in mind, pondering vaguely his future and its apparent absence of design, when he pauses in a shaft of pink sunlight to study the unexpected splendour of a discarded comb. It is strewn amid the filth of an open gutter, the fish heads and carrot tops, the effervescing sludge, and he is certain the comb is made of pure tortoiseshell. He crouches down to look closer, for he is appalled and euphoric. Suddenly he's convinced all the world's gladness can be explained by the three blonde hairs in a tortoiseshell comb in the gutters of a Santa Fe market. It has always been this way, and he is strangely relieved.

"I've been saving it for you," he says. "I always knew it was yours. Even before we met."

"It's beautiful," she says.

"You are beautiful."

"Stop it," she says, squeezing him tighter that he might go on.

They park the horse beside the spring, halfway to the coalmines. The water lies still and black with the heavens

overhead and countless stars stamped upon the pool's dark
surface like the blueprint of a duplicate universe.

Francis spreads his wool poncho on the ground. Penny sits
at his side. She appears peaceful, poised, content — in essence
unaware of her body. The calamitous effects of its nearness.

How, wonders Francis with genuine sincerity, does she
remain so close to herself without getting distracted?

Presently she looks at the moon, her skin glowing in the
chill, and Francis clears his throat.

"Sure is a pretty night," he offers.

"Yes. It sure is," she replies.

He looks up at the sky. "Lots of stars."

She follows his gaze. "That there are."

"What did you say?" asks Francis.

"I just said there certainly —"

"Oh, right, I thought —"

"That is what you said, isn't it? About the stars?"

"Yes," he agrees. "About the stars."

They both fall quiet.

A difficult interval follows wherein even the horse seems
uneasy, pawing noisily at the dirt. Francis settles on a small
detour.

"Listen, I didn't want to bring this up tonight," he says,
"but you haven't seen a friend of mine, have you? A big guy,
named Bob Temple?"

"No, why?" she asks.

"It's nothing. Just making sure."

"Oh."

They again fall quiet. They again look at the sky, their situation essentially unchanged.

Eventually Francis can't help but say it. "Penny, I think you are the prettiest girl I've ever seen. I can't believe I even know you. I can't believe you're here right now. And you're so peaceful too. You seem so relaxed and peaceful."

Penny smiles, keeping her eyes on the sky. "I'm as anxious as you."

"Anxious?" he says. "About what?"

Penny hugs her knees to her chest. She rests her cheek on one knee, looking sideways at Francis. She holds his gaze for some time, perhaps considering her words. A long time she looks.

She says, "You know what."

The way his heart bangs in his chest, Francis is either very alive or very near death. If only love in its extremes did not feel so much like both.

Penny kisses him again, and she tastes like tomorrow.

Her skin is electric, alive. It speaks without speaking.

�֎

Penny lies back on the poncho. She lies very still.

Just looking up at the stars. Waiting to discover whatever in the world comes next.

Harmony of the Planets

Penny lies asleep on the poncho. Francis watches her. They lie facing one another, just inches apart. They are breathing in harmony. Francis breathes in and feels the soft brush of her exhale. Francis breathes out and her hair flutters against her cheek. Overhead, a bank of clouds drifts by. The air grows cool. The stars wink out and then the moon, and in the darkness that follows, a light.

It starts as a faint lustre beneath her blouse, growing brighter by increments until the fabric is positively glowing.

Francis watches, mesmerized, the concealed movement of stars and planets. The whizzing of bright things behind a luminous white veil, and little points of light — distant wonders too delicate to name — flashing, flashing.

the streets of Nowhere are empty and muffled with darkness, the buildings indistinct. Francis walks the horse slowly. Penny sits in the saddle before him. She is very quiet.

To Francis' mind, this quiet is a physical thing, streaming off her like waves. And it seems to him the deeper, the brighter, the more scenic it becomes, the more he wants to engage it. And therein the conundrum.

By and by, Francis resolves to add to this quiet — as there is always room for more — and sinks back into the saddle with a small, contented grin as they ride down the road toward the Whitmore building, where the moon is a weeping yellow mass upon the windows.

"You don't enter through the saloon, do you?"

"Around that way," she says, unclasping her hands from the pommel. "The residence is around back."

"Never tried that way."

They sit the horse in the road, neither speaking for a while.

"So you're my girl?"

Penny doesn't answer at first. She dismounts. She reaches up and takes Francis' hand. She studies his hand, saying nothing, and Francis feels his chest cave in. His belly fills with gravel.

"You know I love you," she begins. "In my heart I'm yours."

"Then it's settled. Let's stop right there."

She shakes her head, still avoiding his eyes. "It's not up to me, Francis. It never was."

"Why not?" he demands. "This is real, what's between us. Why can't it be that simple?"

"Because it's not." Her chin begins to tremble. "And you know it. Even if you weren't some wanted outlaw, you have no money. No way to provide. My father would never even let you through the door."

"Just let me take care of that. I'll speak with him today."

She looks askance. "Please don't."

"What? Why?"

"It will only make things worse."

"So that's it? You're giving up?"

"I just don't see how it can work, Francis. My heart is yours. But without any—"

And then she is sobbing. Her whole body is wracked with sobbing and Francis goes still, staring at his hands in his lap. Never in his life has he felt less capable of tackling a situation. He can't even see where it starts.

After some time of this, Penny's weeping diminishes. Her breath comes and goes in little hitches. She dabs at her eyes.

She says, "I think maybe this was a mistake."

Francis' heart pounds in his throat. "No," he says.

"But I think it is."

"No, you're . . . but some mistakes can be right, can't they?"

"But no less a mistake," she says, pressing a palm to her eye.

"Wait, Penny, don't cry. Look, you don't like this mistake, just pick another. I'll make any mistake you want."

She smiles a little.

"I'm serious. Name it and it's yours."

Despite the tears a muffled laugh escapes her. "Anything?"

Francis takes a breath. He places a hand upon his heart. "Penny. I am promising you now. If it is within my power to screw it up—I will screw it up for you. You don't believe me, just take a look at my life and you'll see I've done it already."

She smiles for real now, if sadly, and reaches up to Francis, taking his hand in her own. She kisses his fingers. She presses his palm to her cheek. "That is the sweetest, dumbest thing I've ever heard."

Now it's Francis' turn to beam.

"But Francis. It still doesn't fix anything," she says. "It doesn't change anything I've said." And the momentary spell is broken.

Francis continues to look at her. Then he pulls abruptly away, turning his horse about.

"Wait, Francis, don't go away mad. Not like this!"

"I want you to listen," he says. "I rode over three thousand miles to beat a path to your heart. If you think I'm stopping here then it's you who's mistaken. This is the beginning. You got that? The beginning."

"Francis—"

But he is already leading his horse away. "I love you, and I'll be back in the morning," he calls over his shoulder. "I'll speak with your father. And that's all there is to it."

Francis' departure is the most dignified, straight-backed, grandly picturesque bit of nonsense he will ever regret. Because when everything unravels, and it will, he'll be able to trace it all back to here. The moment he walked away, sincerely believing everything would be fine. And that Penny would be waiting for his return after sunup.

✺

Francis takes shelter beneath a gnarled, lightning-struck juniper tree a good four hundred yards from town. He unsaddles the horse and piles the saddlebags beneath the tree, all the while watching the hotel in the distance. He's thinking about the morning. He's thinking about Penny's father, and what he'll say in the morning.

At some point, he knows, he'll have to mention Bob Temple. Maybe he should even start with that — explain that Penny is in danger, and therefore must be bundled away...

Francis is still tending to his horse, stroking its long velvet jaw, when a number of wagons materialize from the darkness. He digs out his telescope. He watches as the wagons rattle in from the north and proceed to drop gear in tremendous, abstract heaps at the outskirts of town. Almost immediately a fantastic bustling ensues, lanterns everywhere, muted calls in the distance. An army of bow-legged roustabouts carry lumber and poles, shouting, cursing, raising pavilions like mushroom caps bursting from the earth.

Francis watches all this. How can he not?

Before long a cluster of carnival rides stand in partial assembly at the northern entrance to the town. The arcade becomes a hive of hammering and commotion. In addition to the usual fare of shooting gallery and automatons and dunking games Francis notes the trundling of a large catapult, fully medieval in design, as several horses haul it along on gigantic wheels. He's already wondering about that when a dozen old pianos are wheeled in. Next, a sandwich board is displayed, and if Francis could read it from this distance, he would know that for the hefty fee of ten dollars, a person might launch a broken piano via catapult into the surrounding desert.

Despite his fascination Francis can remain awake no longer. Besides, it feels wrong, somehow, to be here, watching the formation of a circus without Lily. If it turns out there is even one monkey in there, even one, he is certain he will weep.

Francis kicks out a flat area in the dirt and unrolls his bedding. He stretches out on the blanket and looks up at the stars—the black bays of space that go on and on. He thinks about Penny. He thinks about her voice. He wonders if she can sense him now, reaching out with his thoughts, caressing the memory of her voice in his head. Of course she can. There is no escaping what they've become.

Francis has every intention of a nap and no more, returning after sunup to conduct his negotiations with the governor.

He closes his eyes. The dark charisma of sleep tugs him down, down.

The Day We've Been Waiting For

Sometime before noon Francis wakes to an improbable incident with a piano, a catapult, a rain of ivory keys from above. He is slow to rise, despite this chaos, for he's in large part doubtful of the actuality of these occurrences, so closely do they mimic the fiery visions in his head. The only thing clear is that someone has lost their mind. Whether himself or another he can't yet say.

It's not until the third piano, the flaming one, erupts overhead like some meteor from the end times, that Francis apprehends the gravity of this moment, this occasion — it's finally here.

The day we've been waiting for.

And somehow he overslept.

A Frightening Revelation

Francis gathers his horse and saddles it. He doesn't even bother with his bedroll. His eyes water with the alkaline glare and he chides himself as he rides toward town. How could he allow himself to oversleep? Today of all days?

A discordant sickly light reverberates off stones, off pale, stricken shrubs and even the sheen of his horse's pelt. The red clay bluffs to the east are ringing.

Francis sidesteps the wreckage of exploded pianos, riding toward Nowhere at a canter, and then slows in order to navigate the circus. It's going full tilt, the spectacles whirling about him. The smell of taffy, screaming children, the nightmarish melody of the carousel; it's as though the momentary chaos of his heart no longer halts at the breast and now extends to the condition of his life.

With effort he steers free of the crowds, emerging into the relative calm of Main Street, its familiar facades and pedestrians, the Chinese laundry, the post, the windows of the mercantile blinding with glare.

For the first time Francis doesn't stop out front of the Hotel Whitmore but goes straight around back. From this new perspective he observes an impressive three-storey building with an iron fence of pointed knobs and a doublewide stair to the entrance framed by elaborate wind chimes.

Francis charges up the porch steps. He knocks on the front doors, his own heart knocking in cadence. He takes a deep breath in an attempt to calm himself. Over the course of his life he's wanted many things and gone after each in turn but never from a less advantageous position. He looks down at himself, his travel-worn appearance, the filthy bandage on his hand.

Francis removes his hat. By way of his shadow upon the gravel walk, he discovers his hair is standing on end. He hurriedly combs it out with his fingers, watching its effect upon the ground as though gazing into a mirror. Meanwhile his belly has tightened into a knot. He hears footsteps beyond.

The double doors swing wide.

A somewhat severe-looking elderly maid stands formally at the threshold. She clasps her hands before her. She wears a navy-blue uniform, crisp and tidy. Her grey hair is pulled back into a bun so tight that it moves in unison with her eyebrows as she arches them.

"You are?" she queries.

"Francis Blackstone, ma'am."

"You are expected?"

"Hard to say."

The maid says nothing at first. She appears suspicious, bordering on flustered, perhaps by some event prior to his arrival. This makes it altogether difficult for Francis to read his welcome. With nothing to lose, he officially makes his call upon the governor.

"You say Governor Whitmore is not expecting you?"

"No, ma'am. I doubt it."

"We've had an unusual morning, Mr. Blackstone. I don't know that he'll be available."

"That's fine, ma'am. I'll try my luck."

"You will try your luck."

"Yes, ma'am."

On top of everything else she's now skeptical too, her features struggling to include this unexpected crowding of sentiment.

"Am I to understand this is your strategy?"

"Yes, ma'am."

"Luck."

"Yes, ma'am. That was the idea."

"Your idea."

Francis sighs.

"An idea will not break your fall, Mr. Blackstone."

"No, ma'am. I wouldn't think so."

"It will hold no tea."

"No."

"Nor will it get you through a door."

Francis catches himself studying the soft folds of her throat. "May I ask what will?"

She regards him a moment, head to toe and back again, her gaze coming to rest unsettlingly upon the very tip of his nose. After some consideration she says:

"You will follow me."

She turns sharply on her heel, leaving Francis speechless in the doorway.

"You cannot stand upon an idea," she calls out, moving deeper into the foyer, "and expect to gain a better view!"

"No, ma'am." Francis hurries to catch up. Her workaday heels click among the plush velvet couches, the oil paintings on the walls. She mounts the stairs two at a time.

"Put six in your pocket and you still have squat."

Francis actually likes that one. "Where are you getting these?"

The maid directs him up the stairs, and up the stairs again to the den of Governor Whitmore on the third floor.

The maid knocks.

This is Penny's home, thinks Francis, taking in the wallpaper, the oval-framed pictures along the stair. And this bannister, Penny touches this bannister. He can imagine her right hand running its smooth, varnished length as she descends the stairs each morning; her left hand as she returns to her room.

Upon that thought, Francis glances down the long hall with its oriental runners. It's just a door at the far end, an ordinary white door. But knowledge of what lies beyond gives it a mesmeric quality.

"Would that be Miss Penny's room?" asks Francis for no better reason than to hear her name spoken aloud.

The maid scowls at him and knocks again.

Francis' nervousness returns. And with it a kind of foreboding, vague and untraceable. He tries to focus his attention on the voices in the den.

Governor Whitmore is bellowing at another man.

The maid knocks a third time, louder than before.

"A moment!" yells Whitmore. And then, "Come back later!"

Francis returns his attention to Penny's door. Comprehension sets in.

"Is she here?" Francis asks the maid, and the maid clucks with disapproval.

"Just tell me! Is Penny here?"

Francis charges down the hall and the maid calls for him to stop. Francis throws the door wide.

Penny's room is empty, its contents in violent disarray. Francis' heart drops into his belly.

Francis Barges into the Governor's Den

"Who are you?" barks Whitmore, standing in outrage. He's a florid, barrel-chested man with white hair slicked back and meaty jowls, sideburns like two puffs of cotton. A large bay window holds the morning light at his back. Seated opposite the Governor is Sheriff Hicks on the settee. One knee crossed over the other.

"I know where she is," says Francis.

"You what?" Whitmore's face goes red with rage. Sheriff Hicks glares coldly.

"What I mean to say is, I know who's got Penny. Who took her away. His name is Bob Temple."

Something brightens in the sheriff's eye. "Which makes you the Blackstone boy," he says, rising from the couch and drawing his pistol. "Welcome home, son. I believe you are under arrest."

Francis continues as though Hicks hasn't spoken. "I can get Penny back. I can stop him."

The sheriff cocks his pistol. "Like hell you can."

"Hold up," says Whitmore, raising a hand. He looks at Francis. "Speak what you know. I'll hear it."

"I can get her back. Just turn me loose."

Sheriff Hicks sneers with contempt. "Boy, you got some sand. Marching in here, still wearing that belt. What can you do that a sheriff and three deputies can't? A posse is forming as we speak."

"It's me Bob Temple is trying to get to. He doesn't care about your daughter."

"So she's safe then," says Whitmore. "She'll be all right."

"No he'll hurt her. He'll hurt her dead. Listen, you have to let me go, there's no time to lose. He's waiting for me out there. I know that now. I have to meet him."

"This boy is a bona fide outlaw," says Hicks, his pistol still levelled. "No different from Temple."

Governor Whitmore steps closer — so close Francis has to blink twice to refocus. He says, "I should jail you right now. For getting my Penny mixed up in all this."

"That's understandable," says Francis. "In your position I'd feel the same."

"But sand is sand," says Whitmore. "And for some god-damn reason I believe you."

"I appreciate that."

"You say you can get her back?"

"I can and I will. Just cut me loose."

"You get Penny back and I'll see your name is cleared. End of story."

Sheriff Hicks curses in dismay. "Governor Whitmore, this boy is in with Temple. It's a fix. They've been riding together for months."

Whitmore turns on the sheriff. "As long as I get my daughter back, I don't give a cold damn about the past. Just see to it my word is a promise. You got that?"

"I don't know what you want me to do about it. I'm just the sheriff. I work for you."

"That's right you work for me, and you are the law. Now see the law does what I pay it to do. Make up a story, for godsake. Say it was all this Temple fellow. I don't care. Just see it gets done."

"Perhaps this isn't the best time, sir," says Francis. "But about my intentions."

"I already know your intentions son, or you wouldn't have come here at all. But there I cannot help you."

"I'm here to ask for her hand."

Whitmore shakes his head in dismay. "You got nerve, son. And that is something. Now I've met your father and he's a decent man. But there is a difference between my Penny and young men like yourself. You know what I'm speaking of. I'm afraid no amount of heroics can fix that."

They look at each other.

"You look after my Penny," says Whitmore, "and I'll see about your name. That's the best I can do. Now get going."

Fate Is a Monkey in an Impresario's Vest

Francis mounts his horse in the street. He has no idea where Bob Temple is, only the sense that he's out there, and likely not far. Temple will have Penny for one thing. That'll slow him down. More importantly, Bob is waiting for Francis.

How does Francis know?

Francis came out of Nowhere. He ventured into the world and shook its tree and returned to Nowhere once again. There is a compass in his blood he can do nothing about. It points where it points. Whether guided by depth or love or some other immaculate thing, it's at the root of his bearing and that's all he understands — all he's ever understood.

Francis starts out along Main Street and heads, without much prudence or planning, toward the edge of town. Where desert once began there are now teeming hordes, vendors, impromptu lanes of diversion. Francis halts his horse before a signboard, hammered direct into the earth, its lettering huge and lurid and red:

Plutus Brothers Menagerie
and Circus of Fate!

Ah, thinks Francis, staring at the words. So that's how it is.

Francis is no great admirer of fate: The swindler. The hangman. The gambler. The whore. He has come to know providence in its many guises. But the spectacle? Surely this is the worst. And all the more diabolical for its resemblance to family fun.

Francis remains horsed, wading into the crowd. The whole town has turned out. Here a clown menaces small children, who cling to one another like frog's eggs. There a sinister contraption whirls hapless farmers through the sky.

Francis weaves and veers as celebrants clutch at his bridle, and all the while, floating significantly above the clamour, the music of an organ. A very particular organ. It reaches out through the din like a beckoning finger.

Francis has heard this music before. But where?

Oddly curious, he follows. The drifting notes lead him first to the pavilions, and then the big top, where the crowds have grown wild. They are deranged with merriment. They bruise the air with their voices, their shouts, children looping their parents with senseless vitality. He passes a procession on stilts, their sequins shimmering in the sun. Then a row of caged beasts: ostriches, lions, an eohippus, a bear. They spit and growl and flap madly about.

In time Francis comes to the midway.

The various rides and amusements form a corridor of sorts. Francis spies a Ferris wheel up ahead, slowly creaking on its axis. A carousel beside it. Ticketholders sweat and stamp like cattle at the gate. They wave handmade fans. Their detritus lies everywhere, scattered in the dirt: peanut shells, beermud, bales of hay, ticket stubs, corncobs, candied apples, cups and bags and wooden crates, abandoned prizes, a lady's hat, and then that something else: elusive, cloying, lingering in the air like... how to put it?

It's their sorrow. The sadness of so many people trying desperately to have fun.

Francis directs his horse through the middle of the crowd and the crowd opens like a zipper. The organ grows louder, closer; so familiar it hurts. Francis can almost see the individual notes as they trouble the air.

Up ahead is a small cart, offering popcorn by the bag, and when the cart moves aside, there he is, standing directly before Francis: the Organ Grinder himself.

The Organ Grinder is a fat man in a derby and a walrus-style mustache. He clenches a bullet-shaped cigar between his teeth. He stands alone in the dust, surrounded by fabulous rides. The box-organ hangs from a strap about his neck, balanced upon the girth of his round belly. He rotates the crank and the music issuing from the box is like the unholy piping of trained geese.

And hopping atop the organ is a little monkey in an impresario's vest and matching red fez. The monkey screeches and shakes a tin cup.

"Francis!" cries Penny.

Francis turns to find Penny seated atop Temple's horse, not twenty yards away. She appears terrified and confused. Bob Temple stands grinning beside her, holding the horse by the reins.

Fate Is That Song
You Can't Get Out of Your Head

Francis draws his Cooper and aims it. "Let her go," he says.

The crowd erupts into yells. They disperse on the instant.

Temple hauls the girl down from the saddle. But instead of turning her loose he presses a long knife to her side. "I suggest you holster that."

"We've been here before," says Francis. "This has already happened."

"I said you better holster that thing."

"It was always coming to this. Right now."

By some wordless consensus that speaks volumes nonetheless, the onlookers have reassembled themselves neatly along the edges of the strip. It's like they're waiting for a parade. They hold bags of peanuts, cotton candy, tiny flags in their hands.

Only the Organ Grinder remains, roving about on the midway. He's a wandering planet, his orbit unique. He's playing that song. No one recalls where they first heard it.

"Just look at yourself," says Temple, giving the girl a hard shake. "Look what you've done. Is this what love looks like?"

"When it's got nothing to lose, maybe." Francis cocks the pistol.

"You think she agrees? Looking down the barrel of your own gun?"

"Like I said."

"I think you made a big mistake. And you know it," says Temple. "I think behind that calm, you are quaking in your boots."

"Prepare yourself, Bob. We are about to part company."

"Oh, I'm prepared."

Francis slips the Cooper back into its holster. He dismounts the horse and takes his stance on the midway.

Temple snorts in response. He pushes the girl aside and she runs to the safety of the crowd.

Temple looks at Francis. He, too, takes his stance, hand hovering at his hip. "I can see by the way you're standing—you've never done this before."

"Maybe."

"No maybe about it. You're a greenhorn."

"That's fine."

"Is it? You keep saying that and yet here I stand. Testament to your delusion."

"Bob, I got something in my heart you can never take away."

Temple scoffs. "Love again? Are we back to that?"

Francis shakes his head. "Bigger."

Now Look

Do you see this leaf? This acorn? These dewdrops, like jewels, quavering upon a spider's web? They are each a world, and you are a world, and within these worlds are many others and their gateways too. This is what my people say. These worlds, they come from Nothing. And Nothing has no end.

Now drop deeper, beneath the clean light. Dredge up the deer and the bloodborn bull. Unearth like a jaw the coal-black dream from its peat.

Listen, this quieted, this eventless trail calling. One step in and you're gone.

Your Dream Is Bleeding

Bob Temple lies for some time on his side in the dust. The crowd is silent. Francis remains standing where he fired.

"You aren't dead," says Francis. "I can see you breathing."

"Yup."

Temple struggles to sit upright, cursing quietly to himself. He places an exploratory palm against the side of his chest and pulls it away, looking with some consternation at the blood there. It's as though he's received an unwanted card at the table and must now account for it among his hand. He coughs suddenly into the crook of his arm and the crowd gasps and cringes at the dark, wet arc of blood jumping from his chest, twice, in rhythm with his coughing.

Francis watches.

"Shit," says Temple. He sits there a bit. He looks around in bewilderment. "Where'd you learn to do that?"

"I don't know, Bob. Just thought of it on the spot."

"Well . . . shit," says Temple again, staring at the dirt before him. "Never seen that before."

Presently Temple winces, bracing himself in preparation to stand. He leans slowly to one side and then groans, freezing in a grimace. "Starting to hurt," he narrates. "Can really feel it now."

The crowd watches in silence.

Temple takes a deep breath, and it comes loud and strident. He pats at his chest. "Little hard to breathe."

A woman in the crowd clucks and turns away. A small child begins to cry.

Temple pushes himself heavily to his feet and staggers to his horse. He stands there, leaning against the saddle, a faint, burbling wheeze audible not from his mouth but the chest itself. After collecting himself, Temple grunts and heaves himself indelicately atop his horse and positions himself in the saddle, staring dazedly ahead.

Francis approaches him. He stands beside the horse, one hand on the bridle, Temple still staring ahead. Francis looks up at him. "Where's my money?"

Temple coughs again, glancing with disgust at the result on his shirt. He groans involuntarily. "Spent it all on cigars."

Francis regards him. After a moment he opens the horse's saddlebag and digs about, retrieving the lamp. He handles it briefly, satisfying himself that the lamp is unharmed, and places it into his pocket.

"This doesn't belong to you," he says. "Or even to me for that matter. I promised to return it."

Temple wheezes, his eyes glassy and dim as he sits his saddle, staring into some haunted distance that isn't desert and isn't sky but another place altogether, and not a bad one. "It's the strangest thing, Francis. I feel very...strange."

Francis pats him on the thigh. "You're just not used to dying, Bob. You'll be all right."

Francis slaps the horse's rump. It starts at a slow walk. The crowd parts to allow Temple's passage as his horse ambles out of town.

"See you, Bob Temple."

A Harder Farewell

The Organ Grinder halts his song as Governor Whitmore comes at a run. Whitmore grabs Penny in one arm, pulling her close and pointing after Bob Temple with the other.

"The hell are you all doing?" yells Whitmore. "Finish him! Shoot him! Someone, please shoot that man before he rides away!"

"Let him be," says Francis. He watches Temple grow smaller as his horse wanders away. "He won't go far."

Penny pushes loose from her father and runs into Francis' arms and kisses his neck, his face, her hands pressed to his chest.

"Francis," she says. "Francis."

She is crying. Francis strokes her hair. Her back. Her shoulders are narrow as a child's.

Governor Whitmore arrives at their periphery. He doesn't speak, though his paternity calls to Penny all the same.

"Say goodbye, Penny," says her father.

She clutches Francis tighter. "Francis," she says.

"Say goodbye, dear."

"I can't. I just can't."

With Penny still in his arms, Francis looks at her father, who gazes sternly back.

"We had an agreement," says Whitmore. "Which I am prepared to keep."

Francis slowly nods. He releases Penny. "It's all right," he tells her.

"Don't go, Francis."

"It's all right, you'll see," he says.

"Francis, don't go."

"There's something I have to do," he says.

"If I let you go now you'll never come back."

"If you don't let me go I can't come back."

"You're coming back?"

Francis glances at her father. "I'm sorry, Penny."

She whispers the word *no*.

Francis climbs his horse and walks it out of town.

The Organ Grinder resumes his tune.

Last Ride

Bob Temple has no thought whatsoever where he's going. Just somewhere else, somewhere he can feel the air upon his face and the quiet of the desert and breathe. His horse senses this and walks unhurriedly in no particular direction. Just walking, as horses sometimes do. All the while Temple's gaze remains fixed on the barbiturate brown distance — at some hazy point not fully in this world, though he is headed there with intent. The very promise of his demise is oddly consoling.

In time Temple becomes aware of others around him. They are upon horses. Though he does not count, they are thirty-eight in number. He knows who they are. Things happen, none of them pleasant. The main thing is to breathe, which is no small task when drowning in lungblood.

With great effort, he manages to ask, "How did you find me?"

Bursula Carter peers down at him.

"Portal," she says, pointing with her thumb.

Hovering vertically in the air is a disk of liquid blue light, shimmering with galactic allure.

Or maybe it was, "Your trail wasn't hard to follow." Temple can't be sure. Either way he grunts in response. He's finding it all the more difficult to remain both lucid and alive, hanging upside down as he is. They've stripped him naked, strung him up by the ankles and tied the rope to his horse's saddle after heaving the length of it over two tree limbs. Lungblood is trickling steadily up his throat, out his mouth, his nose.

"What was that?" says Bursula, bending closer.

Temple wheezes. He sputters.

"If these are your last words you better spit them out. I have little tolerance for mouth sounds."

"I didn't know it was an angel," he says.

"What's that?"

"When I did it. That thing I did. I didn't know it was an angel."

"You are wasting your breath," she says. "In five minutes' time, ten at the outside, you can tell them yourself. Now is this really what you want to talk about?"

"No."

"Go on then. Let's get to it."

He waves Bursula nearer. Temple wants to explain. But the world is never more real in your body, more clamorous and exacting, than the moment you're preparing to leave. With great difficulty he makes it understood that Francis Blackstone possesses the one thing Bursula Carter wants most in this world, despite her not knowing it exists. He tells Bursula where she can expect to find it. Temple's only and final request involves instructions—highly detailed, more than you'd think—regarding what Bursula should do to Francis upon catching him.

After the Carter Gang departs, Bob Temple, who is still naked and inverted, twists slowly in place. He looks at himself, his situation. So here it is, he thinks. No denying it. Each of us has a body that will at some point betray our pride. He figures anyone who lives long enough will eventually reach this conclusion, if not these circumstances exactly.

Temple notices they've made a knife available to him, secured to the saddle of his horse beside the rope knot. Temple tries to whistle to his horse and ends up making a hideous mess. He wipes his eyes. He tries snapping his fingers and the horse nickers.

He snaps his fingers again. The horse blows softly and treads forward to meet Bob Temple, who is consequently pulled higher on the rope and just out of reach of the knife.

Bob Temple rotates in place, his arms hanging limply to the ground.

The bells are different this time. They no longer call from someplace else, somewhere far away. They don't call at all.

They are simply shining. They are here, and they are shining.

Incredibly Francis

As Francis walks the trail from Nowhere toward the coal-mines he actually sees another horseman. The horse walks slowly, indeterminately, and though the figure sitting the horse is too distant to identify without glass, he rightly presumes it is Bob Temple taking his last ride on earth.

Upon reaching the mines Francis hobbles his horse. He stows the clay lamp in his satchel and slings it over his shoulder. This time he brings plenty of matches and a second lantern. He descends the rope ladder and retraces his steps past the canary cage with its suggestive photograph, down the tunnel and past the trolley, until he reaches the rift in the ceiling. He repositions the satchel at his side, ensuring its contents won't be damaged. He leaves the lantern burning on the floor to offer what light it will. He gets a foothold in the wall and inserts himself into the crevice and begins the slow, laborious wiggling that will see him to the top.

Inside the burial chamber, he lights a match.

Nothing appears disturbed. It's all just as he left it.

Francis lights a second match and this time sets the clay lamp aglow. He places the lamp among the middlemost niche in the wall.

"There you go," he says aloud. "That's my end of the bargain."

He waits a moment but there is no response.

"I can't say I got what I asked for," says Francis. "You were there when I needed you, that much is true. But I never did get that fortune we discussed—the one I needed to get the girl."

Again, no response.

"Because that was the deal, right? I take you around, give you one last run, you give me the girl in the end?"

He clears his throat. He rubs the back of his neck.

"Anyhow I brought the lamp back, just like I promised."

He turns in place, awaiting something, anything at all, but there's only silence. He nods to himself, to the darkness all around.

"All right then. Guess that makes it farewell."

Incredibly Francis feels very little in this moment. There's no outrage, no disbelief—just a hollowness inside. A tender sense of what might have been.

He removes a single stick of dynamite from his satchel. He touches the fuse to the lampflame and watches the powder fizz and sparkle. When the fuse is half spent he holds the stick aloft, just above the crevice he climbed. When it reaches three-quarters he drops it into the crevice.

A moment later there is a spectacular quaking as the tunnel in its entirety, including the entrance to this very chamber, is collapsed and forever sealed beneath him.

Francis makes his way to the surface much as he did before. When he gets there he seals this second, smaller exit as well, filling it first with a crosshatch of sticks and then stones and finally sand atop that until even he could not find this location again.

Francis walks the short distance to the mine's original entrance, where his horse remains hobbled. He's not surprised to see the entrance to the mine is completely caved in, a cloud of dust lingering above it, slowly dissipating in the desert breeze. He is surprised to find thirty-eight other horses alongside his own. Their riders are nowhere to be seen. He stands there a while, just looking at that. A long while he looks, his gaze sweeping between the variously coloured steeds and the collapsed entrance to the mine, not ten feet away.

Finally he locates a coil of rope on one of his new horses and strings them all together.

He doesn't know how much treasure thirty-nine horses can carry but figures it's quite a lot. More than enough anyway.

He glances briefly at the town of Nowhere, small and squat in the distance, and then at the trail he has come to know. He sorts through the contents of his own saddlebag, reassuring himself all is there, everything he needs; water, compass, the map to the Carter cave, a bit of jerky, and so forth.

He mounts up and nudges his lead horse into a trot, thinking it's time she had a name. A good horse name. Something to set her apart from the rest. He's still pondering names when he merges onto the main trail, a long string of horses in tow, and aligns his bearing with the westering sun.

EPILOGUE
OR
Happiness, to the Accompaniment
of Descending Scales

Francis Blackstone is an old man.

He's lived long enough to speak on a telephone, get zapped by the capacitor on a faulty fan, and twice he crashed an opentop motorcar — once in San Francisco, and once in London when he travelled there by steamer with the Wildest West Show. He learned to play a piano and tune it by ear and even shook hands with the boy who would later marry the woman who gave birth to Richard Milhous Nixon. Looking back on his life Francis has few regrets. He actually has difficulty recalling many of the events in this story. It was that long ago. That much has happened since.

Today is his birthday. It's evening and he sits in his rocker on the porch of his estate just outside Tucson, Arizona, with all four of his daughters and their families gathered on the steps below. His wife, Penelope, the one true love of his life, sits in an identical rocker beside him while insects dance about the electric lightbulbs dangling either side of the steps.

And just above the door, the first thing a visitor sees, a little broken guitar. It's inscribed with the words:

She cut a path to the stars
That the horses might follow

There is a grandchild in his lap. Francis forgets which one. He's watching a storm gather over the desert; the distinct smell of it, which has not changed and will not change no matter how many years go by. Lightning branches soundlessly on the horizon.

His eldest daughter, Meredith-Wonder, sets her drink on the step. She stands ceremoniously and a hush descends. All present look at Francis and Penelope, their hands bridging the distance between rockers.

Meredith says, "Eighty-four years old, Dad. How does it feel?"

He says, "Lot of shoes."

He rocks back in his chair. He feels the faint tremble of its squeaking.

"Lotta lotta shoes."

He's deaf as a hammer and has trouble reading lips in poor light.

In the Beginning

Robert Temple is a boy.

He's in the meadow beyond the barn, wandering freely through the grass. It's late afternoon and the sun is falling. Its light on the earth is a new colour, some shade of gold he's never seen or noticed. He feels it on his skin, his face, on the tiniest hairs of his arm.

Robert rambles slowly, hands outstretched, capturing seedpods and ladybugs. He makes finger-shadows against the sun. He lies down in the grass, arms resting at his side. He shuts his eyes. Sunlight filters through, webbed and pulsing. He imagines he is deep in the earth. He imagines he was never born at all. Insects buzz and buzz.

They say, Long ago, there were fish roaming here.

Robert pictures in his mind the great vast oceans towering high above him.

They say, Now the fish are all gone, and only little boys remain.

After a while Robert opens his eyes. Insects streak through the sky like tiny comets.

His mother's voice reaches him from across the field. He lifts his head and sees her slight figure on the distant porch, hands cupped to her mouth, calling his name for supper.

Robert wonders what would happen if he stayed right here — if he never went home. Would his mother remain on the porch? Would she ever stop calling? For the first time in his life, Robert understands he has a choice. His life is his own, or could be if he wills it. His heart thunders in his chest. He is a little bit frightened, though he doesn't know why.

From over the field and all around, the evening crickets begin to sing.

They sing, And now, in the dirt, in the sleep of brown dirt, we have important bones for you to touch and remember.

Robert feels a quickening in his blood. As though something new has been put there, and something else has gone away. As though all the mothers of the world will keep calling and calling. And all the little boys will keep turning, turning.

Their eyes already fixed on the places they will go.

Acknowledgements

I offer my sincere thanks to the following people for their help in creating *Like Rum-Drunk Angels*.

Shaun Bradley, my agent, who had the wherewithal to get behind this story and steer its earliest development.

Bethany Gibson, my kind and brilliant editor, for gently shaping the manuscript into its polished form.

Thank you to Alan Sheppard, and everyone at Goose Lane Editions for their hard work and support, and also to freelance copy editor Peter Norman for his keen eye.

For their key input at early stages, I thank Dave Carpenter, Thomas Trofimuk, Travis Enfield, and Gail Greenwood.

For their love and encouragement, I thank Leala, Anika, Indigo, Susan, Travis, Raigan, Dennis, and Marian. And for sharing our family's history of the magical cherry tree, I thank my grandmother, Fonda Spooner.

I'd also like to acknowledge writer Rhonda Kronyk for her insight and assistance with regards to Indigenous cultural sensitivity, as well as the many individuals who offered their accounts of sacred medicine use with Indigenous Elders.

Additionally, this story pays tribute to many giants from the past. Among them I heartily acknowledge the classical tales of *Arabian Nights*, William Faulkner's *As I Lay Dying*, and William Goldman's *Butch Cassidy and the Sundance Kid*. Last of all, for their timeless lyrics and inspiration, I thank the musical creators behind:

A writer, photographer, and filmmaker, Tyler Enfield is the author of *Madder Carmine*, winner of the High Plains Book Award. He is also the author of *Wrush*, an award-winning teen fantasy series. His films include the NFB-produced *Invisible World*, an interactive film about the Cambodian civil war, which won Alberta Screen Awards for Best Director and Best Interactive Media. Born and raised in California, Tyler Enfield now lives in Edmonton. *Like Rum-Drunk Angels* is his second novel.